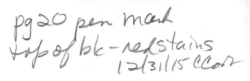

DARK LORD

THE RISE OF DARTH VADER

DARK LORD

THE RISE OF DARTH VADER

JAMES LUCENO

DEL REY BALLANTINE BOOKS
NEW YORK

Published in the United States by Del Rey Books, an imprint of The Random
House Publishing Group, a division of Random House, Inc., New York.

DEL REY is a registered trademark and the Del Rey colophon
is a trademark of Random House, Inc.

ISBN 0-345-47732-4

Printed in the United States of America on acid-free paper

www.starwars.com
www.starwarskids.com
www.delreybooks.com

1 3 5 7 9 8 6 4 2

First Edition

For Abel Lucero Lima, ace guide at Tikal
(aka Yavin 4), with whom I've left bootprints
throughout the Mundo Maya

Acknowledgments

Sincere thanks to Shelly Shapiro, Sue Rostoni, Howard Roffman, Amy Gary, Leland Chee, Pablo Hidalgo, Matt Stover, Troy Denning, and Karen Traviss. Special thanks to Ryan Kaufman, formerly of LucasArts, who described what it felt like to wear the Suit.

DARK LORD

THE RISE OF DARTH VADER

PART I

The Outer Rim Sieges

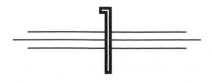

MURKHANA. FINAL HOURS OF THE CLONE WARS

Dropping into swirling clouds conjured by Murkhana's weather stations, Roan Shryne was reminded of meditation sessions his former Master had guided him through. No matter how fixed Shryne had been on touching the Force, his mind's eye had offered little more than an eddying whiteness. Years later, when he had become more adept at silencing thought and immersing himself in the light, visual fragments would emerge from that colorless void—pieces to a puzzle that would gradually assemble themselves and resolve. Not in any conscious way, though frequently assuring him that his actions in the world were in accord with the will of the Force.

Frequently but not always.

When he veered from the course on which the Force had set him, the familiar white would once again be stirred by powerful currents; sometimes shot through with red, as if he were lifting his closed eyes to the glare of a midday sun.

Red-mottled white was what he saw as he fell deeper into Murkhana's atmosphere. Scored to reverberating thunder; the rush of the wind; a welter of muffled voices . . .

He was standing closest to the sliding door that normally sealed the troop bay of a Republic gunship, launched moments earlier from the forward hold of the *Gallant*—a *Victory*-class Star Destroyer, harried by vulture and droid tri-fighters and awaiting High Command's word to commence its own descent through Murkhana's artificial ceiling. Beside and behind Shryne stood a platoon of clone troopers, helmets fitting snugly over their heads, blasters cradled in their arms, utility belts slung with ammo magazines, talking among themselves the way seasoned warriors often did before battle. Alleviating misgivings with inside jokes; references Shryne couldn't begin to understand, beyond the fact that they were grim.

The gunship's inertial compensators allowed them to stand in the bay without being jolted by flaring anti-aircraft explosions or jostled by the gunship pilots' evasive maneuvering through corkscrewing missiles and storms of white-hot shrapnel. Missiles, because the same Separatists who had manufactured the clouds had misted Murkhana's air with anti-laser aerosols.

Acrid odors infiltrated the cramped space, along with the roar of the aft engines, the starboard one stuttering somewhat, the gunship as battered as the troopers and crew it carried into conflict.

Even at an altitude of only four hundred meters above sea level the cloud cover remained dense. The fact that Shryne could barely see his hand in front of his face didn't surprise him. This was still the war, after all, and he had grown accustomed these past three years to not seeing where he was going.

Nat-Sem, his former Master, used to tell him that the goal of the meditative exercises was to see clear through the swirling whiteness to the other side; that what Shryne saw was only the shadowy expanse separating him from full contact with the Force. Shryne had to learn to ignore the clouds, as it were. When he had learned to do that, to look through them to the radiant expanse beyond, he would be a Master.

Pessimistic by nature, Shryne's reaction had been: *Not in this lifetime.*

Though he had never said as much to Nat-Sem, the Jedi Master had seen through him as easily as he saw through the clouds.

Shryne felt that the clone troopers had a better view of the war than he had, and that the view had little to do with their helmet imaging systems, the filters that muted the sharp scent of the air, the earphones that dampened the sounds of explosions. Grown for warfare, they probably thought the Jedi were mad to go into battle as they did, attired in tunics and hooded robes, a lightsaber their only weapon. Many of them were astute enough to see comparisons between the Force and their own white plastoid shells; but few of them could discern between armored and unarmored Jedi—those who were allied with the Force, and those who for one reason or another had slipped from its sustaining embrace.

Murkhana's lathered clouds finally began to thin, until they merely veiled the planet's wrinkled landscape and frothing sea. A sudden burst of brilliant light drew Shryne's attention to the sky. What he took for an exploding gunship might have been a newborn star; and for a moment the world tipped out of balance, then righted itself just as abruptly. A circle of clarity opened in the clouds, a perforation in the veil, and Shryne gazed on verdant forest so profoundly green he could almost taste it. Valiant combatants scurried through the underbrush and sleek ships soared through the canopy. In the midst of it all a lone figure stretched out his hand, tearing aside a curtain black as night . . .

Shryne knew he had stepped out of time, into some truth beyond reckoning.

A vision of the end of the war, perhaps, or of time itself.

Whichever, the effect of it comforted him that he was indeed where he was supposed to be. That despite the depth to which the war had caused him to become fixed on death and destruction, he was still tethered to the Force, and serving it in his own limited way.

Then, as if intent on foiling him, the thin clouds quickly conspired to conceal what had been revealed, closing the portal an errant current had opened. And Shryne was back where he started, with gusts of superheated air tugging at the sleeves and cowl of his brown robe.

"The Koorivar have done a good job with their weather machines," a speaker-enhanced voice said into his left ear. "Whipped up one brute of a sky. We used the same tactic on Paarin Minor. Drew the Seps into fabricated clouds and blew them to the back of beyond."

Shryne laughed without merriment. "Good to see you can still appreciate the little things, Commander."

"What else is there, General?"

Shryne couldn't make out the expression on the face behind the tinted T-visor, but he knew that shared face as well as anyone else who fought in the war. Commander of the Thirty-second air combat wing, the clone officer had somewhere along the line acquired the name Salvo, and the sobriquet fit him like a gauntlet.

The high-traction soles of his jump boots gave him just enough added height to stand shoulder-to-shoulder with Shryne, and where his armor wasn't dinged and scored it was emblazoned with rust-brown markings. On his hips he wore holstered hand blasters and, for reasons Shryne couldn't fathom, a version of the capelike command skirt that had become all the rage in the war's third year. The left side of his shrapnel-pitted helmet was laser-etched with the motto LIVE TO SERVE!

Torso markings attested to Salvo's participation in campaigns on many worlds, and while he wasn't an ARC—an Advanced Reconnaissance Commando—he had the rough edges of an ARC, and of their clone template, Jango Fett, whose headless body Shryne had seen in a Geonosian arena shortly before Master Nat-Sem had fallen to enemy fire.

"Alliance weapons should have us in target lock by now," Salvo said as the gunship continued to descend.

Other assault ships were also punching through the cloud cover, only to be greeted by flocks of incoming missiles. Struck by direct hits, two, four, then five craft were blown apart, flaming fuselages and mangled troopers plummeting into the churning scarlet waves of Murkhana Bay. From the nose of one gunship flew a bang-out capsule that carried the pilot and co-pilot to within meters of the water before it was ripped open by a resolute heat seeker.

In one of the fifty-odd gunships that were racing down the well, three other Jedi were going into battle, Master Saras Loorne among them. Stretching out with the Force, Shryne found them, faint echoes confirming that all three were still alive.

He clamped his right hand on one of the slide door's view slots as the pilots threw their unwieldy charge into a hard bank, narrowly evading a pair of hailfire missiles. Gunners ensconced in the gunship's armature-mounted turrets opened up with blasters as flights of Mankvim Interceptors swarmed up to engage the Republic force. The anti-laser aerosols scattered the blaster beams, but dozens of the Separatist craft succumbed to missiles spewed from the gunships' top-mounted mass-drive launchers.

"High Command should have granted our request to bombard from orbit," Salvo said in an amplified voice.

"The idea is to *take* the city, Commander, not vaporize it," Shryne said loudly. Murkhana had already been granted weeks to surrender, but the Republic ultimatum had expired. "Palpatine's policy for winning the hearts and minds of Separatist populations might not make good military sense, but it makes good political sense."

Salvo stared at him from behind his visor. "We're not interested in politics."

Shryne laughed shortly. "Neither were the Jedi."

"Why fight if you weren't bred for it?"

"To serve what remains of the Republic." Shryne's brief green vision of the war's end returned, and he adopted a rueful grin. "Dooku's dead. Grievous is being hunted down. If it means anything, I suspect it'll be over soon."

"The war, or our standing shoulder-to-shoulder?"

"The war, Commander."

"What becomes of the Jedi then?"

"We'll do what we have always done: follow the Force."

"And the Grand Army?"

Shryne regarded him. "Help us preserve the peace."

Murkhana City was visible now, climbing into steep hills
that rose from a long crescent of shoreline, the sheen of over-
lapping particle shields dulled by the gray underbelly of the
clouds. Shryne caught a fleeting glimpse of the Argente Tower
before the gunship dropped to the crests of the frothing waves
and altered course, pointing its blunt nose toward the stacked
skyline and slaloming through warheads fired from weapons em-
placements that lined the shore.

In a class with Mygeeto, Muunilinst, and Neimoidia, Murkhana was not a conquered planet but a host world—home to
former Senator and Separatist Council member Passel Argente,
and headquarters of the Corporate Alliance. Murkhana's deal
makers and litigators, tended to by armies of household droids
and private security guards, had fashioned a hedonistic domain of
towering office buildings, luxurious apartment complexes, exclusive medcenters, and swank shopping malls, casinos, and night-
clubs. Only the most expensive speeders negotiated a vertical
cityscape of graceful, spiraling structures that looked as if they
had been grown of ocean coral rather than constructed.

Murkhana also housed the finest communications facility in that part of the Outer Rim, and was a primary source of the "shadowfeeds" that spread Separatist propaganda among Republic and Confederacy worlds.

Arranged like the spokes of a wheel, four ten-kilometer-long bridges linked the city to an enormous offshore landing platform. Hexagonal in shape and supported on thick columns anchored in the seabed, the platform was the prize the Republic needed to secure before a full assault could be mounted. For that to happen, the Grand Army needed to penetrate the defensive umbrellas and take out the generators that sustained them. But with nearly all rooftop and repulsorlift landing platforms shielded, Murkhana's arc of black-sand beach was the only place where the gunships could insert their payloads of clone troopers and Jedi.

Shryne was gazing at the landing platform when he felt someone begin to edge between him and Commander Salvo, set on getting a better look through the open hatch. Even before he saw the headful of long black curls, he knew it was Olee Starstone. Planting his left hand firmly on the top of her head, he propelled her back into the troop bay.

"If you're determined to make yourself a target, Padawan, at least wait until we hit the beach."

Rubbing her head, the petite, blue-eyed young woman glanced over her shoulder at the tall female Jedi standing behind her. "You see, Master. He does care."

"Despite all evidence to the contrary," the female Jedi said.

"I only meant that it'll be easier for me to bury you in the sand," Shryne said.

Starstone scowled, folded her arms across her chest, and swung away from both of them.

Bol Chatak threw Shryne a look of mild reprimand. The raised cowl of her black robe hid her short vestigial horns. An Iridonian Zabrak, she was nothing if not tolerant, and had never taken Shryne to task for his irascible behavior or interfered with his teasing relationship with her Padawan, who had joined Chatak in the Murkhana system only a standard week earlier, arriving with Master Loorne and two Jedi Knights. The demands of the Outer Rim Sieges had drawn so many Jedi from Coruscant that the Temple was practically deserted.

Until recently, Shryne, too, had had a Padawan learner . . .

For the Jedi's benefit, the gunship pilot announced that they were closing on the jump site.

"Weapons check!" Salvo said to the platoon. "Gas and packs!"

As the troop bay filled with the sound of activating weapons, Chatak placed her hand on Starstone's quivering shoulder.

"Use your unease to sharpen your senses, Padawan."

"I will, Master."

"The Force will be with you."

"We're all dying," Salvo told the troopers. "Promise yourselves you'll be the last to go!"

Access panels opened in the ceiling, dropping more than a dozen polyplast cables to within reach of the troopers.

"Secure to lines!" Salvo said. "Room for three more, General," he added while armored, body-gloved hands took tight hold of the cables.

Calculating that the jump wouldn't exceed ten meters, Shryne shook his head at Salvo. "No need. We'll see you below."

Unexpectedly, the gunship gained altitude as it approached the shoreline, then pulled up short of the beach, as if being reined in. Repulsorlifts engaged, the gunship hovered. At the same time, hundreds of Separatist battle droids marched onto the beach, firing their blasters in unison.

The intercom squawked, and the pilot said, "Droid buster away!"

A concussion-feedback weapon, the droid buster detonated

at five meters above ground zero, flattening every droid within a radius of fifty meters. Similar explosions underscored the ingress of a dozen other gunships.

"Where were these weapons three years ago?" one of the troopers asked Salvo.

"Progress," the commander said. "All of a sudden we're winning the war in a week."

The gunship hovered lower, and Shryne leapt into the air. Using the Force to oversee his fall, he landed in a crouch on the compacted sand, as did Chatak and Starstone, if less expertly.

Salvo and the clone troopers followed, descending one-handed on individual cables, triggering their rifles as they slid to the beach. When the final trooper was on the ground, the gunship lifted its nose and began to veer away from shore. Up and down the beach the same scenario was playing out. Several gunships failed to escape artillery fire and crashed in flames before they had turned about.

Others were blown apart before they had even off-loaded.

With projectiles and blaster bolts whizzing past their heads, the Jedi and troopers scurried forward, hunkering down behind a bulkhead that braced a ribbon of highway coursing between the beach and the near-vertical cliffs beyond. Salvo's communications specialist comlinked for aerial support against the batteries responsible for the worst of the fire.

Through an opening in the bulkhead hastened the four members of a commando team, with a captive in tow. Unlike the troopers, the commandos wore gray shells of *Katarn*-class armor and carried heftier weapons. Hardened against magnetic pulses, their suits allowed them to penetrate defensive shields.

The enemy combatant they had captured wore a long robe and tasseled headcloth but lacked the sallow complexion, horizontal facial markings, and cranial horns characteristic of the Koorivar. Like their fellow Separatists the Neimoidians, Passel

Argente's species had no taste for warfare, but felt no compunction about employing the best mercenaries credits could buy.

The burly commando squad leader went immediately to Salvo.

"Ion Team, Commander, attached to the Twenty-second out of Boz Pity." Turning slightly in Shryne's direction, the commando nodded his helmeted head.

"Welcome to Murkhana, General Shryne."

Shryne's dark brows beetled. "The voice is familiar . . . ," he began.

"The face even more so," the commando completed.

The joke was almost three years old but still in use among the clone troopers, and between them and the Jedi.

"Climber," the commando said, providing his sobriquet. "We fought together on Deko Neimoidia."

Shryne clapped the commando on the shoulder. "Good to see you again, Climber—even here."

"As I told you," Chatak said to Starstone, "Master Shryne has friends all over."

"Perhaps they don't know him as well as I do, Master," Starstone grumbled.

Climber lifted his helmet faceplate to the gray sky. "A good day for fighting, General."

"I'll take your word for it," Shryne said.

"Make your report, squad leader," Salvo interrupted.

Climber turned to the commander. "The Koorivarr are evacuating the city, but taking their sweet time about it. They've a lot more faith in these energy shields than they should have." He beckoned the captive forward and spun him roughly to face Salvo. "Meet Idis—human under the Koorivar trappings. Distinguished member of the Vibroblade Brigade."

"A mercenary band," Bol Chatak explained to Starstone.

"We caught him . . . with his trousers down," Climber continued, "and persuaded him to share what he knows about the shoreline defenses. He was kind enough to provide the location of the landing platform shield generator." The commando indicated a tall, tapered edifice farther down the beach. "Just north of the first bridge, near the marina. The generator's installed two floors below ground level. We may have to take out the whole building to get to it."

Salvo signaled to his comlink specialist. "Relay the building coordinates to *Gallant* gunnery—"

"Wait on that," Shryne said quickly. "Targeting the building poses too great a risk to the bridges. We need them intact if we're going to move vehicles into the city."

Salvo considered it briefly. "A surgical strike, then."

Shryne shook his head no. "There's another reason for discretion. That building is a medcenter. Or at least it was the last time I was here."

Salvo looked to Climber for confirmation.

"The general's correct, Commander. It's still a medcenter."

Salvo shifted his gaze to Shryne. "An *enemy* medcenter, General."

Shryne compressed his lips and nodded. "Even at this point in the war, patients are considered noncombatants. Remember what I said about hearts and minds, Commander." He glanced at the mercenary. "Is the shield generator accessible from street level?"

"Depends on how skilled you are."

Shryne looked at Climber.

"Not a problem," the commando said.

Salvo made a sound of distaste. "You'd trust the word of a merc?"

Climber pressed the muzzle of his DC-17 rifle into the small of the mercenary's back. "Idis is on our side now, aren't you?"

The mercenary's head bobbed. "Free of charge."

Shryne looked at Climber again. "Is your team carrying enough thermal detonators to do the job?"

"Yes, sir."

Salvo still didn't like it. "I strongly recommend that we leave this to the *Gallant*."

Shryne regarded him. "What's the matter, Commander, we're not killing the Separatists in sufficient numbers?"

"In sufficient numbers, General. Just not quickly enough."

"The *Gallant* is still holding at fifty kilometers," Chatak said in a conciliatory tone. "There's time to recon the building."

Salvo demonstrated his displeasure with a shrug of indifference. "It's your funeral if you're wrong."

"That's neither here nor there," Shryne said. "We'll rendezvous with you at rally point Aurek-Bacta. If we don't turn up by the time the *Gallant* arrives, feed them the building's coordinates."

"You can count on it, sir."

M urkhana had been a dangerous world long before it had become a treacherous one. Magistrate Passel Argente had been content to allow crime to flourish, under the condition that the Corporate Alliance and its principal subsidiary, Lethe Merchandising, received their fair share of the action. By the time Argente had joined Count Dooku's secessionist movement and drawn Murkhana into the Confederacy of Independent Systems there was almost no distinguishing the Corporate Alliance's thug tactics from those of Black Sun and similar gangster syndicates, save for the fact that the Alliance was more interested in corporate acquisitions than it was in gambling, racketeering, and the trade in illegal spice.

Where persuasion failed, the Corporate Alliance relied on the tank droid to convince company owners of the wisdom of acceding to offers of corporate takeover, and scores of those treaded war machines had taken up positions on the steep streets of Murkhana City to thwart Republic occupation.

Shryne knew the place about as well as anyone, but he let the commandos take the point. Dodging blasterfire from battle droids and roving bands of mercenaries, and trusting that the captive fighter had known better than to steer them wrong, the three Jedi followed the four special ops troopers on a circuitous course through the switchbacked streets. High overhead, laser and ion bolts splashed against the convex energy shields, along with droid craft and starfighters crippled in the furious dogfights taking place in the clouds.

Shortly the allied team reached the approach avenues of the southernmost of the quartet of bridges that joined the city and the landing platform. Encountering no resistance at the med-center, they infiltrated the building's soaring atrium. Wan light streamed through tall permaplex windows; dust and debris wafted down to a mosaic floor as the building trembled in concert with the intensifying Republic bombardment.

The particle-filled air buzzed with current from the shield generator, raising the hairs on the back of Shryne's neck. The place looked and felt deserted, but Shryne sent Chatak, Star-stone, and two of the commandos to reconnoiter the upper floors, just in case. Still trusting to the captive's intelligence, Shryne, Climber, and Ion Team's explosives specialist negotiated a warren of faintly lighted corridors that led to a turbolift the captive had promised would drop them into the shield generator room.

"Sir, I didn't want to say anything in front of General Chatak," Climber said as they were descending, "but it's not often you find a Jedi and a commander at odds about tactics."

Shryne knew that to be true. "Commander Salvo has good instincts. What he lacks is patience." He turned fully to the hel-meted commando. "The war's changed some of us, Climber. But the Jedi mandate has always been to keep the peace without killing everyone who stands in the way."

Climber nodded in understanding. "I know of a few com-manders who were returned to Kamino for remedial training."

"And I know a few Jedi who could use as much," Shryne said. "Because all of us want this war over and done with." He touched Climber on the arm as the turbolift was coming to a halt. "Apologies up front if this mission turns out to be a waste of time."

"Not a problem, sir. We'll consider it leave."

Outside the antigrav shaft, the deafening hum of the generator made it almost impossible to communicate without relying on comlinks. Prizing his from a pouch on his utility belt, Shryne set it to the frequency Climber and his spec-three used to communicate with each other through their helmet links.

Warily, the three of them made their way down an unlighted hallway and ultimately onto a shaky gantry that overlooked the generator room. Most of the cavernous space was occupied by the truncated durasteel pyramid that fed power to the landing platform's veritable forest of dish-shaped shield projectors.

Macrobinoculars lowered over his tinted visor, Climber scanned the area.

"I count twelve sentries," he told Shryne through the comlink.

"Add three Koorivar technicians on the far side of the generator," the spec-three said from his position.

Even without macrobinoculars, Shryne could see that the majority of the guards were mercenaries, humans and humanoids, armed with blaster rifles and vibroblades, the brigade's signature weapon. Cranial horns—a symbol of status, especially among members of Murkhana's elite—identified the Koorivar among the group. Three Trade Federation battle droids completed the contingent.

"Generator's too well protected for us to be covert," Climber said. "Excuse me for saying so, but maybe Commander Salvo was right about letting the *Gallant* handle this."

"As I said, he has good instincts."

"Sir, just because the guards aren't here for medical care doesn't mean we can't make patients of them."

"Good thinking," Shryne said. "But we're three against twelve."

"You're good for at least six of them, aren't you, sir?"

Shryne showed the commando a narrow-eyed grin. "On a good day."

"In the end you and Salvo both get to be right. Even better, we'll be saving the *Gallant* a couple of laser bolts."

Shryne snorted a laugh. "Since you put it that way, Climber."

Climber flashed a series of hand gestures at his munitions expert; then the three of them began to work their way down to the greasy floor.

Surrendering thought and emotion, Shryne settled into the Force. He trusted that the Force would oversee his actions so long as he executed them with determination rather than in anger.

Taking out the guards was merely something that needed to be done.

At Climber's signal he and the spec-three dropped four of the sentries with precisely aimed blaster bolts, then juked into return fire to deal with those who were still standing.

As tenuous as his contact with the Force sometimes was, Shryne was still a master with a sword, and almost thirty years of training had honed his instincts and turned his body into an instrument of tremendous speed and power. The Force guided him to areas of greatest threat, the blue blade of his lightsaber cleaving the thick air, deflecting fire, severing limbs. Moments expanded, allowing him to perceive each individual energy bolt, each flick of a vibroblade. Unfaltering intention gave him ample time to see to every danger, and to carry out his task.

His opponents fell to his clean slashes, even one of the droids, whose melted circuitry raised an ozone reek. One mercenary whimpered as he fell backward, air rasping through a hole in his chest, blood leaking from vessels that hadn't been cauterized by the blade's passing.

Another, Shryne was forced to decapitate.

He sensed Climber and the spec-three to either side of him, meeting with similar success, the sibilant sound of their weapons punctuating the shield generator's ceaseless hum.

A droid burst apart, flinging shrapnel.

Shryne evaded a whirling storm of hot alloy that caught a Koorivar full-on, peppering his sallow face and robed torso.

Tumbling out of the reach of a tossed vibroblade, he noticed two of the technicians fleeing for their lives. He was willing to let them go, but the spec-three saw them, as well, and showed them no quarter, cutting both of them down before they had reached the safety of the room's primary turbolift.

With that, the fight began to wind down.

Shryne's breathing and heartbeat were loud in his ears but under control. Thought, however, intruded on his vigilance, and he lowered his guard before he should have.

The shivering blade of a mercenary's knife barely missed him. Spinning on his heel, he swept his attacker's feet out from under him, and in so doing rid the human of his left foot. The merc howled, his eyes going wide at the sight, and he lashed out with both hands, inadvertently knocking the lightsaber from Shryne's grip and sending it skittering across the floor.

Some distance away, Climber had been set upon by a battle droid and two mercenaries. The droid had been taken out, but its sparking shell had collapsed on top of Climber, pinning his right hand and blaster rifle, and the pair of mercs were preparing to finish him off.

Climber managed to hold one of his would-be killers at bay with well-placed kicks, even while he dodged a blaster bolt that ricocheted from the floor and the canted face of the shield generator. Rushing onto the scene, the spec-three went hand-to-hand with the merc Climber had booted aside, but Climber was out of tricks for dealing with his second assailant.

Vibroblade clasped in two hands, the enemy fighter leapt.

Shryne moved in a blur—not for Climber, because he knew that he could never reach him in time—but for the still-spinning lightsaber hilt, which he toed directly into Climber's gloved and outstretched left hand. In the same instant the merc was leaning over Climber to deliver what would have been a fatal blow, the commando's thumb hit the lightsaber's activation stud. A column of blue energy surged from the hilt, and through the Separatist's chest, impaling him.

Shryne hurried to Climber's side while the spec-three was moving through the room, making certain no further surprises awaited them.

Yoda or just about any other Jedi Master would have been able to rid Climber of the battle droid with a Force push, but Shryne needed Climber's help to move the sparking carcass aside. Years back, he would have been able to manage it alone, but no longer. He wasn't sure if the weakness was in him or if, with the death of every Jedi, the war was leaching some of the Force out the universe.

Climber rolled the mercenary's body to one side and sat up. "Thanks for the save, General."

"Just didn't want you to end up like your template."

Climber stared at him.

"Headless, I mean."

Climber nodded. "I thought you meant killed by a Jedi."

Shryne held out his hand out for the lightsaber, which Climber was regarding as if noticing it for the first time. Then, feeling Shryne's gaze on him, he said, "Sorry, sir," and slapped the hilt into Shryne's hand.

Shryne hooked the lightsaber to his belt and yanked Climber

to his feet, his eyes falling on Chatak, Starstone, and Ion Team's other two commandos, who had rushed into the room with weapons drawn.

Shryne gestured to them that everything was under control.

"Find any patients?" he asked Chatak when she was within earshot.

"None," she said. "But we hadn't checked out the entire building when we heard the blasterfire."

Shryne turned to Climber. "Set your thermal charges. Then contact Commander Salvo. Tell him to alert airborne command that the landing platform energy shield will be dropping, but that someone is still going to have to take out the shore batteries on the bridge approaches before troops and artillery can be inserted. General Chatak and I will finish sweeping the building and catch up with you at the rally point."

"Affirmative, sir."

Shryne started off, then stopped in his tracks. "Climber."

"General?"

"Tell Commander Salvo for me that we probably could have done things his way."

"You certain you want me to do that?"

"Why not?"

"For one thing, sir, it's only going to encourage him."

Ras says you made a kill with General Shryne's lightsaber," one of the commandos who had accompanied Bol Chatak said to Climber while all four members of Ion Team were slaving thermal detonators to the shield generator's control panels.

"That's right. And knowing that you'd want to see it, I had my helmet cam snap a holo."

Climber's sarcasm was lost on the small-arms expert, a spec-two who went by the name Trace.

"How'd it handle?"

Climber sat still for a moment. "More like a tool than a weapon."

"Good tool for opening up mercenaries," Ras said from nearby.

Climber nodded. "No argument. But give me a seventeen any day."

"Shryne's all right," Trace said after they had gone back to placing the charges.

"I'll take him over Salvo in a firefight," Climber said, "but not on a battlefield. Shryne's too concerned about collateral damage."

Completing his task, he walked with purpose through the control room, assessing everyone's work. Ion Team's comlink specialist hurried over while Climber was adjusting the placement of one of the detonators.

"Has Commander Salvo been updated?" Climber asked.

"The commander is on the freq now," the spec-one said. "Wants to speak to you personally."

Climber distanced himself from the rest of the team and chinned the helmet comlink stud to an encrypted frequency. "Spec-zero Climber secure, Commander."

"Are the Jedi with you?" Salvo said abruptly.

"No, sir. They're sweeping the rest of the building in case we overlooked anyone."

"What's your situation, squad leader?"

"We're out of here as soon as the rest of the thermals are set. T-five, at most."

"Retain a couple of those thermals. Your team is to rejoin us soonest. We have a revised priority."

"Revised, how?"

"The Jedi are to be killed."

Climber fell silent for a long moment. "Say again, Commander."

"We're taking out the Jedi."

"On whose orders?"

"Are you questioning my authority?"

"No, sir. Just doing my job."

"Your job is to obey your superiors."

Climber recalled Shryne's actions in the generator room; his speed and accuracy, his skill with the lightsaber.

"Yes, sir. I'm just not too keen about going up against three Jedi."

"None of us is, Climber. That's why we need your team here. I want to set up an ambush short of the rally point."

"Understood, Commander. Will comply. Out."

Climber rejoined his three teammates, all of whom were watching him closely.

"What was all that about?" Trace asked.

Climber sat on his haunches. "We've been ordered to spring an ambush on the Jedi."

Ras grunted. "Odd time for a live-fire exercise, isn't it?"

Climber turned to him. "It's not an exercise."

Ras didn't move a muscle. "I thought the Jedi were on our side."

Climber nodded. "So did I."

"So what'd they do?" Trace asked.

Climber shook his head. "Salvo didn't say. And it's not a question we're supposed to ask, are we clear on that?"

The three specs regarded one another.

"How do you want to handle it?" Ras said finally.

"The commander wants us to blow an ambush," Climber said in a determined voice. "I say we give him what he wants."

From the sheer heights above the medcenter, Shryne, Chatak, and Starstone watched the towering building tremble as the shield generator buried at its base exploded. Clouds of smoke billowed into the chaotic sky, and the structure swayed precariously. Fortunately it didn't collapse, as Shryne feared it might, so the bridges that spanned the bay suffered no damage. Ten kilometers away, the shimmering energy shield that umbrellaed the landing platform winked out and failed, leaving the huge hexagon open to attack.

Not a moment passed before squadrons of Republic V-wing starfighters and ARC-170 bombers fell from the scudding clouds, cannons blazing. In defense, anti-aircraft batteries on the landing field and bridges opened up, filling the sky with hyphens of raw energy.

Far to the south the *Gallant* hung motionless, five hundred meters above the turbulent waters of the bay. Completing quick-turn burns, Republic gunships were streaking from the Star Destroyer's docking bays and racing shoreward through storms of intense fire.

"Now it begins in earnest," Shryne said.

The three Jedi struck west, moving deeper into the city, then south, angling for the rendezvous point. They avoided engagements with battle droids and mercenaries when they could, and won their skirmishes when evasion wasn't an option. Shryne was relieved to see that Chatak's curly-haired Padawan demonstrated remarkable courage, and was as deft at handling a lightsaber as many full-fledged Jedi Knights. He suspected that she had a stronger connection with the Force than he had had even during his most stalwart years as an eager learner.

When he wasn't seeking ways to avoid confrontation, Shryne was obsessing over his wrong call regarding the medcenter.

"A surgical strike would have been preferable," he confessed to Chatak as they were hurrying through a gloomy alley Shryne knew from previous visits to Murkhana.

"Ease up on yourself, Roan," she told him. "The generator was there precisely because the Corporate Alliance knew that we would show the medcenter mercy. What's more, Commander Salvo's opinion of you hardly matters in the scheme of things. If both of you weren't so hooked on military strategy, you could be off somewhere sharing shots of brandy."

"If either of us drank."

"Never too late to start, Roan."

Starstone loosed a loud sigh. "This is the wisdom you impart to your Padawan—that it's never too late to start drinking?"

"Did I hear a voice?" Shryne said, glancing around in theatrical concern.

"Not an important one," Chatak assured him.

Starstone was shaking her head back and forth. "This is not the apprenticeship I expected."

Shryne threw her a look. "When we get back to Coruscant, I'll be sure to slip a note into the Temple's suggestion box that

Olee Starstone has expressed disappointment with the way she's being trained."

Starstone grimaced. "I was at least under the impression that the hazing would stop once I became a Padawan."

"That's when the hazing *begins,*" Chatak said, suppressing a smile. "Wait till you see what you have to endure at the trials."

"I didn't realize the trials would include psychological torture."

Chatak glanced at her. "In the end, Padawan, it all comes down to that."

"The war is trial enough for anyone," Shryne said over his shoulder. "I say that all Padawans automatically be promoted to Jedi Knights."

"You won't mind if I quote you to Yoda?" Starstone said.

"That's *Master* Yoda to you, Padawan," Chatak admonished.

"I apologize, Master."

"Even if Yoda and the rest of the High Council members have their heads in the clouds," Shryne muttered.

Starstone bit her lip. "I'll pretend I'm not hearing this."

"You'd better hear it," Shryne said, turning to her.

They held to their southwesterly course.

The fighting along the shoreline was becoming ferocious. Starfighters and droid craft flying well below optimum altitudes were disappearing in balls of flame. Overwhelmed by ranged ion cannon fire from the *Gallant,* energy shields throughout the city were beginning to fail and a mass exodus was under way, with panicked crowds of Koorivar fleeing shelters, homes, and places of business. Mercenary brigades, reinforced by battle droids and tanks, were fortifying their positions in the hills. Shryne surmised that the fight to occupy Murkhana was going to be long and brutal, perhaps at an unprecedented cost in lives.

Two hundred meters shy of the rendezvous, he was shaken by a sudden restiveness that had nothing to do with the overarching battle. Feeling as if he had unwittingly led his fellow Jedi into the sights of enemy snipers, he motioned Chatak and Starstone to a halt, then guided them without explanation to the refuge of a deserted storefront.

"I thought I was the only one sensing it," Chatak said quietly.

Shryne wasn't surprised. Like Starstone, the Zabrak Jedi had a deep and abiding connection to the Force.

"Can you get to the heart of it?" he asked.

She shook her head no. "Not with any clarity."

Starstone cut her eyes from one Jedi to the other. "What's wrong? I don't sense anything."

"Exactly," Shryne said.

"We're close to the rendezvous, Padawan," Chatak said in her best mentor's voice. "So where is everyone? Why haven't the troopers set up a perimeter?"

Starstone mulled it over. "Maybe they're just waiting for us to arrive."

The young woman's offhand remark went to the core of what Shryne and Chatak were feeling. Trading alert glances, they unclipped their lightsabers and activated the blades.

"Be mindful, Padawan," Chatak cautioned as they were leaving the shelter of the storefront. "Stretch out with your feelings."

Farther on, at a confluence of twisting streets, Shryne perceived Commander Salvo and a platoon of troopers dispersed in a tight semicircle. Not, however, to provide the Jedi with cover fire in case they were being pursued. Shryne's earlier sense of misgiving blossomed into alarm, and he shouted for Chatak and Starstone to drop to the ground.

They no sooner did when a series of concussive detonations shook the street. But the blasts had been shaped to blow at Salvo's position rather than at the Jedi.

Shryne grasped instantly that the flameless explosions had

been produced by ECDs—electrostatic charge detonators. Used to disable droids, an ECD was a tactical version of the magnetic-pulse weapon the gunships had released on reaching the beach. Caught in the detonators' indiscriminate blast radius, Salvo and his troopers yelled in surprise as their helmet imaging systems and weapons responded to the surge by going offline. Momentarily blinded by light-flare from heads-up displays, the troopers struggled to remove their helmets and simultaneously reach for the combat knives strapped to their belts.

By then, though, Captain Climber and the rest of Ion Team had rushed into the open from where they had been hiding, two of the commandos already racing toward the temporarily blinded troopers.

"Gather weapons!" Climber instructed. "No firing!"

Blaster in hand and helmet under one arm, Climber advanced slowly on the three Jedi. "No mind tricks, General," he warned.

Shryne wasn't certain that the Jedi technique was even included in his repertoire any longer, but he kept that to himself.

"My specs have their white-noise hardware enabled," Climber went on. "If they hear me repeat so much as a phrase of what you say to me, they have orders to waste you. Understood?"

Shryne didn't deactivate his lightsaber, but allowed it to drop from his right shoulder to point at the ground. Chatak and Starstone followed suit, but remained in defensive stances.

"What's this about, Climber?"

"We received orders to kill you."

Shryne stared at him in disbelief. "Who issued the order?"

Climber gave his jaw a flick, as if to indicate something behind him. "You'll have to ask Commander Salvo, sir."

"Climber, where are you?" Salvo shouted as Climber's spec-two was escorting the commander forward. The commander's helmet was off and he had his gloved hands pressed to his eyes. "You blew those ECDs?"

"We did, sir. To get to the bottom of this."

Sensing Shryne's approach, Salvo raised his armored fists.

"At ease, Commander," Shryne told him.

Salvo relaxed somewhat. "Are we your prisoners, then?"

"You gave the order to kill us?"

"I won't answer that," Salvo said.

"Commander, if this has anything to do with our earlier head-butting—"

"Don't flatter yourself, General. This is beyond both of us."

Shryne was confused. "Then the order didn't originate with you. Did you ask for verification?"

Salvo shook his head no. "That wasn't necessary."

"Climber?" Shryne said.

"I don't know any more than you know, General. And I doubt that Commander Salvo will be as easily persuaded to part with information as our captive merc was."

"General Shryne," the spec-one interrupted, tapping his forefinger against the side of his helmet. "Comlink from forward operations. Additional platoons are on their way to Aurek-Bacta to reinforce."

Climber looked Shryne in the eye. "Sir, we're not going to be able to stop all of them, and if it comes to a fight, we're not going to be able to help you any more than we have. We don't kill our own."

"I understand, Climber."

"This has to be a mistake, sir."

"I agree."

"For old times' sake, I'm giving you a chance to escape. But orders are orders. If we find you, we will engage." Climber held Shryne's gaze. "Of course, sir, you could kill all of us now, and increase your odds of surviving."

Salvo and the spec-two made nervous movements.

"As you put it," Shryne said, "we don't fire on our own."

Climber nodded in relief. "Exactly what I would have expected you to say, General. Makes me feel all right about disobeying a direct order, and accepting whatever flak flies our way as a result."

"Let's hope it doesn't come to that, Climber."

"Hope is not something we store in our kit, General."

Shryne touched him on the upper arm. "One day you may have to."

"Yes, sir. Now get a move on before you're forced to put those lightsabers to the test."

A chorus of ready tones announced that helmet imaging systems, heads-up displays, and weapons had recovered from the magnetic-pulse effects of the ECDs and were back online.

The troopers, also recovered, didn't waste a moment in arming their rifles and leveling them at the four commandos, who had their DC-17s raised in anticipation of just such a standoff.

Arms outstretched, Commander Salvo rushed to position himself between the two groups before a blaster bolt could be fired.

"Stand down, all of you!" he snapped. "That's an order!" He glanced menacingly at Climber. "You had better comply this time."

While weapons were being lowered all around and the first of the reinforcement platoons was arriving—the troopers plainly confused by the scene unfolding in front of them—Salvo motioned the squad leader off to one side.

"Has your programming been wiped?" Salvo asked. "Our orders came down from the top of the command chain."

"I thought the Jedi were the top of the chain."

"From the Commander in Chief, Climber. Do you copy?"

"Supreme Chancellor Palpatine?"

Salvo nodded. "Evidently you and your team need reminding that we serve the Chancellor, not the Jedi."

Climber considered it. "Were you apprised of what the Jedi have done to prompt an order of execution?"

Salvo's upper lip curled. "That doesn't concern me, Climber, and it shouldn't concern you."

"You're right, Commander. I must have been misprogrammed. All this time I've accepted that the Grand Army and the Jedi Knights served the *Republic*. No one said anything to me about serving Palpatine first and foremost."

"Palpatine *is* the Republic, Climber."

"Palpatine issued the orders personally?"

"His command was to execute an order that has been in place since before the start of the war."

Climber took a moment to consider it. "Here's my take on it, Commander. It all comes down to serving the ones who are fighting alongside you, watching your back, putting a weapon in your hand when you need it most."

Salvo sharpened his tone. "We're not going to argue this now. But I promise you this much: if we don't catch them, you'll pay for your treason—you and your entire team."

Climber nodded. "We knew that going in."

Salvo took a breath and gave his head a rueful shake. "You shouldn't be thinking for yourself, brother. It's more dangerous than you know."

He swung to the members of his platoon and the recent arrivals.

"Platoon leaders, switch your comlinks to encrypted command frequency zero-zero-four. Have your troopers fan out. Grid search. Every building, every nook and cranny. You know what you're up against, so keep your wits about you."

"Ever see a Jedi run, Commander?" a platoon leader asked. "My guess is they're already ten klicks from here."

Salvo turned to his comlink specialist. "Contact the *Gallant*. Inform command that we have a situation, and that we're going to need whatever seeker droids and BARC detachments can be spared."

"Commander," the same platoon leader said, "unless the Seps are in on this hunt, we're going to have our hands full. Are we here to take Murkhana or the Jedi?"

Climber smirked. "Don't make matters worse by trying to confuse him, Lieutenant."

Gesturing with his forefinger, Salvo said: "Worse for you if they escape."

Shryne knew Murkhana City by heart.

"This way . . . Down here . . . Up there," he instructed as they made their escape, using the speed granted by the Force to put kilometers between themselves and their new enemy.

The city was wide open to bombardment now. The energy shields were down and the anti-laser aerosols had diffused. Two additional Star Destroyers hung over the bay, but Republic forces were continuing to show restraint. Most of the intense fighting was still occurring around the landing platform, although the hexagonal field itself was not being targeted, as it and the three bridges that remained were essential for moving troopers and matériel into the city. Shryne figured that once the landing platform was taken, the Separatists would probably blow the rest of the bridges, if only to slow the inevitable occupation, while residents continued to flee for their lives.

In the streets, firefights were undergoing a conspicuous change now that the clone troopers had been issued a new priority. Separatist mercenaries and battle droids were making the most of the confusion. Shryne, Chatak, and Starstone had witnessed several instances when platoons of clones disengaged from fighting, presumably to continue the hunt for the Jedi.

When Shryne felt that the three of them had a moment to spare he led them into a deserted building and pulled his comlink from his belt.

"The troopers have changed frequencies to prevent our eavesdropping on them," he said.

"That doesn't affect our knowing their methods for conducting a search," Chatak said.

"We can avoid them for however long it takes to clear this up. If it comes down to worst cases, I have contacts in the city who might be able to help us escape."

"Whose lives are we protecting here," Starstone asked in an edgy voice, "ours or the troopers'? I mean, aren't we the ones who had them grown?"

Shryne and Chatak traded secret glances.

"I'm not going to start killing troopers," Shryne said emphatically.

Chatak glanced at her Padawan. "That's what battle droids were created for."

Starstone gnawed at her lower lip. "What about Master Loorne and the others?"

Shryne made adjustments to his comlink. "Still no response from any of them. And not because of signal jamming."

Knowing that Chatak was doing the same, he stretched out with the Force, but no reverberations attended his call.

Chatak's shoulders slumped. "They've been killed."

Starstone sighed and hung her head.

"Draw on your training, Padawan," Chatak said quickly. "They're with the Force."

They're dead, Shryne thought.

Starstone looked up at him. "Why have they turned on us?"

"Salvo implied that the order came from high up."

"That can only mean the Office of the Supreme Chancellor," Chatak said.

Shryne shook his head. "That doesn't make sense. Palpatine owes his life to Skywalker and Master Kenobi."

"Then this has to be a miscommunication," Starstone chimed in. "For all we know, the Corporate Alliance broke the High Command code and issued counterfeit orders to our company commanders."

"Right about now that would be a *best*-case scenario," Shryne said. "If our comlinks were powerful enough to contact the Temple . . ."

"But the Temple can contact us," Starstone said.

"And it might yet," Chatak said.

"Maybe Passel Argente cut a deal with the Supreme Chancellor to spare Murkhana," Starstone said.

Shryne glanced at her. "How many more theories are you planning to offer?" he said, more harshly than he meant to.

"I'm sorry, Master."

"Patience, Padawan," Chatak said in a comforting voice.

Shryne slipped the comlink back into its pouch. "We need to avoid further engagements with droids or mercenaries. Lightsaber wounds are easy to identify. We don't want to leave a trail."

Exiting the building, they resumed their careful climb into the hills.

Everywhere they turned, the streets were crowded with clone troopers, battle droids, and masses of fleeing Koorivar. Before they had gone even a kilometer, Shryne brought them to a halt once more.

"We're getting nowhere fast. If we ditch our robes, we might have better luck at blending in."

Chatak regarded him dubiously. "What do you have in mind, Roan?"

"We find a couple of mercenaries and take their robes and headcloths." He gazed at Chatak and Starstone in turn. "If the troopers can switch sides, then so can we."

7

Salvo ended his helmet comlink communication with Murkhana's theater commanders and joined Climber at what had become the troopers' forward command base. The other three commandos were searching for the escaped Jedi, but Salvo didn't want the squad leader out of his sight.

"General Loorne and the two Jedi Knights he arrived with were ambushed and killed," Salvo shared with Climber. "Apparently no troopers among the Twenty-second staked a claim to the moral high ground."

Climber let the remark go. "Did you report our actions to High Command?"

Salvo shook his head. "But don't think I won't. Like I told you, it depends on whether we're able to kill them. Just now I don't want your actions reflecting negatively on my command."

"Did you learn anything about what prompted the execution order?"

Salvo spent a moment arguing with himself about what he should and should not reveal. "Theater command reports that four Jedi Masters attempted to assassinate Supreme Chancellor

Palpatine in his chambers on Coruscant. The reason is unclear, but it appears that the Jedi have been angling from the start to assume control of the Republic, and that the war may have been engineered to help bring that about."

Climber was stunned. "So Palpatine's order was put in place because he anticipated that the Jedi might try something?"

"It's not unusual to have a contingency plan, Climber. You should know that better than anyone."

Climber thought hard about it. "How does it make you feel, Commander—about what the Jedi did, I mean?"

Salvo took a moment to respond. "As far as I'm concerned, their treachery just adds more enemies to the list. Other than that, I don't feel one way or another about it."

Climber studied Salvo. "You know, word among some of the troopers is that the Jedi had a hand in ordering the creation of the Grand Army. Were they figuring we'd side with them when they grabbed control, or would they have turned on us eventually?"

"No way to know."

"Except they made their move too soon."

Salvo nodded. "Even now, troopers and Jedi are battling it out inside the Temple on Coruscant. Thousands are believed dead."

"I've never been to Coruscant," Climber said, breaking a brief silence. "Closest I ever came was training on one of the inner worlds of that system. You've been there?"

"Once. Before the start of the Outer Rim Sieges."

"Who would you rather be serving, Commander—Palpatine or the Jedi?"

"That's outside the scope of the part we were created to play, Climber. When this war ends, we'll be sitting pretty. I wouldn't have thought so even twelve hours ago, but now, with the Jedi out of the picture, I suspect we're in for a promotion."

Climber glanced at the sky. "Going to be dark soon. Puts our search teams at high risk of being ambushed by Seps."

Salvo shrugged. "More than a hundred seeker droids have been deployed. Shouldn't be hard to find three Jedi."

Climber blew his breath out in derision. "You know as well as I do that they're too smart to be caught."

"Granted," Salvo said. "By now, they're probably wearing bodysuits and armor."

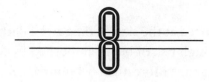

E at," Shryne said, forcing some of the rations he had taken from his utility belt on a distracted Olee Starstone. "We don't know when we'll have another chance."

Several hours had passed since they had fled the ambush site, and they'd traveled clear across the city to an empty warehouse close to the access ramps of the northernmost of the landing platform bridges. It was midnight, and they were attired in the garb of three mercenaries they had taken by surprise behind the Argente Tower.

Shryne continued. "There may come a point when we'll have to get rid of our comlinks, beacon transceivers, and lightsabers. Being taken prisoner could be our way off Murkhana."

"Should we use Force influence?" Starstone said.

"That might work on a couple of troopers at a time," Shryne said, "but not an entire platoon, much less a full company."

Chatak eyed her Padawan with clear intent. "It's a matter of surviving until the Republic is victorious."

Shryne had a ration pack lifted to his mouth when his beacon transceiver began to vibrate. He fished the device from the deep pocket of the Koorivar robe and regarded it in silence.

"Could be troopers, tapping into our frequencies," Chatak said.

Shryne studied the beacon's small display screen. "It's a coded burst-transmission from the Temple."

Chatak hurried to his side to peer over his shoulder. "Can you decipher it?"

"It's not a simple Nine Thirteen," Shryne said, referring to the code the Jedi used to locate one another in emergency situations. "Give me a moment." When the burst-transmission began to recycle, he turned to Chatak in stark incredulity. "The High Council is ordering all Jedi back to Coruscant."

Chatak was dumbfounded.

"No explanation," Shryne said.

Chatak stood up and paced away from him. "What could have happened?"

He thought about it. "A follow-up attack on Coruscant by Grievous?"

"Perhaps," Chatak said. "But that doesn't account for the clone troopers' disloyalty."

"Maybe there's been a universal clone trooper revolt," Starstone suggested. "The Kaminoans could have betrayed us. All these years, they could have been in league with Count Dooku. They could have programmed the troopers to revolt at a predetermined time."

Shryne was glancing at Chatak. "Does she ever stop?"

"I haven't been able to find the off switch."

Shryne moved to the nearest window and watched the night sky.

"Republic starfighters will be setting down on the landing platform by late morning," he said.

Chatak joined him at the window. "Then Murkhana is won."

Shryne turned to face her. "We have to reach the platform. The troopers have their orders, and now we have ours. If we can seize a transport or starfighters, we may yet be able to return to Coruscant."

Throughout the long night and morning, explosive light strobed through the warehouse's arched windows as Republic and Separatist forces clashed at sea and in the air. The battle for the landing platform raged well into the afternoon. But now the Separatist forces were in full retreat, streaming across the two intact bridges, leaving the platform's defense to homing spider droids, hailfire weapons platforms, and tanks.

By the time the Jedi managed to reach the more northern of the pair of bridges, the wide avenue was so closely packed with fleeing mercenaries and other Separatist fighters they could scarcely make any headway against the flow. A crossing that should have taken an hour required more than three, and the sun was low on the horizon when they reached the end of the bridge.

They were just short of the platform itself when a succession of powerful explosions took out the final hundred meters of the span and split the massive hexagon into thirds, sending hundreds of clone troopers, mercenaries, and Separatist droids plummeting into the churning water.

Shryne knew that the Separatists were responsible for the explosions. Before too long, munitions planted under the final bridge would be detonated, as well. By then, though, there would be no stopping the Republic onslaught.

While mercenaries shouldered past him in a frenzy, Shryne surveyed the forest of bridge pylons left exposed by the explosions, calculating their distance from one another and the odds of accomplishing what he had in mind.

Finally he said: "Either we frog-leap for the platform or we head back into the city." He looked at Starstone. "You decide."

Her blue eyes sparkled and she put on a brave face. "Not a problem, Master. We leap for it."

Shryne almost grinned. "Right. One at a time."

Chatak put her arm around her Padawan's shoulder. "Let's just hope no clone troopers are watching."

Shryne gestured to his pilfered outfit of robe and head-cloth. "We're just a bunch of very agile mercs."

Chatak took the lead, with Starstone right on her heels. Shryne waited until they were halfway along before following. The first few leaps were easy, but the closer he got to the platform, the greater the distance between the pylons, many of which had been left with jagged tops. On his penultimate jump, he nearly lost his balance, and on his final leap for the edge of the platform his hands arrived well in front of his feet.

A last-moment grab from Starstone was all that saved him from a plunge into the waves.

"Remind me to mention this to the Council, Padawan," he told her.

The platform was being hammered, but not past the point of utility. On one fractured section gunships were beginning to land, along with a vanguard flight of troop transports. Elsewhere, battle droids were being flattened by magpulse busters, then picked off before they had a chance to reactivate by V-wings and ARC-170s performing lightning-fast strafing runs.

With night falling, the Jedi wove through firefights and fountaining explosions, using their captured blasters rather than their lightsabers to defend themselves against teams of clone troopers and commandos, though without killing any.

They came to a halt at a ruined stretch of permacrete, at the far end of which a squadron of starfighters was touching down.

"Can you pilot a ship?" Shryne asked Starstone in a rush.

"Only an interceptor, Master. But without an astromech droid I doubt I could fly one to Coruscant. And I've never even seen the cockpit of a V-wing."

Shryne considered it. "Then it'll have to be an ARC-one-seventy." He pointed to a bomber that was just landing, probably to refuel. "That's our ship. It's our best bet, anyway. Enough chairs for the three of us, and hyperspace-capable."

Chatak watched the crew for a moment. "We may have to stun the copilot and tail gunner."

Shryne was on the verge of moving when he felt the beacon transceiver vibrate again, and he pawed it from the deep pocket of the robe.

"What is it, Roan?" Chatak asked while he was staring in stupefaction at the device. *"What?"* she repeated.

"Another coded burst from the beacon," he said without moving his gaze from the screen.

"Same order?"

"The opposite." Eyes wide, he looked up at Chatak and Starstone. "All Jedi are ordered to avoid Coruscant at all costs. We're to abandon whatever missions we're involved in, and go into hiding."

Chatak's mouth fell open.

Shryne made his lips a thin line. "We still need to get off Murkhana."

They double-checked their blasters and again were on the verge of setting out for the starfighter when every Separatist droid and war machine on the landing platform abruptly began to power down. At first Shryne thought that another droid buster had been delivered without his being aware of it. Then he realized his mistake.

This was something different.

The droids hadn't simply been dazzled. They had been deactivated, even the hailfires and tanks. Red photoreceptors lost their glow, alloy limbs and antennas relaxed, every soldier and war machine stood motionless.

At once, a full wing of gunships dropped out of the noon sky, releasing almost a thousand clone troopers, riding polyplast cables to the platform's ruined surface.

Shryne, Chatak, and Starstone watched helplessly as they were almost instantly surrounded.

"Capture is infinitely preferable to execution," Shryne said. "It could still be our way out."

Closest to the ragged edge of the platform, he allowed his blaster, comlink, beacon transceiver, and lightsaber to slip from his hands into the dark waters far below.

PART II
THE EMPEROR'S EMISSARY

The Star Destroyer *Exactor,* second in a line of newly minted *Imperator*-class naval vessels, emerged from hyperspace and inserted into orbit, its spiked bow aimed at the former Separatist world of Murkhana. At sixteen hundred meters in length, the *Exactor,* unlike its *Venator*-class predecessors, was a product of Kuat Drive Yards, and featured gaping ventral launching bays rather than a dorsal flight deck.

Moved by gravity rather than by their ion drives, the carcasses of Banking Clan and Commerce Guild warships were grim reminders of the Republic invasion that had been launched in the concluding weeks of the war. Murkhana, however, had fared far better than some contested worlds, and the Corporate Alliance elite had decamped for remote systems in the galaxy's Tingel Arm, taking much of the planet's wealth with it.

In his quarters aboard the capital ship now under his personal command, Darth Vader, gloved and artificial right hand clamped on the hilt of his new lightsaber, knelt before a larger-than-life hologram of Emperor Palpatine. Only four standard weeks had elapsed since the war had ended and Palpatine had proclaimed himself Emperor of the former Republic, to the adulation of the leaders of countless worlds that had been drawn into the protracted conflict, and to the sustained acclaim of nearly the entire Senate.

Palpatine wore a voluminous embroidered robe of rich weave, the cowl of which was raised, concealing in shadow the scars he had suffered at the hands of the four treasonous Jedi Masters who had attempted to arrest him in his chambers in the Senate Office Building, as well as other deformations resulting from his fierce battle with Master Yoda in the Rotunda of the Senate itself.

"This is an important time for you, Lord Vader," Palpatine was saying. "You are finally free to make *full* use of your powers. If not for us, the galaxy would never have been restored to order. Now you must embrace the sacrifices you made to bring this about, and revel in the fact that you have fulfilled your destiny. It can all be yours, my young apprentice, anything you wish. You need only have the determination to *take it,* at whatever cost to those who stand in your way."

Palpatine's disfigurements were really nothing new; nor was his deliberate, vaguely contemptuous voice. The Emperor had used the same voice to procure his first apprentice; to ensnare Trade Federation Viceroy Nute Gunray in facilitating his dark designs; to persuade Count Dooku to unleash a war; and finally to seduce Vader—former Jedi Knight Anakin Skywalker—to the dark side, with the promise that he could keep Anakin's wife from dying.

Few among the galaxy's trillions were aware that Palpatine was also a Sith Lord, known by the title Darth Sidious, or that he had manipulated the war in order to bring down the Republic, crush the Jedi, and place the entire galaxy under his full control. Fewer still knew of the crucial role Sidious's current apprentice had played in those events, having helped Sidious defend himself against the Jedi who had sought his arrest; having led the assault on the Jedi Temple on Coruscant; having killed in cold blood the half dozen members of the Separatist Council in their hidden fortress on volcanic Mustafar.

And who there had suffered even more gravely than Palpatine.

Down on one knee, his black-masked face raised to the hologram, tall, fearsome Vader was wearing the bodysuit and armor, helmet, boots, and cloak that both camouflaged the evidence of his transformation and sustained his life.

Without revealing his distress at being unable to maintain the kneeling posture, Vader said: "What are your orders, Master?"

And asked himself: *Is this poorly designed suit the source of my distress, or is something else at work?*

"Do you recall what I told you about the relationship between power and understanding, Lord Vader?"

"Yes, Master. Where the Jedi gained power through understanding, the Sith gain understanding through power."

Palpatine smiled faintly. "This will become clearer to you as you continue your training, Lord Vader. And to that end I will provide you with the means to increase your *power*, and broaden your *understanding*. In due time, power will fill the vacuum created by the decisions you made, the acts you carried out. Married to the order of the Sith, you will need no other companion than the dark side of the Force . . ."

The remark stirred something within Vader, but he was unable to make full sense of the feelings that washed through him: a commingling of anger and disappointment, of grief and regret . . .

The events of Anakin Skywalker's life might have occurred a lifetime ago, or to someone else entirely, and yet some residue of Anakin continued to plague Vader, like pain from a phantom limb.

"Word has reached me," Palpatine was saying, "that a group of clone troopers on Murkhana may have deliberately refused to comply with Order Sixty-Six."

Vader tightened his hold on the lightsaber. "I had not heard, Master."

He knew that Order Sixty-Six had not been hardwired into the clones by the Kaminoans who had grown them. Rather, the troopers—the commanders, especially—had been programmed to demonstrate unfailing loyalty to the Supreme Chancellor, in his role as Commander in Chief of the Grand Army of the Republic. And so when the Jedi had revealed their seditious plans, they had become a threat to Palpatine, and had been sentenced to death.

On myriad worlds Order 66 had been executed without misfortune—on Mygeeto, Saleucami, Felucia, and many others. Taken by surprise, thousands of Jedi had been assassinated by troopers who had for three years answered almost exclusively to them. A few Jedi were known to have escaped death by dint of superior skill or accident. But on Murkhana, apparently unique events had played out; events that were potentially more dangerous to the Empire than the few Jedi who had survived.

"What was the cause of the troopers' insubordination, Master?" Vader asked.

"Contagion." Palpatine sneered. "Contagion brought about by fighting alongside the *Jedi* for so many years. Clone or otherwise, there is only so much a being can be programmed to do. Sooner or later even a lowly trooper will become the sum of his experiences."

Light-years distant in his inner sanctum, Palpatine leaned toward the holotransceiver's cam.

"But you will demonstrate to them the peril of independent thinking, Lord Vader, the refusal to obey orders."

"To obey you, Master."

"To obey *us,* my apprentice. Remember that."

"Yes, my Master." Vader paused with purpose. "It's possible, then, that some Jedi may have survived?"

Palpatine adopted a look of consummate displeasure. "I am not worried about your pathetic former *friends,* Lord Vader. I want those clone troopers punished, as a reminder to all of them that for the rest of their abbreviated lives they would do well to understand whom they truly serve." Retracting his face into the hood of his robe, he said in a seething tone: "It is time that you were revealed as my authority. I leave it to you to drive the point home."

"And the escaped Jedi, Master?"

Palpatine fell silent for a moment, as if choosing his words carefully. "The escaped Jedi . . . yes. You may kill any you come across during the course of your mission."

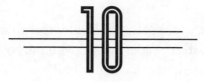

Vader didn't rise until the Emperor's holoimage had de-rezzed entirely. Then he stood for a long moment with his sheathed arms dangling at his sides, his head mournfully bowed. Finally he turned and moved for the hatch that opened onto the *Exactor*'s ready room.

To the galaxy at large, Jedi Knight Anakin Skywalker—poster boy for the war effort, the "Hero with No Fear," the *Chosen One*—had died on Coruscant during the siege of the Jedi Temple.

And to some extent that was true.

Anakin is dead, Vader told himself.

And yet, if not for events on Mustafar, Anakin would sit now on the Coruscant throne, his wife by his side, their child in her arms . . . Instead, Palpatine's plan could not have been more flawlessly executed. He had won it all: the war, the Republic, the fealty of the one Jedi Knight in whom the entire Jedi order had placed its hope. The revenge of the self-exiled Sith had been complete, and Darth Vader was merely a minion, an errand boy, allegedly an apprentice, the public face of the dark side of the Force.

While he retained his knowledge of the Jedi arts, he felt uncertain about his place in the Force; and while he had taken his first steps toward awakening the power of the dark side, he felt uncertain about his ability to sustain that power. How far he might have been now had fate not intervened to strip him of almost everything he possessed, as a means of remaking him!

Or of humbling him, as Darths Maul and Tyranus had been humbled before him; as indeed the Jedi order itself had been humbled.

Where Darth Sidious had gained everything, Vader had lost everything, including—for the moment, at least—the self-confidence and unbridled skill he had demonstrated as Anakin Skywalker.

Vader turned and moved for the hatch.

But this is not walking, he thought.

Long accustomed to building and rebuilding droids, supercharging the engines of landspeeders and starfighters, upgrading the mechanisms that controlled the first of his artificial limbs, he was dismayed by the incompetence of the medical droids responsible for his resurrection in Sidious's lofty laboratory on Coruscant.

His alloy lower legs were bulked by strips of armor similar to those that filled and gave form to the long glove Anakin had worn over his right-arm prosthesis. What remained of his real limbs ended in bulbs of grafted flesh, inserted into machines that triggered movement through the use of modules that interfaced with his damaged nerve endings. But instead of using durasteel, the medical droids had substituted an inferior alloy, and had failed to inspect the strips that protected the electromotive lines. As a result, the inner lining of the pressurized bodysuit was continually snagging on places where the strips were anchored to knee and ankle joints.

The tall boots were a poor fit for his artificial feet, whose claw-like toes lacked the electrostatic sensitivity of his equally false fingertips. Raised in the heel, the cumbersome footgear canted him slightly forward, forcing him to move with exaggerated caution lest he stumble or topple over. Worse, they were so heavy that he often felt rooted to the ground, or as if he were moving in high gravity.

What good was motion of this sort, if he was going to have to call on the Force even to walk from place to place! He may as well have resigned himself to using a repulsor chair and abandoned *any* hope of movement.

The defects in his prosthetic arms mirrored those of his legs.

Only the right one felt *natural* to him—though it, too, was artificial—and the pneumatic mechanisms that supplied articulation and support were sometimes slow to respond. The weighty cloak and pectoral plating so restricted his movement that he could scarcely lift his arms over his head, and he had already been forced to adapt his lightsaber technique to compensate.

He could probably adjust the servodrivers and pistons in his forearms to provide his hands with strength enough to crush the hilt of his new lightsaber. With the power of his arms alone, he had the ability to lift an adult being off the ground. But the Force had always given him the ability to do that, especially in moments of rage, as he had demonstrated on Tatooine and elsewhere. What's more, the sleeves of the bodysuit didn't hug the prostheses as they should, and the elbow-length gloves sagged and bunched at his wrists.

Gazing at the gloves now, he thought: *This is not seeing.*

The pressurized mask was goggle-eyed, fish-mouthed, short-snouted, and needlessly angular over the cheekbones. Coupled with a flaring dome of helmet, the mask gave him the forbidding appearance of an ancient Sith war droid. The dark hemispheres that covered his eyes filtered out light that might have caused further injury to his damaged corneas and retinas, but in enhanced mode the half globes reddened the light and prevented him from being able to see the toes of his boots without inclining his head almost ninety degrees.

Listening to the servomotors that drove his limbs, he thought: *This is not hearing.*

The med droids rebuilt the cartilage of his outer ears, but his eardrums, having melted in Mustafar's heat, had been beyond repair. Sound waves now had to be transmitted directly to implants in his inner ear, and sounds registered as if issuing from underwater. Worse, the implanted sensors lacked sufficient discrimination, so that too many ambient sounds were picked up, and their distance and direction were difficult to determine. Sometimes the sensors needled him with feedback, or attached echo or vibrato effects to even the faintest noise.

Allowing his lungs to fill with air, he thought: *This is not breathing.*

Here the med droids had truly failed him.

From a control box he wore strapped to his chest, a thick cable entered his torso, linked to a breathing apparatus and heartbeat regulator. The ventilator was implanted in his hideously scarred chest, along with tubes that ran directly into his damaged lungs, and others that entered his throat, so that should the chest plate or belt control panels develop a glitch, he could breathe unassisted *for a limited time.*

But the monitoring panel beeped frequently and for no reason, and the constellation of lights served only as steady reminders of his vulnerability.

The incessant rasp of his breathing interfered with his ability to rest, let alone sleep. And sleep, in the rare moments it came to him, was a nightmarish jumble of twisted, recurrent memories that unfolded to excruciating sounds.

The med droids had at least inserted the redundant breathing tubes low enough so that, with the aid of an enunciator, his scorched vocal cords could still form sounds and words. But absent the enunciator, which imparted a synthetic bass tone, his own voice was little more than a whisper.

He could take food through his mouth, as well, but only when he was inside a hyperbaric chamber, since he had to remove the triangular respiratory vent that was the mask's prominent feature. So it was easier to receive nourishment through liquids, intravenous and otherwise, and to rely on catheters, collection pouches, and recyclers to deal with liquid and solid waste.

But all those devices made it even more difficult for him to move with ease, much less with any *grace*. The pectoral armor that protected the artificial lung weighed him down, as did the electrode-studded collar that supported the outsize helmet, necessary to safeguard the cybernetic devices that replaced the uppermost of his vertebrae, the delicate systems of the mask, and the ragged scars in his hairless head, which owed as much to what he had endured on Mustafar as to attempts at emergency trephination during the trip back to Coruscant aboard Sidious's shuttle.

The synthskin that substituted for what was seared from his bones itched incessantly, and his body needed to be periodically cleansed and scrubbed of necrotic flesh.

Already he had experienced moments of claustrophobia—moments of desperation to be rid of the suit, to emerge from the shell. He needed to build, or have built, a chamber in which he could feel human again . . .

If possible.

All in all, he thought: *This is not living.*

This was solitary confinement. Prison of the worst sort. Continual torture. He was nothing more than wreckage. Power without clear purpose . . .

A melancholy sigh escaped the mouth grille.

Collecting himself, he stepped through the hatch.

* * *

Commander Appo was waiting in the ready room, the special ops officer who had led the 501st Legion against the Jedi Temple.

"Your shuttle is prepared, Lord Vader," Appo said.

For reasons that went beyond the armor and helmets, the imaging systems and boots, Vader felt more at home among the troopers than he did around other flesh-and-bloods.

And Appo and the rest of Vader's cadre of stormtroopers seemed to be at ease with their new superior. To them it was only reasonable that Vader wore a bodysuit and armor. Some had always wondered why the Jedi left themselves exposed, as if they had had something to prove by it.

Vader looked down at Appo and nodded. "Come with me, Commander. The Emperor has business for us on Murkhana."

Shryne squinted against the golden wash of Murkhana's primary, which had just climbed from behind the thickly forested hills that walled Murkhana City to the east. By his reckoning he had spent close to four weeks confined with hundreds of other captives to a windowless warehouse somewhere in the city. Hours earlier all of them had been marched through the dark to a red-clay landing field that had been notched into one of the hills and was currently swarming with Republic troops.

On its hardstand sat a military transport Shryne surmised would deliver everyone to a proper prison on or in orbit around some forlorn Outer Rim world. Thus far, though, none of the prisoners had been ordered to board the transport. Instead, a head count was being conducted. More important, the clone troopers were obviously waiting for someone or something to arrive.

When his eyes had adjusted fully to the light, Shryne scanned the prisoners to all sides of him, relieved to find Bol Chatak and her Padawan standing some fifty meters away, among a mixed group of indigenous Koorivar fighters and an assortment of

Separatist mercenaries. He called to them through the Force, figuring that Chatak would be first to respond, but it was Starstone
who turned slightly in his direction and smiled faintly. Then
Chatak looked his way, offering a quick nod.

On their capture at the landing platform, the three of them
had been separated. The fact that Chatak had managed to retain
her headcloth perhaps explained why her short cranial horns
hadn't singled her out as Zabrak and raised an alert among her
captors.

Assuming that the conditions of her captivity had been similar to his, Chatak's being overlooked made perfect sense to
Shryne. Rounded up with hundreds of enemy fighters following
the still-puzzling deactivation of Murkhana's battle droids and
other war machines, Shryne had been searched, roughed up, and
marched into the dark building that would become his home for
the next four weeks—a special torment reserved for mercenaries.
Any who hadn't willingly surrendered their weapons had been
executed, and dozens more had died in fierce fights that had broken out for the few scraps of food that had been provided.

It hadn't taken long for Shryne to grasp that winning the
hearts and minds of Separatist fighters was no longer tops on
Chancellor Palpatine's list.

It also hadn't taken long for him to give up worrying about
being found out, since he had been placed in the custody of low-
ranking clone troopers whose armor blazes identified them as
members of companies other than Commander Salvo's. The
troopers had rarely spoken to any of the prisoners, so there had
been no news of the war or of events that might have prompted
the High Council to order the Jedi to go into hiding. Shryne
knew only that the fighting on Murkhana had stopped, and that
the Republic had triumphed.

He was considering the advantage of edging himself closer to
where Chatak and Starstone stood when a convoy of military

speeders and big-wheeled juggernauts arrived on the scene. Commander Salvo and some of his chief officers stepped from one of the landspeeders; from the hatch of one of the juggernauts emerged commando squad leader Climber, and the rest of Ion Team.

Shryne wondered about the timing of the commander's arrival. Perhaps Salvo was determined to have a close look at each and every prisoner before any were loaded into the transport. That Shryne was farther back from the leading edge of the crowd than Chatak and Starstone were meant nothing. Given the amount of time they had spent with Salvo, he would have no trouble identifying all of them.

Oddly, though, the commander wasn't paying much attention to the prisoners. His T-visor gaze was fixed instead on a Republic shuttle that was descending toward the landing field.

"*Theta*-class," one of the prisoners said quietly to the mercenary standing alongside him.

"You don't see many of those," the second human said.

"Must be one of Palpatine's regional governors."

The first man sniffed. "When they care enough to send the very best . . ."

The shuttle had commenced its landing sequence. With ion drive powering down and repulsorlift engaged, the craft folded its long wings upward to provide access to the main hold, then settled gently to the ground. No sooner had the boarding ramp extended than a squad of elite troopers filed out, the red markings on their armor identifying them as Coruscant shock troopers.

A much taller figure followed, attired head-to-foot in black.

"What in the moons of Bogden—"

"New breed of trooper?"

"Only if someone furnished the cloners with a donor a lot taller than the original."

Salvo and his officers hastened over to the figure in black.

"Welcome, Lord Vader."

"Vader?" the merc closest to Shryne said.

Lord, Shryne thought.

"That's no clone," the first human said.

Shryne didn't know what to make of Vader, although it was evident from the reaction of Salvo and his officers that they had been told to expect someone of high rank. With his large helmet and flowing black cape, Vader looked like something borrowed from the Separatists—a grotesque, Grievous-like marriage of humanoid and machine.

"Lord Vader," Shryne repeated under his breath.

Like Count Dooku?

Salvo was gesturing to Climber and the other commandos, who had remained at the juggernaut. From inside the enormous vehicle floated a large antigrav capsule with a transparent lid, which two of the commandos began to guide toward Vader's shuttle. As the capsule passed close to Shryne, he caught a glimpse of brown robes, and his stomach lurched into his throat.

When the capsule finally reached Salvo, the commander opened an access panel in its base and removed three gleaming cylinders, which he proffered to Vader.

Lightsabers.

Vader nodded for the commander of his shock troopers to accept them, then, in a deep, synthesized voice, said to Salvo: "What were you saving the bodies for, Commander—posterity?"

Salvo shook his head. "We weren't issued any instructions—"

Vader's gloved right hand waved him silent. "Dispose of them in any fashion you see fit."

Salvo was motioning Climber to remove the antigrav coffin when Vader stopped him.

"Have you forgotten anyone, Commander?" Vader asked.

Salvo regarded him. "Forgotten, Lord Vader?"

Vader folded his arms across his massive chest. "*Six* Jedi were assigned to Murkhana, not three."

Shryne traded brief glances with Chatak, who was also close enough to Vader to hear the remark.

"I'm sorry to report, Lord Vader, that the other three evaded capture," Salvo said.

Vader nodded. "I already know that, Commander. And I haven't come halfway across the galaxy to chase them down." He drew himself erect with a haughty air. "I've come to deal with the ones who allowed them to escape."

Climber immediately stepped forward. "That would be me."

"And us," the rest of Ion Team announced in unison.

Vader stared down at the commandos. "You disobeyed a direct order from High Command."

"The order made no sense at the time," Climber answered for everyone. "We thought it might be a Separatist trick."

"What you 'thought' has no bearing on this," Vader said, pointing at Climber. "You are expected to follow orders."

"And we follow any reasonable ones. Killing our own didn't qualify."

Vader continued to point his forefinger at Climber's chest. "They weren't your allies, squad leader. They were traitors, and you sided with them."

Climber stood his ground. "Traitors how? Because a few of them tried to arrest Palpatine? I still don't see how that warrants a death penalty for the lot of them."

"I'll be sure to notify the Emperor of your concerns," Vader said.

"You do that."

Shryne closed his mouth and swallowed hard. *Jedi had tried to arrest Palpatine.* The Republic now had an *Emperor*!

"Unfortunately," Vader was saying, "you won't be alive to learn of his response."

In one swift motion he drew aside his cloak and pulled a lightsaber from his belt. Igniting with a *snap-hiss,* the hilt projected a crimson blade.

If Shryne had been confused earlier, he was now overwhelmed.

A Sith blade?

The four commandos fell back, raising their weapons.

"We'll accept execution for our actions," Climber said. "But not from some lapdog of the Emperor."

Quickly Salvo and his officers stepped forward, but Vader only showed them the palm of his hand. "No, Commander. Leave this to me."

With that he moved on the commandos.

Spreading out, they fired, but not a single bolt made it past Vader's blade. Deflected bolts went straight through the helmet visors of two of the commandos, and in two furious sweeps Vader opened the pair from shoulder to hip, as if they were flimsy ration containers. Climber and the third commando took advantage of the moment to break for the nearby tree line, firing as they fled. A deflection shot from Vader caught Climber in the left leg, but the bolt didn't so much as slow him down.

Vader tracked them, then motioned to his cadre of troopers. "I want them *alive,* Commander Appo."

"Yes, Lord Vader."

Appo's shock troopers raced off in pursuit of the commandos. Not one of Salvo's officers had fired a weapon, but now all of them were regarding Vader with vigilant uncertainty, their rifles half raised.

"Don't let my weapon fool you," Vader told them, as if reading their thoughts. "I am not a Jedi."

From off to Shryne's left, a familiar voice shouted. "But *I* am!"

Bol Chatak had unwound her headcloth, revealing her vestigial horns, and had ignited the lightsaber Shryne thought she'd had sense enough to ditch when they were captured.

Vader whirled, watching Chatak as she began to stalk him, prisoners and troopers alike giving her wide berth.

"So much the better that one of you survived," he said, waving his lightsaber back and forth in front of him. "The commandos saved your life, and now you hope to save theirs, is that it?"

Chatak held her blue blade at shoulder height. "My only intent is to take you out of the hunt."

Vader's angled his blade to point toward the ground. "You won't be the first Jedi I've killed."

Their blades met with an explosion of light.

Fearing that the prisoners would use the distraction to scatter, Salvo's men hurried in to form a cordon around them. Pressed in among everyone, Shryne lost sight of Chatak and Vader, but he could tell from the angry clashes of their blades that the duel was fast and furious. Momentarily immobilized, he allowed himself to be swept up in the surge of the crowd, so that he might be raised up over the heads of those in front of him.

For a moment he was.

Just long enough to glimpse Chatak, all grace and speed, working her way into her opponent's space. Her moves were broad and circular, and the lightsaber seemed an extension of her. Vader, by contrast, was clumsy, and his strikes were mostly vertical. He was, however, a full head taller than Chatak and incredibly powerful. At various times his stances and techniques mimicked those of Ataro and Soresu, but Vader appeared to lack a style of his own, and executed his moves stiffly.

With a whirling motion Chatak got far enough inside Vader's long reach to inflict a forearm wound. But Vader scarcely reacted to the hit, and instead of seeing cauterized flesh

Shryne saw sparks and smoke fountain through Vader's slashed glove.

Then he lost sight of them again.

Wedged into the crowd, he wondered if he could use the Force to call one of the trooper's blaster rifles into his grip. At the same time he hoped that Starstone had abandoned her lightsaber at the landing platform, and wouldn't attempt to join her Master against Vader.

We need to learn what happened to the Jedi, he tried to send to her. *Our time for dealing with Vader will come. Be patient.*

He wondered if he was right. Maybe he should attempt to reach Chatak, weapon or no. Maybe his life was meant to end here, on Murkhana.

He looked to the Force for guidance, and the Force restrained him.

A pained cry cut through the chaos, and the crowd of prisoners parted just long enough for Shryne to see Chatak down on her knees in front of Vader, her sword arm amputated at the elbow. Vader had simply beaten her into submission, and now, with a flick of his bloodshine blade, he decapitated her.

Sorrow lanced Shryne's heart.

Unreadable behind his mask, Vader gazed down at Chatak's slack body.

The clone troopers relaxed the cordon somewhat, allowing the prisoners to spread out. And the moment they did, Vader began to scan faces in the crowd.

There were techniques for concealing one's Force abilities, and Shryne employed them. He also prepared for the possibility that he could be found out. But Vader's black gaze moved right past him. Instead, it appeared to focus on Olee Starstone.

Vader took a step in her direction.

Now I have no choice, Shryne thought.

He was ready to lunge when a shock trooper called to Vader,

reporting that the commandos had been captured. Vader stopped in his tracks, glancing in Starstone's direction before turning to Salvo.

"Commander, see to it that the prisoners are loaded into the transport." Again, Vader scanned the crowd. "A less accommodating dungeon awaits them on Agon Nine."

Vader had no sooner turned his back to the prisoners than Shryne was in motion, edging, elbowing, shouldering his way through the crowd to Starstone, whose narrow shoulders heaved as she attempted to suppress her grief at her Master's death. Realizing Shryne was at her side, she turned into his comforting but brief embrace.

"Your Master is with the Force," he told her. "Rejoice for that."

She narrowed her eyes at him. "Why didn't you help her?"

"I thought we'd agreed to abandon our lightsabers."

She nodded. "I abandoned mine. But you could have done *something*."

"You're right. Maybe I should have challenged 'Lord Vader' to a fistfight." Shryne's nostrils flared. "Your Master reacted in anger and in vengeance. She would have been more use to us alive."

Starstone reacted as if she had been slapped. "That's a heartless remark."

"Don't confuse emotion with truth. Even if Bol Chatak had defeated Vader, she would have been killed."

Starstone gestured vaguely in Vader's direction. "But that monster would be *dead*."

Shryne held her accusing gaze. "Vengeance isn't becoming in a Jedi, Padawan. Your Master died for nothing."

The prisoners were on the move now, troopers herding them toward the boarding ramp of the military transport.

"Fall back," Shryne said into Starstone's ear.

The two of them slowed down, allowing other captives to maneuver around them.

"Who is Vader?" Starstone asked after a moment.

Shryne shook his head in ignorance. "That's something we might be able to learn if we can remain alive."

Starstone took her lower lip between her teeth. "I'm sorry about what I said, Master."

"Don't worry about that. Tell me how Bol Chatak was able to keep the lightsaber hidden from the guards."

"Force persuasion," Starstone said quietly. "At first we thought we might be able to escape, but my Master wanted to wait until she knew what had happened to you. We were locked away in a building and left to fend for ourselves. Very little food, and troopers everywhere. Even if my Master had used her lightsaber then, I don't know how far we would have gotten before troopers were all over us."

"Did you use Force persuasion at any time?"

She nodded. "That's how I was able to hold on to my Master's beacon transceiver."

Shryne eyed her in surprise. "You have it with you?"

"Master Chatak told me to keep it."

"Foolish," he said, then asked: "Were you able to learn anything about the war?"

"Nothing." Starstone let her misgiving show. "Did you hear Vader say that he would tell the 'Emperor'?"

"I heard him."

"Could the Senate have named Palpatine Emperor?"

"Seems like something the Senate would do."

"But Emperor of what Empire?"

"I've been asking myself that." He glanced at her. "I think the war has ended."

She thought about it for a moment. "Then why were the troopers ordered to kill us?"

"Jedi on Coruscant may have attempted to arrest Palpatine *before* he was promoted—or crowned, I suppose I should say."

"That's why we were ordered into hiding."

"Good theory—for a change."

They were closing on the lip of the boarding ramp now, almost at the end of the line. Accepting of the inevitable, most of the prisoners were demonstrating remarkable discipline, and many of the troopers were drifting away as a result. Two troopers were stationed at the top of the ramp, one to either side of the rectangular hatch, and three more were moving more or less alongside the two Jedi.

"Vader is a *Sith*, Master," Starstone said.

Shryne showed her a long-suffering look. "What do you know of the Sith?"

"Before Master Chatak chose me as her Padawan, I trained under Master Jocasta Nu in the Temple archives. For my review, I elected to be tested in Sith history."

"Congratulations. Then I don't need to remind you that a crimson blade doesn't guarantee that the wielder is a Sith, any more than every person strong in the Force is a Jedi. Asajj Ventress was a mere apprentice to Dooku, not a true Sith. A crimson blade can owe to nothing more than a synthetic power crystal. Then crimson is simply a color, like Master Windu's amethyst blade."

"Yes, but Jedi normally don't wield crimson blades," Starstone argued, "if only because of their *association* with the Sith. So even if Vader was nothing more than another apprentice of Count Dooku, why is he now serving Palpatine—*Emperor* Palpatine—as an executioner?"

"You're assuming too much," Shryne said. "Even if you're right, why is that so hard to believe, when Dooku did just the opposite—went from serving the Jedi order to serving the Sith?"

Starstone shook her head. "I suppose it shouldn't be hard to believe, Master. But it is."

He looked at her. "Here is what matters: Vader suspects that two Jedi are going to be aboard the prison transport. Eventually he'll identify us and we'll be killed, unless we take our chances, here and now."

"How, Master?"

"Drop back with me to the end of the line. I'm going to try something, and I hope the Force is with me. If I fail, we board as instructed. Understood?"

"Understood."

The last of the captive mercenaries and Koorivar moved past the two reluctant Jedi, up the ship's ramp and through the hatch. At the top Shryne made a passing motion with his hand to one of the troopers.

"There's no reason to detain us," he said.

The trooper gazed at him from inside the helmet. "There's no reason to detain them," he told his comrades.

"We're free to return to our homes."

"They're free to return to their homes."

"Everything's fine. It's time for you to board the ship."

"Everything's fine. It's time for us to board the ship."

Shryne and Starstone waited until the final trooper had filed inside; then they leapt from the ramp onto the clay field and concealed themselves behind one of the landing gear pods.

When an opportunity presented itself, they hurried from beneath the ship and escaped into the thick vegetation, heading for what remained of Murkhana City.

In his personal quarters aboard the *Exactor,* Vader examined the damage the Zabrak Jedi's lightsaber had done to his left forearm. After assuring himself that the pressure suit had self-sealed above the burn, he had peeled off the long glove and used a fine-point laser cutter to remove flaps of armorweave fabric that had been fused to the alloy beneath. The Jedi's lightsaber had sliced through the shielding that bulked the glove and had melted some of the artificial ligaments that allowed the hand to pronate. Permanent repairs would have to wait until he returned to Coruscant. In the meantime he would have to entrust his arm to the care of one of the Star Destroyer's med droids.

His own lightsaber rested within reach, but the longer he gazed at it, and at the blackened furrow in the alloy, the more disheartened he became. Had the hand been flesh and blood it would be shaking now. Only Dooku, Asajj Ventress, and Obi-Wan had been good enough with a blade to injure him, so how had an undistinguished Jedi Knight been able to do so?

With the loss of my limbs, have I also lost strength in the Force?

Vader recognized the voice of the one who posed the question as the specter of Anakin. Anakin telling him that he was not as powerful as he thought he was. The little slave boy, cowering because he was not the master of his fate. A mere accessory in the world, owned by another, passed over.

And now newly enslaved!

He lifted his masked face to the cabin's ceiling and growled in torment. Sidious's inept med droids had done this to him! Slowed his reflexes, burdened him with armor and padding. He relished having destroyed them.

Or . . . had Sidious deliberately engineered this prison?

Again, it was Anakin who asked, that small node of fear in Vader's heart.

Was this punishment for having failed at Mustafar? Or had Mustafar merely provided Sidious with an excuse to weaken him? Perhaps all along the promise of apprenticeship had been nothing more than a ploy, when, in fact, Sidious merely needed someone to command his army of stormtroopers.

Another *Grievous,* while Sidious reaped the real rewards of power, confident that his newest minion posed no threat to his rule.

Vader dwelled on it, fearing he would drive himself mad, and at last reached an even more disheartening conclusion. Grievous was *duped* into serving the Sith. But Sidious had sent Anakin to Mustafar for one reason only: to kill the members of the Separatist Council.

Padmé and Obi-Wan were the ones who had sentenced him to his black-suit prison.

Sentenced by his wife and his alleged best friend, their love for him warped by what they had perceived as betrayal. Obi-Wan, too brainwashed by the Jedi to recognize the power of the dark side; and Padmé, too enslaved to the Republic to understand that Palpatine's machinations and Anakin's defection to the Sith had been essential to bringing peace to the galaxy! Essential to placing power in the hands of those resourceful enough to use it properly, in order to save the galaxy's myriad species from themselves; to end the incompetence of the Senate; to dissolve the bloated, entitled Jedi order, whose Masters were blind to the decay they had fostered.

And yet their Chosen One had seen it; so why hadn't they followed his lead by embracing the dark side?

Because they were too set in their ways; too inflexible to adapt.

Vader mused.

Anakin Skywalker had died on Coruscant.

But the Chosen One had died on Mustafar.

Blistering rage, as seething as Mustafar's lava flows, welled up in him, liquefying self-pity. This was what he saw behind the mask's visual enhancers: bubbling lava, red heat, scorched flesh—

He had only wanted to save them! Padmé, from death; Obi-Wan, from ignorance. And in the end they had failed to recognize his power; to simply accede to him; to accept on faith that he knew what was best for them, for *everyone*!

Instead Padmé was dead and Obi-Wan was running for his life, as stripped of everything as Vader was. Without friends, family, purpose . . .

Clenching his right hand, he cursed the Force. What had it ever provided him but pain? Torturing him with foresight, with visions he was unable to prevent. Leading him to believe that he had great power when he was little more than its *servant*.

But no longer, Vader promised himself. The power of the dark side would render the *Force* subservient, minion rather than ally.

Extending his right arm, he took hold of the lightsaber and turned it about in his hand. Just three standard weeks old, assembled—as Sidious had wished—in the shadow of the moonlet-size terror weapon he was having constructed, it had now tasted first blood.

Sidious had provided the synthcrystal responsible for the crimson blade, along with his own lightsaber to serve as a model. Vader, though, had no fondness for antiques, and while he could appreciate the handiwork that had gone into fashioning the inlaid, gently curved hilt of Sidious's lightsaber, he prefered a weapon with more ballast. Determined to please his Master, he had tried to create something novel, but had ended up fashioning a black version of the lightsaber he had wielded for more than a decade, with a thick, ridged handgrip, high-output diatium power cell, dual-phase focusing crystal, and forward-mounted adjustment knobs. Down to the beveled emitter shroud, the hilt mimicked Anakin's.

But there was a problem.

His new hands were too large to duplicate the loose grip Anakin had favored, right hand wrapped not on the grip but around the crystal-housing cylinder, close to the blade itself. Vader's hands required that the grip be thicker and longer, and the result was an inelegant weapon, verging on ungainly.

Another cause of the injury to his left arm.

The Sith grew past the use of lightsabers, Sidious had told him. *But we continue to use them, if only to humiliate the Jedi.*

Vader yearned for the time when memories of Anakin would fade, like light absorbed by a black hole. Until that happened, his life-sustaining suit would be an ill fit. Even if it was well suited to the darkness in his invulnerable heart . . .

The comlink chimed.

"What is it, Commander Appo?"

"Lord Vader, I've been informed of a discrepancy in the prisoner count. Allowing for the Jedi you killed on Murkhana, two prisoners are unaccounted for."

"The others who survived Order Sixty-Six," Vader said.

"Shall I instruct Commander Salvo to initiate a search?"

"Not this time, Commander. I will handle it myself."

Down there?" Starstone said, halting at the head of a creepy stairway Shryne was already descending. The stairs led to the basement of a rambling building that had been left unscathed by the battle, and was typical of those that crowned the verdant hills south of Murkhana City. But she had a bad feeling about the stairway.

"Don't worry. This is only Cash's way of keeping out the riffraff."

"Doesn't appear to be slowing you down any," she said, following him into the stairway's dark well.

"Glad to see that your sense of humor has returned. You must have been the life of the dungeon."

And Shryne meant it, because he didn't want her dwelling on Bol Chatak's death. In the long hours it had taken them to get from the landing field to Cash Garrulan's headquarters Starstone seemed to have made peace with what had happened.

"How is it you know this person?" she asked over his shoulder.

"Garrulan's the reason the Council first sent me to Murkhana. He's a former Black Sun vigo. I came here to put him out of business, but he turned out to be one of our best sources of intelligence on Separatist activities in this quadrant. Years before Geonosis, Garrulan was warning us about the extent of Dooku's military buildup, but no one on the Council or in the Senate seemed to take the threat seriously."

"And in return for the intelligence you allowed Garrulan to remain in business."

"He's not a Hutt. He deals in, well, wholesale commodities."

"So not only are we on the run, we're turning to gangsters for help."

"Maybe you have a better idea?"

"No, Master, I don't."

"I didn't think so. And stop calling me 'Master.' Someone will either make the Jedi connection or get the impression you're my servant."

"Force forbid," Starstone muttered.

"I'm Roan. Plain and simple."

"I'll try to remember that—*Roan.*" She laughed at the sound of it. "I'm sorry, it just doesn't ring true."

"You'll get used to it."

At the foot of the stairs was an unadorned door. Shryne rapped his knuckles on the jamb, and to the droid eyeball that poked through a circular portal in response said something in what Starstone surmised was Koorivar. A moment later the door slid into its housing to reveal a muscular and extensively tattooed human male, cradling a DC-17 blaster rifle. Smiling at Shryne, he ushered them into a surprisingly opulent foyer.

"Still sneaking up on people, huh, Shryne?"

"Old habits."

The man nodded sagely, then gave Shryne and Starstone the once-over. "What's with the getups? You look like you've spent a month in a trash compactor."

"That would have been a step up," Starstone said.

Shryne peered into the back room. "Is he here, Jally?"

"He's here, but not for long. Just packing up what we couldn't move before the invasion. I'll tell him—"

"Let's make it a surprise."

Jally laughed shortly. "Oh, he'll be surprised, all right."

Shryne motioned for Starstone to follow him. On the far side of a beaded-curtain entryway a mixed group of humans, aliens, and labor droids were hauling packing crates into a spacious turbolift. Even more well appointed than the foyer, the room was cluttered with furniture, infostorage and communications devices, weapons, and more. The humanoid standing in the midst of it and dispensing orders to his underlings was a Twi'lek with fatty lekku and a prominent paunch. Sensing someone behind him, he turned and stared openmouthed at Shryne.

"I heard you'd been killed."

"Wishful thinking," Shryne said.

Cash Garrulan moved his head from side to side. "Perhaps." He extended his fat arms and shook both of Shryne's hands, then gestured to Shryne's filthy robe. "I love the new look."

"I got tired of wearing brown."

His gazed shifted. "Who's your new friend, Roan?"

"Olee," Shryne said without elaboration. He aimed a glance at the packing crates. "Clearance sale, Cash?"

"Let's just say that peace has been bad for business."

"Then it is over?" Shryne asked solemnly.

Garrulan inclined his large head. "You hadn't heard? It was all over the HoloNet, Roan."

"Olee and I have been out of touch."

"Apparently so." The Twi'lek turned to bark instructions at two of his employees, then motioned Shryne and Starstone into a small and tidy office, where Garrulan and Shryne sat down.

"Are you two in the market for blasters?" Garrulan asked. "I've got BlasTechs, Merr-Sonns, Tenloss DXs, you name it. And

I'll let you have them cheap." When Shryne shook his head no, Garrulan said: "What about comlinks? Vibroblades? Tatooine handwoven carpets—"

"Fill us in on how the war ended."

"How it ended?" Garrulan snapped his fat fingers. "Just like that. One moment Chancellor Palpatine has been kidnapped by General Grievous; the next, Dooku and Grievous are dead, the Jedi are traitors, the battle droids shut down, and we're one big happy galaxy again, more united than before—an Empire, no less. No formal surrender by the Confederacy of Independent Systems, no bogged-down Senate, no trade embargoes. And whatever the Emperor wants, the Emperor gets."

"Any comments from the members of the Separatist Council?"

"Not a peep. Although rumors abound. The Emperor had them put to death. They're still on the run. They're holed up in the Tingel Arm, in the company of Passel Argente's cronies . . ."

Shryne extended his arm to prevent Starstone from pacing. "Sit down," he said. "And stop chewing on your lip."

"Yes, Mas—Roan."

"I have to say," Garrulan went on, "I never would have guessed that the Jedi would be held accountable."

"For attempting to arrest Palpatine, you mean," Shryne said.

"No—for the *war.*" Garrulan stared at Shryne for a long moment. "You really don't know what's happened, do you? Maybe you two should have a drink."

Garrulan was halfway to his feet when Shryne said: "No drinks. Just tell us."

The Twi'lek looked genuinely dismayed. "I hate to be the bearer of bad news, Roan—especially to you, of all people—but the war has been laid at the feet of the Jedi. You manipulated the whole charade: vat-grown troopers on one side, Master Dooku on the other, all in an attempt to overthrow the Republic and place yourselves in charge. That's why Palpatine ordered your execution, and why the Jedi Temple was sacked."

Shryne and Starstone traded looks of dread.

Reading their expressions, the crime boss adopted a somber tone. "From what I understand, nearly all of the Jedi were killed—in the Temple, or on one world or another."

Shryne put his arm around Starstone's quaking shoulders. "Steady, kid," he said, as much to himself as to Olee.

The second beacon transmission, ordering all Jedi to go to ground, suddenly made sense. The Temple, defenseless in the absence of so many Jedi Knights, had been attacked and plundered; teachers and younglings slaughtered by Coruscant's shock troopers—stormtroopers, as they were now being called. How many Jedi had returned to the Core, Shryne wondered, only to be killed on arrival?

The order was finished. Not only was there nothing for Shryne and Starstone on Coruscant, there was nothing for them *anywhere*.

"For what it's worth," Garrulan said, "I don't believe a word of it. Palpatine is behind this. He has been from the start."

Starstone was shaking her head back and forth in disbelief. "It's not possible that every Jedi has been killed." She turned to Shryne. "Some Jedi weren't even with clone troopers, Master. Other commanders may have refused to obey High Command's execution orders."

"You're right," Shryne said, trying to sound comforting.

"We'll find other survivors."

"Sure we will."

"The order will rebuild itself."

"Absolutely."

Garrulan waited for them to fall silent before saying: "A lot of others have had the carpet yanked out from under them— even those of us at the bottom of the food chain." He laughed regretfully. "War has always been better for us than peace. At least the Corporate Alliance was willing to tolerate us for a share of the profits. But the regional governors the Emperor installed are out to cast us as the new enemy. And between you and me, I'd sooner deal with the Hutts."

Shryne studied him. "Where's that leave you, Cash?"

"Not on Murkhana, that much is certain. My Koorivar competitors in crime have my blessings, and my sympathy." Garrulan returned Shryne's look. "What about you, Roan? Any ideas?"

"Not right now," Shryne said.

"Perhaps you should consider working for me. I could use people with your special talents, especially now. I owe you a favor, in any case."

Starstone glared at him. "We haven't fallen so low as to—" she started to say when Shryne clamped his hand over her mouth.

"Maybe I will consider it. But first you've got to get us off Murkhana."

Garrulan showed Shryne the palms of his hands. "I don't owe you *that* much."

"Make it happen, and I'll owe *you.*"

Starstone looked from Shryne to Garrulan and back again. "Is this the way you were before the war? Cutting deals with anyone you pleased?"

"Don't mind her," Shryne said. "What about it, Cash?"

Garrulan sat back in his oversize chair. "Shouldn't be too hard to equip you with false identities and outwit the local garrison troopers."

"Normally, I'd agree," Shryne cut in. "But someone new has been added to the mix. A Lord Vader." When Garrulan didn't react to the name, he continued. "A sort of black-armored version of Grievous, only more dangerous, and apparently in charge of doing Palpatine's dirty work."

"Really," Garrulan said, clearly interested. "I haven't heard anything about him."

"You will," Shryne said. "And he could present a problem to our getting off this rock."

Garrulan stroked his lekku. "Well, then, I may have to rethink my offer—in the interest of avoiding Imperial complications. Or we may simply need to take additional precautions."

Black armorweave and feats of strength weren't the only things that distinguished Darth Vader from Anakin Skywalker. Where Anakin had had limited access to the Jedi Temple data room, Vader—even light-years from Coruscant—could peruse any data he wished, including archival records, ancient texts, and holocrons fashioned by past Masters. Thus was he able to learn the identities of the six Jedi who had been assigned to Murkhana at the end of the war; the four who had been killed—Masters Loorne and Bol Chatak, and two Jedi Knights—and the two who remained at large: Roan Shryne and Chatak's Padawan, Olee Starstone, now presumably in the care of the older and more experienced Shryne.

A petite young woman with dark curly hair and an engaging smile, Starstone until recently had seemed destined to become a Temple acolyte, having been selected by Master Joscasta Nu to serve as her apprentice in the archives room. Shortly before the start of the war, and in the interest of broadening her understanding of the rest of the galaxy, Starstone had asked to be allowed to do fieldwork, and it was during a brief visit to Eriadu that she had attracted the attention of Bol Chatak.

Chatak hadn't accepted her as a learner, however, until the war's second year, and only then at the behest of the High Council. With so many Jedi Knights participating in military campaigns on far-flung worlds, the Temple was no place for an able-bodied young Jedi who could be of greater service to the Republic as a warrior than as a librarian.

By all accounts Starstone had shown great promise. Candid, smart as a vibro-whip, and a brilliant researcher, she should probably have never been allowed to leave the Temple. Although she would have died there, a victim of Darth Vader's blade or the blaster bolts of Commander Appo's shock troopers.

Roan Shryne was another matter, and it was Shryne's holo-image Vader was circling, as data about the long-haired rogue Jedi Knight scrolled in a separate holoprojector field.

Shryne had originally been encountered on the Outer Rim world of Weytta, which happened to be in the same galactic neighborhood as Murkhana. His file contained passing references to an "incident" that had attended his procurement, but Vader hadn't been able to locate a detailed account of what had occurred.

At the Temple he had demonstrated an early talent for being able to sense the presence of the Force in others, and so had been encouraged to pursue a course that would have landed him in the Temple's Acquisition Division. When he was old enough to understand what acquisition entailed, however, he had steadfastly refused further tutelage, for reasons the records also didn't make clear.

The matter was brought before the High Council, which ultimately decided that Shryne should be allowed to find his own path rather than be pressed into service. The path Shryne eventually followed was the study of weapons of war, both ancient and modern, from which had grown an interest in the role played by crime syndicates in the spread of illegal arms.

Shryne's condemnation of the loopholes in Republic laws that had allowed the Trade Federation and similar groups to amass droid armies was what had brought him initially to Murkhana, shortly before the outbreak of the war. There he had had dealings with a crime boss of local repute, who had gradually become Shryne's informant on the Separatist military buildup. As a result, Shryne had made frequent journeys to Murkhana, even during the war, both as an undercover singleton and with a Padawan learner.

A couple of years older than Obi-Wan Kenobi, Shryne, like Obi-Wan, had been a peripheral member of what some Jedi had referred to as the "Old Guard"—a select group that had included Dooku, Qui-Gon Jinn, Sifo-Dyas, Mace Windu, and others, many of whom had been or would be named to sit on the High Council. But unlike Obi-Wan, Shryne had never been privy to Council discussions or decisions.

Interestingly, Shryne had been among those Jedi sent to Geonosis on the rescue mission that had wound up becoming the spark that ignited the war. During the battle there, his former Master, Nat-Sem, had been killed, along with Shryne's first Padawan.

Then, two and a half years into the war, Shryne lost a *second* learner at the Battle of Manari.

It was noted in the records that Shryne's fellow Jedi began to see a change in him after Manari, not only with regard to the war, but also with regard to the role the Jedi had been constrained to play—*manipulated* to play, Vader now understood—and many Jedi had expected him to leave the order, as several other Jedi Knights had done, either finding their way to the Separatist side or simply vanishing from sight.

Continuing to study the ghostly image of Shryne, Vader activated the cabin comm.

"What have you learned?" he asked.

"Still no sign of either Jedi, Lord Vader," Appo said. "But the Twi'lek crime boss has been located."

"Good work, Commander. He will prove to be all the lead we need."

Cash Garrulan was trying to figure out how he could unload eight hundred pairs of knockoff Neuro-Saav electrobinoculars in a hurry when Jally burst into his office to draw his attention to the security monitors.

In mounting annoyance, Garrulan watched twenty clone troopers climb from a wheeled transport and take up positions around the aged, sprawling structure that was his headquarters.

"Stormtroopers, no less," Garrulan said. "Probably sent by the regional governor to grab whatever they can before we depart." Pushing himself upright, he swept a stack of data cards from his desk into an open attaché case. "Give the troopers our munitions overstock. Don't make a stand, whatever you do. If things get rough, offer them more—the electrobinoculars, for instance." He grabbed his cloak and threw it over his shoulders. "I, however, am not about to suffer the indignity of an arrest. I'll take the back stairs and meet you at the docking bay."

"Good choice. We'll handle the clones."

Hurrying out of his office and through the stockroom, he pressed the release for the back door, only to find a towering figure filling the entryway. Dressed in black from outsize helmet to knee-high boots, the masked figure had his gloved fists planted on his hips in a way that spread his cloak wide.

"Going somewhere, *Vigo*?"

The slightly bass voice was enhanced by a vocoder of some sort and underscored by deep, rhythmical breathing, obviously regulated by the control box strapped to the figure's broad and armored chest.

Vader, Garrulan told himself. The Grievous-like monstrosity Shryne said had been "added to the mix."

"May I inquire who wishes to know?"

"You're free to ask," Vader said, but left it at that.

Garrulan tried to compose his thoughts. Vader and his stormtroopers hadn't come for handouts. They were hot on Shryne's trail. Still, he thought there might be a way to win Vader over.

"I'm not and never have been a Separatist. I just happen to be living on a Sep world."

"Your former allegiances don't concern me," Vader said.

Stretching out his right hand, Vader yanked Garrulan off his feet and carried him through the foyer and into the office, where he deposited him in a castered chair, which rolled backward and struck the wall.

"Make yourself comfortable," Vader said.

Garrulan rubbed the back of his head. "It's going to be like that, is it?"

"Yes. Like that."

Garrulan forced a breath. "Well, I'd offer you a chair, as well, but I don't think I have another one large enough."

The commander of Vader's troopers entered from the front room while Vader was taking in the office's lavish appointments.

"You've done well for yourself, Vigo."

"I get by," Garrulan said.

Vader stood over him. "I'm searching for two Jedi who escaped a transport that was to have delivered them to Agon Nine."

"Enchanting spot. But what makes you think—"

"Before you say another word," Vader cut him off, "be advised that I know that you and one of the Jedi go back a long way."

Garrulan immediately revised his plans. "You're talking about Roan Shryne and the girl."

"Then they did come here."

Garrulan nodded. "They asked for my help in leaving Mur-khana."

"What arrangements did you make?"

"Arrangements?" Garrulan gestured broadly to the room. "I didn't come by all this by accident. I was surprised even to see Shryne alive. I told them that I don't help traitors. In fact, I reported their visit to local authorities."

Vader turned to the stormtrooper commander, who nodded his head and moved into the packing room.

"You wouldn't lie to me, Vigo." Vader didn't make it a question.

"Not until I get to know you better."

The commander returned. "He did contact the local garrison commander, Lord Vader."

It was impossible to determine if Vader was at all satisfied. At last, Vader said: "Do you know where Shryne was headed from here?"

Garrulan shook his head. "He didn't say. But he knows Murkhana well, and I'm only one of his local contacts. But, of course, you already know that."

"I wanted to hear it from you," Vader said.

Garrulan smiled to himself. Vader had taken the bait. "Happy to oblige . . . Lord Vader."

"If you were Shryne, what would be your next move?"

"Well, now we're speculating, aren't we," Garrulan said, relaxing somewhat. "I mean, you appear to be asking my professional opinion on the matter."

"And if I am?"

"I only thought there might be something in it for me."

"What is it you want, Vigo? You already appear to have more than you need."

Garrulan adopted a more serious tone. "Material things," he

said in a dismissive manner. "I need you to put in a good word for me with the regional governor."

Vader nodded. "That can be arranged—providing that your professional opinion amounts to anything."

Garrulan leaned forward. "There's this Koorivar by the name of Bioto. Dabbles in smuggling and other ventures. Owns a very fast ship called the *Dead Ringer.*" He paused while the commander disappeared once more, undoubtedly to communicate with Space Traffic Control. "If *I* were in a hurry to get offworld with the least amount of problems, Bioto's the one I'd turn to."

"Lord Vader," the commander said suddenly, "STC reports that the *Dead Ringer* recently launched from Murkhana Landing. We have the projected flight path."

Vader turned, his cloak swirling. "Contact the *Exactor,* Commander. Order that the ship be moved into a position to inter-cept." Without further word he moved into the front room, only to stop short after a few long strides. "You're very clever, Vigo," he said, turning partway to Garrulan. "I won't forget this."

Garrulan inclined his head in a bow of respect. "Nor will I, Lord Vader."

A moment after Vader exited, Jally returned, blowing out his breath in relief.

"Not someone I'd feel good about crossing, boss."

"He does have a way," Garrulan said, getting to his feet. "Forget the rest of this junk. Have our ship readied for launch. We're done with Murkhana."

Wings folded above its fuselage and running lights powering down, Vader's shuttle entered the *Exactor*'s main docking bay and alighted on the lustrous deck. Nearby, and surrounded by clone troopers, sat the *Dead Ringer,* a somewhat boxy cargo transport, heavily armed with turbolaser cannons and outfitted with a state-of-the-art hyperdrive. Also under guard, the transport's mostly Koorivar crew of seven stood with their hands clasped atop their horned heads while troopers completed a search of the ship. Already off-loaded cargo containers were stacked outside the *Dead Ringer*'s starboard docking ring, awaiting scans.

Vader and Appo descended the shuttle's boarding ramp and strode over to where the crew had been gathered. A trooper indicated the captain, and Vader approached him.

"What is your cargo, Captain?"

The Koorivar glowered up at him. "I demand to speak to the officer in charge."

"You are speaking to him."

The captain blinked in surprise, but managed to hold on to

his angry tone. "I don't know who you are, but be forewarned that if my ship suffered any damage as a result of being targeted by your tractor beam, I will lodge a formal complaint with the regional governor."

"Duly noted, Captain," Vader said. "And I'm certain that the regional governor will take a keen interest in you once he learns that you are transporting proscribed weapons." He swung to the officer in charge of the troopers. "Escort them to the brig!"

"Lord Vader," Appo said while the crew was being whisked away, "security reports that two humans have been found in a secret compartment beneath the ship's galley."

Vader turned in the direction of the transport. "Interesting. Let's see what security has uncovered."

By the time Vader and Appo had moved around to the transport's port side, a detail of troopers was emerging from the ship, with two humans in custody. The man was tall and long-haired, and very protective of the young woman by his side. The pair were dressed alike in robes and headcloths typical of the mercenary brigade that had fought for the Separatists on Murkhana.

Their eyes widened on seeing Vader.

"They are unarmed, Lord Vader," one of the troopers announced.

"We stowed away without the captain's knowledge," the man said. "We're only trying to get to Ord Mantell."

"You're not stowaways," Vader said. "The captain was well paid to take you aboard his ship, and you have been promised payment, as well."

The girl began to quake in fear. "We didn't know we were doing anything illegal! We're not smugglers or criminals. I'm telling you the truth. We did it only for the credits!"

Vader appraised her. "I will consider sparing your lives if you tell me who hired you to carry out this deception."

The man firmed his lips, then swallowed hard and spoke. "Some of Cash Garrulan's goons."

Vader nodded. "Just as I suspected." He swung to Appo. "Commander, have the *Exactor*'s scanners detected anything yet?"

"Nothing yet."

"They will, soon enough."

Vader turned to the head of the trooper detail. "Lock these two away with the crew."

All color drained from the girl's face. "But you said—"

"That I would *consider* sparing you," Vader cut her off.

"Lord Vader, our sensors may have found something," Appo said suddenly. "The craft is only a CloakShape that launched from the outskirts of Murkhana City. But it is pursuing a course that will take it close to the *Exactor*'s previous position, and it is attempting to evade our scans."

"The Jedi are aboard that craft. Can we interdict from our present position, Commander?"

"No. The CloakShape is out of the range of our tractor beam."

Vader growled in displeasure. "We will need to remedy that. Is my starfighter prepared?"

"It's waiting in launching bay three."

"Assign two pilots to serve as my wingmates. Tell them to rendezvous with me in the launching bay." Vader shrugged his cloak behind his shoulders. "And, Commander, the vigo will be attempting to flee Murkhana. Don't bother capturing him. Target his vessel, and make certain that everyone on board is killed."

The CloakShape, a broad-winged craft with a transverse maneuvering fin, had been modified for spaceflight. The cockpit had been enlarged to accommodate pilot and copilot, and a rear-facing gunner's chair had been installed in the tail section. Shryne was forward; Starstone, aft; and in the pilot's seat was Brudi Gayn, a freelancer who made occasional runs for Cash Garrulan. A rangy, dark-haired human a few years older than Shryne, he spoke Basic with a strong Outer Rim accent.

Shryne had already decided that Gayn was the most casual pilot he had ever flown with. Any farther from the instrument panel and his chair would have been adjacent to Starstone's. His hold on the yoke was negligent. Yet he handled the craft masterfully, and didn't miss a trick.

"Well, they've got a good fix on us," he told Shryne and Starstone through their helmet comlinks. "Definitely going to have to upgrade our countermeasures at some point."

Hanging far to starboard, Vader's massive warship was just visible through the CloakShape's triangle of transparisteel viewport.

"I hate the look of these new mass-produced *Imperator*-class Destroyers," Gayn continued. "None of the artistry that went into the old Acclamators and Venators—even the Victory Twos." He shook his head in disappointment. "So goes elegance."

"Wars'll do that," Shryne said into his helmet comm.

The console issued an alert chime, and Gayn leaned forward a bit to study one of the display screens.

"Three bandits closing on our tail. Signatures ID them as two V-wings and what might be a modified Jedi Interceptor. This Vader character?"

"Good bet."

"Guess the Empire isn't any more choosy about commandeering Jedi hardware than it is Sep gear."

"Obviously, we're still serving Palpatine in our own way."

"Are you two aware that three starfighters are chasing us?" Starstone broke in.

"Thanks for the heads-up, sweetheart, but we're on it," Gayn said.

"Here's another heads-up for you, *flyboy*. They're gaining on us. Can't you coax any more speed out of this junker? It's about as lethargic as you are."

Gayn laughed shortly. "I suppose I could try jettisoning the tail gunner. That ought to lighten us up."

"First you might try letting some of the hot air out of yourself," Starstone fired back.

"Ouch," Gayn said. "Is she always like this, Shryne?"

"She was a librarian. You know how they can be."

"A librarian with the Force . . . Very dangerous combination." He chuckled to himself, then asked: "What happens to the Force now? Without the Jedi order, I mean?"

"I don't know," Shryne said. "Maybe it goes into hibernation."

Gayn rocked his head from side to side. "Well, here's a little something to show you that the Force isn't the only game in town."

Gazing in the direction indicated by Brudi Gayn's gloved right hand, Shryne saw a swift space skiff approaching the Cloak-Shape on an intercept course.

"Hope it's on our side."

Gayn laughed again. "It's our ticket out of here."

All but wedged into the cockpit of his black interceptor, Vader was in full command of the situation. He had the starfighter's inertial compensator dialed down, and felt revitalized by the experience of near weightlessness. In another life he had flown without helmet or flight suit, but those necessary accoutrements notwithstanding, he felt unburdened, released from gravity's reign.

This was not the craft Anakin Skywalker had piloted to

Mustafar, and the starfighter's socketed astromech droid had a black dome. Nor was this the craft he would have chosen to fly. But the interceptor would do, at least until Sienar Fleet Systems completed the starfighter that was being built to his specifications.

After all, despite the manifold losses he had endured, he remained the galaxy's best pilot.

The CloakShape's lead evaporated as he made adjustments and poured on speed. The Jedi's choice of escape vehicles was a reflection of their desperation, since the CloakShape lacked a hyperdrive of any sort. But Vader saw what they had in mind. They hoped to rendezvous with the Sorosuub skiff that even now was angling toward them. The plan would have worked, however, only if Vader had taken the Twi'lek crime boss at his word. And because he hadn't, the Jedi wouldn't have enough time to transfer to the larger ship. By then both the CloakShape and the skiff would be in proton torpedo range.

"Form up on me," he told the clone pilots in the escort V-wings, "and fire on my command. There's no need to take them alive."

"Lord Vader, we have identified the Sorosuub," one of the pilots returned. "The registry is Murkhana. The owner is Cash Garrulan."

"So," Vader said, mostly to himself. "It all ends here."

"But there is something else, Lord Vader. The CloakShape appears to be fitted with external booster-ring adapters."

Glancing at the display screen in which the CloakShape was centered, Vader issued a command to the astromech droid to display the skiff on a secondary screen.

Instantly he understood.

"All speed," he ordered the clone pilots. "This is not a rendezvous. Fire proton torpedoes the moment our targets are in range."

It was going to be close, Vader realized.

He enabled the interceptor's laser cannon. The CloakShape, too, was traveling flat-out, and was faster than he would have thought possible. The pilot was skilled and artful. At this distance it would be difficult to keep him in laser lock.

The astromech sent an update to the cockpit data screen, and at the same time the voice of one of the escort pilots issued through the console comlink.

"Lord Vader, the skiff is positioning a hyperdrive booster in the CloakShape's flight path."

The vision enhancers built into Vader's mask delivered a close-up of the red-and-white hypermatter ring. Quickly he thumbed the triggers on the steering yoke, and a hail of crimson bolts streaked from the interceptor's long-barreled laser cannons. But it was unlikely that the bolts would ever reach their targets, because the targets would be long gone.

Still calling all power from the ion drive, Vader watched the CloakShape slip neatly into the precisely positioned booster ring and make the jump to lightspeed. A split second later Cash Garrulan's skiff engaged its hyperdrive and disappeared.

Allowing the interceptor to power down, Vader gazed in defeat at the distant starfield.

He had much to do to make himself whole once more.

One of the V-wing pilots hailed him. "Escape vectors are being plotted, Lord Vader."

"Delete the calculations, pilot," he said. "If the Jedi are so determined to disappear, then let them."

PART III
IMPERIAL CENTER

You have my full assurance that I will not disband the Senate," the Emperor told the small audience he had summoned to his new chambers. "Furthermore, I don't want you to think of yourselves as mere accessories, ratifying legislation and facilitating the business of governing. I will seek your counsel in enacting laws that will serve the growth and integrity of our Empire."

He fell silent for a moment, then delivered his bombshell.

"The difference now is that when I have taken into account your contributions and those of my advisers, my judgment will be *final*. There will be no debates, no citations of constitutional precedent, no power of veto, no court proceedings or deferrals. My decrees will be issued simultaneously to our constituent worlds, and they will take effect immediately."

The Emperor leaned forward in the high-backed chair that was his temporary throne, but not so far forward that his disfigured face was placed in the light.

"Understand this: you no longer represent your homeworlds solely. Coruscant, Alderaan, Chandrila . . . All these and tens of thousands of worlds far removed from the Core are cells of the

Empire, and what affects one, affects us all. No disturbances will be tolerated. Interplanetary squabbles or threats of secession will meet with harsh reprisals. I have not led us through three years of galactic warfare to allow a resurgence of the old ways. The Republic is *extinct*."

Bail Organa barely managed to keep from squirming in his chair, as some of the Emperor's other invited guests were doing—Senators Mon Mothma and Garm Bel Iblis especially, in what almost amounted to overt defiance. But if the Emperor was taking notes, he was doing so without most of his guests being aware of it.

The Emperor's new chambers—the throne room, for all intents and purposes—occupied an upper floor of Coruscant's tallest building and, in design, more closely resembled what had been Palpatine's holding office below the Senate Rotunda than his former quarters in the Senate Office Building.

Divided into two levels by a short but wide staircase, the sanitized room was longer than it was wide, with large permaplas windows surrounding the upper tier. Flanking the burnished staircase were a pair of cup-shaped duty stations, in each of which stood a Red Guard—an Imperial Guard—with the Emperor's advisers seated behind them. The center of the gleaming dais was occupied by the throne, the back of which arched over Palpatine's head, placing him in perpetual shadow, as the cowl of his cloak did his sallow and deeply lined face. Recessed into the wide arms of the chair were modest control pads into which his slender fingers would enter occasional input.

The corridors of the Senate were rife with rumors that the Emperor had a second and more private suite, along with some sort of medical facility, in the very crown of the building.

"Your Majesty, if I may," the human Senator from Commenor said in a suitably deferential tone. "Perhaps you could shed some light on the matter of why the Jedi betrayed us. As you are undoubtedly aware, the HoloNet seems reluctant to provide details."

Well beyond the need to employ diplomacy or deception to achieve his ends, the Emperor made a derisive sound.

"The Order deserved all that it received for deluding us into believing that they served *me* in serving you. The complexity of their nefarious plan continues to astound me. Why they didn't attempt to kill me three years ago is something I will never understand. As if I could have stood against them. If it were not for the recent actions of my guards and our troopers, I would be dead."

Palpatine's off-color eyes clouded with hatred.

"In fact, the Jedi believed that they could oversee the galaxy better than we could, and they were willing to perpetuate a war simply to leave us defenseless and susceptible to their treason. Their vaunted Temple was a fort, their base of operations. They came to me with tales of having killed General Grievous—a *cyborg,* no less—and sought to arrest me because I refused to take them at their word that the fighting was suddenly over, the Separatists defeated.

"When I dispatched a legion of troopers to reason with them, they drew their lightsabers and the battle was met. We have the Grand Army to thank for our victory. Our noble commanders recognized the truth of the Jedi's treachery, and they executed my commands with vigor. The very fact that they did so, without question, without hesitation, suggests to me that our troopers had some inkling all along that the Jedi were manipulating events.

"After all these weeks, we still lack confirmation that Viceroy Gunray and his powerful allies are dead. That their battle droids and war machines stand motionless on hundreds of worlds we can take as a sign of their surrender. At the same time, however, we must focus our attention on solidifying the Empire world by world."

Palpatine sat back in his chair.

"The Jedi order is a lesson to us that we cannot permit any agency to become powerful enough to pose a threat to our designs, or to the freedoms we enjoy. That is why it is essential we increase and centralize our military, both to preserve the peace and to protect the Empire against inevitable attempts at insurrection. To that end I have already ordered the production of new classes of capital ships and starfighters, suitable for command by nonclone officers and crew, who themselves will be the product of Imperial academies, made up of candidates drawn from existing star system flight schools.

"No less important, our present army of clone troopers is aging at an accelerated rate, and will need to be supplemented, gradually replaced, by new batches of clones. I suspect that the Jedi had a hand in creating a short-lived army in full confidence that there would be no need for troopers once they had overthrown the Republic and instituted their theocracy based on the Force.

"But that is no longer a concern.

"By bringing the known worlds of the galaxy under one law, one language, the enlightened guidance of *one* individual, corruption of the sort that plagued the former Republic will never be able to take root, and the regional governors I have installed will prevent the growth of another Separatist movement."

When everyone in the room was satisfied that Palpatine was finished, the Senator from Rodia said: "Then species other than human need not fear discrimination or partiality?"

Palpatine spread his crooked, long-nailed hands in a placating gesture. "When have I ever shown myself to be intolerant of species differences? Yes, our army is human, I am human, and most of my advisers and military officers are human. But that is merely the result of circumstance."

*   *   *

"The war continues," Mon Mothma said to Bail.

Confident that they were beyond the reach of the building's assortment of eavesdropping devices and far enough from anyone who might be an Internal Security Bureau spy, Bail said: "Palpatine will use his disfigurement to distance himself further from the Senate. We may never get that close to him again."

Mon Mothma lowered her head in sadness as they continued to walk.

Coruscant was already beginning to adapt to its new title of Imperial Center. Red-patched stormtroopers were more present than they had been at the height of the war, and unfamiliar faces and uniformed personnel crowded the corridors of the building. Military officers, regional governors, security agents . . . the Emperor's new minions.

"When I look at that hideous face or survey the damage done to the Rotunda, I can't help thinking, *this* is what's become of the Republic and the Constitution," Mon Mothma said.

"He maintains he has no plans for disbanding the Senate or punishing the various hive species that supported the Confederacy—" Bail started.

"For the moment," Mon Mothma interruped. "Besides, the homeworlds of those species have already been punished. They are disaster areas."

"He can't afford to move against anyone just now," Bail went on. "Too many worlds are still too well armed. Yes, new clone troopers are being grown and new capital ships are coming off the line, but not fast enough for him to risk becoming enmeshed in another war."

She looked at him skeptically. "You're very confident all of a sudden, Bail. Or is that circumspection I hear?"

Bail asked himself the same question.

In the throne room, he had tried to puzzle out which among the Emperor's cabal of advisers, human or otherwise, were aware that Palpatine was a Sith Lord who had manipulated the entire war and eradicated his sworn enemies, the Jedi, as part of a plan to assume absolute power over the galaxy.

Certainly Mas Amedda knew, along with Sate Pestage, and possibly Sly Moore. Bail doubted that Armand Isard or any of Palpatine's military advisers knew. How would their knowing change things, in any case? To the few beings who knew or cared, the Sith were nothing more than a quasi-religious sect that had disappeared a millennium ago. What mattered was that Palpatine was now *Emperor* Palpatine, and that he enjoyed the staunch support of most of the Senate and the unwavering allegiance of the Grand Army.

Only Palpatine knew the full story of the war and its abrupt conclusion. But Bail knew a few things that Palpatine didn't; primarily, that Anakin Skywalker and Padmé Amidala's twin children had not died with her on the asteroid known as Polis Massa; and that in the twins Jedi Masters Obi-Wan Kenobi and Yoda were placing their trust for the eventual defeat of the dark side. Even now infant Luke was on Tatooine, in the care of his aunt and uncle, and being watched over by Obi-Wan. And infant Leia—Bail grinned just thinking about her—infant Leia was on Alderaan, probably in the arms of Bail's wife, Breha.

During Palpatine's brief abduction by General Grievous, Bail had promised Padmé that should anything untoward happen to her, he would do all he could to protect those close to her. The fact that Padmé was pregnant had been something of an open secret, but at the time Bail had been referring to Anakin, never realizing that events would draw him into a conspiracy with Obi-Wan and Yoda that would end with his assuming custody of Leia.

It had taken only days for Bail and Breha to come to love the child, though initially Bail had worried that they may have been entrusted with too great a challenge. Given their parentage, chances were high that the Skywalker twins would be powerful in the Force. What if Leia should show early signs of following in the dark footsteps of her father? Bail had wondered.

Yoda had eased his mind.

Anakin hadn't been *born* to the dark side, but had arrived there because of what he had experienced in his short life, instances of suffering, fear, anger, and hatred. Had Anakin been discovered early enough by the Jedi, those emotional states would never have surfaced. More important, Yoda appeared to have had a change of heart regarding the Temple as providing the best crucible for Force-sensitive beings. The steadfast embrace of a loving family would prove as good, if not better.

But the adoption of Leia was only one of Bail's concerns.

For weeks following Palpatine's decree that the Republic would henceforth be an Empire, he had been concerned for his—indeed, Alderaan's—safety. His name was prominent on the Petition of the Two Thousand, which had called for Palpatine to abrogate some of the emergency powers the Senate had granted him. Worse, Bail had been the first to arrive at the Jedi Temple after the slaughter there; and he had rescued Yoda from the Senate following the Jedi Master's fierce battle with Sidious in the Rotunda.

Holocams at the Temple or in the former Republic Plaza might easily have captured his speeder, and those images could have found their way to Palpatine or his security advisers. Word might have leaked that Bail was the person who had arranged for Padmé to be delivered to Naboo for the funeral. If Palpatine had been apprised of that fact, he might begin to wonder if Obi-Wan, having carried Padmé from distant Mustafar, had informed Bail about Palpatine's secret identity, or about the horrors committed on Coruscant by Anakin, renamed Darth Vader by the Sith Lord, whom Obi-Wan had left for dead on the volcanic world.

And then Palpatine might begin to wonder if Padmé's child, or children, had in fact died with her . . .

Bail and Mon Mothma hadn't seen each other since Padmé's funeral, and Mon Mothma knew nothing of the role Bail had played in the final days of the war. However, she had heard that

Bail and Breha had adopted a baby girl, and was eager to meet baby Leia.

The problem was, Mon Mothma was also eager to continue efforts to undermine Palpatine.

"There's talk in the Senate about building a palace to house Palpatine, his advisers, and the Imperial Guard," she said as they were nearing one of the repulsorlift landing platforms attached to what had become Palpatine's building.

Bail had heard the talk. "And statues," he said.

"Bail, the fact that Palpatine doesn't have full faith in his New Order makes him all the more dangerous." She came to a sudden halt when they reached the walkway to the landing platform and turned to him. "Every signatory of the Petition of the Two Thousand is suspect. Do you know that Fang Zar has fled Coruscant?"

"I do," Bail said, just managing to hold Mon Mothma's gaze.

"Clone army or no, Bail, I'm not going to abandon the fight. We have to act while we still can—while Sern Prime, Enisca, Kashyyyk, and other worlds are prepared to join us."

Bail worked his jaw. "It's *too* soon to act. We have to bide our time," he said, repeating what Padmé had told him in the Senate Rotunda on the day of Palpatine's historical announcement. "We have to place our trust in the future, and in the Force."

Mon Mothma adopted a skeptical look. "Right now there are members of the military who will side with us, who know that the Jedi *never* betrayed the Republic."

"What counts is that the clone troopers believe that the Jedi did betray the Republic," Bail said; then he lowered his voice to add: "We risk everything by placing ourselves in Palpatine's sights just now."

He kept to himself his concerns for Leia.

Mon Mothma didn't say another word until they stepped

onto the landing platform, where stormtroopers and a tall, star-tling figure in black were striding down the boarding ramp of a *Theta*-class shuttle that had just set down.

"Some Jedi must have survived the execution order," Mon Mothma said at last.

For reasons he couldn't fully understand, Bail's attention was riveted on the masked figure, who appeared to be in command of the clones, and who also appeared to glance with clear purpose in Bail's direction. The group passed close enough to Bail for him to hear one of the stormtroopers say: "The Emperor is waiting for you in the facility, Lord Vader."

Bail felt as if someone had let the air out of him.

His legs began to shake and he grabbed hold of the platform railing for support, somehow managing to keep apprehension from his voice when he said to Mon Mothma: "You're right. Some Jedi did survive."

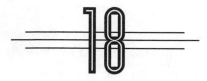

In the capable hands of gangly Brudi Gayn, the modified
CloakShape and the booster ring that had allowed it to enter
hyperspace completed three short jumps in as many hours,
emerging in a remote area of the Tion Cluster, far from any inhabited worlds. Waiting there, however, was a twenty-year-old
Corellian freighter as large as a *Tantive*-class corvette, but with a
circular command module.

Shryne counted five gun turrets; he already knew from Brudi
that the *Drunk Dancer* boasted sublights and a hyperdrive better
suited to a ship twice its size.

Brudi disengaged from the booster ring while they were still
some distance from the freighter, then in his own good time ma-
neuvered the CloakShape through a magnetic containment shield
in the *Drunk Dancer*'s starboard side, and into a spacious docking bay. On their landing disks sat a small drop ship and a swift,
split-winged Incom Relay, not much bigger than the CloakShape.

Brudi popped the canopy, and Shryne and Starstone climbed
down to the deck, slipping out of their helmets and flight suits at
the bottom of the ladder. The two Jedi were wearing the simple

spacer garments that Cash Garrulan had provided. Long accustomed to executing undercover missions, Shryne didn't feel out of place without a tunic and robe, even without a lightsaber. He knew better than to convince himself that, having escaped Murkhana, they were suddenly in the clear. Before and during the war he had had his share of close calls and times when he had been chased, but going into *hiding* was entirely new.

Even newer to Olee Starstone, who looked as if the events of the past couple of weeks, the past thirty-six hours especially, were finally beginning to catch up to her. He could tell from her uncertain gestures that Starstone, who had probably never worn anything but Temple robes or field outfits, was still adjusting to their new circumstances.

Shryne resisted the temptation to console her. Their future was cloudier than the gunship drop into Murkhana City had been, and the sooner Starstone learned to take responsibility for herself, the better.

Alerted to the CloakShape's arrival, several members of the *Drunk Dancer*'s crew were waiting in the docking bay. Shryne had encountered their type before, primarily in those outlying systems that had drifted into Count Dooku's embrace before the Separatist movement had been formalized as the Confederacy of Independent Systems. Just from the look of them Shryne could see that they lacked the discipline of crews belonging to Black Sun or the Hutt syndicates, despite Brudi's disclosure that the *Drunk Dancer* accepted occasional contracts from a variety of crime cartels.

Dressed in bits and pieces of apparel they had obviously obtained on dozens of worlds, they were a ragtag band of freelance smugglers, without star system or political affiliation, or bones to pick with anyone. Determined to maintain their autonomy, they had learned that smugglers didn't get rich by working for others.

In the docking bay Shryne and Starstone were introduced to

the *Drunk Dancer*'s first mate, Skeck Draggle, and the freighter's security chief, Archyr Beil. Both were humanoids as long-limbed as Brudi Gayn, with six-fingered hands and severe facial features that belied cheerful dispositions.

In the ship's main cabin space the two Jedi met Filli Bitters, a towheaded human slicer who took an immediate interest in Starstone, and the *Drunk Dancer*'s communications expert, Eyl Dix, whose hairless dark green head hosted two pair of curling antennae, in addition to a pair of sharp-tipped ears.

Before long everyone, including a couple of inquisitive droids, had gathered in the main cabin to hear Shryne and Starstone's account of their narrow escape from Murkhana. The fact that no one mentioned anything about the hunt for Jedi made Shryne uneasy, but not uneasy enough to pursue the point—at least not until he had a clearer sense of just where he and Starstone stood in the eyes of the smugglers.

"Cash asked that we bring you to Mossak," Skeck Draggle said after the Jedi had entertained everyone with details of the daring flight. "Mossak's just the other side of Felucia, and a decent hub for jumps into the Tingel Arm or just about anywhere up and down the Perlemian Trade Route." He looked directly at Shryne. "We, ah, normally don't offer free transport. But seeing how it was Cash who asked, and, uh, knowing what you folk have had to endure, we'll cover the costs."

"We appreciate that," Shryne said, sensing the sharp-featured Skeck had left something unstated.

"The Twi'lek fix you with new identichips?" Archyr asked, in what seemed to be actual concern.

Shryne nodded. "Good enough to fool agents at Murkhana STC, anyway."

"Then they'll pass muster on Mossak, as well," the lanky security chief said. "You shouldn't have too much trouble finding temporary work, if that's your plan." Archyr regarded Shryne. "You have any contacts you can trust?"

Shryne's eyebrows bobbed. "Good question."

When the assembled crew members fell into a separate conversation, Starstone moved close to Shryne. "Just what is our plan, Mas—"

Shryne's lifted finger stopped her midsentence. "No order; no ranks."

"You don't know that," she said, echoing his quiet tone. "You agreed that other Jedi probably survived."

"Listen, kid," he said, gazing at her for emphasis, "the Climbers of this galaxy are few and far between."

"Jedi could have survived by other means. It's our duty to locate them."

"Our *duty?*"

"To ourselves. To the Force."

Shryne took a deep breath. "How do you propose we do that?"

She gnawed at her lower lip while she considered it, then looked at him pointedly. "We have Master Chatak's beacon transceiver. If we could patch it into the *Drunk Dancer*'s communications suite, we could issue a Nine Thirteen code on encrypted frequencies."

Shryne laughed in spite of himself. "You know, that could actually work." He glanced at the crew members. "Still, I wouldn't get my hopes up if I were you."

She returned the smile. "But you're not me."

When Shryne turned back to the crew, he found Skeck gazing at him. "So I guess your scheme failed, huh?"

"Which scheme would that be, chief?"

Skeck glanced at his crewmates before answering. "Knocking Palpatine off his perch. Fighting the war the way it probably should have been fought all along."

"You've been misinformed," Shryne said flatly.

Skeck sat back in feigned nonchalance. "Really? We've all heard the recordings of what went on in Palpatine's chambers."

The other crew members nodded somberly.

"Don't get me wrong," the first mate continued before Shryne could respond. "I've nothing against any of you personally. But you have to admit, the way some of your people conducted themselves when Republic interests were at stake . . . The prestige you enjoyed. The wealth you amassed."

"I give the Jedi credit for trying," the slicer, Filli Bitters, chimed in. "But you should never have left yourselves so short-handed on Coruscant. Not with so many troopers garrisoned there."

Shryne laughed cheerlessly. "We were needed in the Outer Rim Sieges, you see."

"Don't you get it?" Eyl Dix said. "The Jedi were played." When she shrugged her narrow shoulders, her twin antennae bobbed. "That's what Cash thinks, anyway."

Skeck laughed in derision. "From where I sit, getting played is worse than losing."

"You'll be safe from Imperial reach on Mossak," Bitters said quickly, in an obvious attempt to be cheerful.

Sudden silence told Shryne that none of the *Drunk Dancer*'s crew was buying the slicer's optimism.

"I realize that we're already in your debt," he said at last, "but we've a proposition for you."

Skeck's green eyes widened in interest. "Lay it out. Let's see how it looks."

Shryne turned to Starstone. "Tell them."

She gestured to herself. "Me?"

"It was your idea, kid."

"Okay," Starstone began uncertainly. "Sure." She cleared her voice. "We're hoping to make contact with other Jedi who survived Palpatine's execution orders. We have a transceiver capable of transmitting on encrypted frequencies. Any Jedi who survived will be doing the same thing, or listening for special transmissions. The thing is, we'd need to use the *Drunk Dancer*'s communications suite."

"That's a little like whistling in the stellar wind, isn't it?" Dix said. "From what we hear, the clones got the drop on all of you."

"*Almost* all of us," Starstone said.

Bitters was rocking his head back and forth in uncertainty, but Shryne could tell that the white-haired computer expert was excited by the idea—and perhaps grateful for a chance to win points with Olee. Regardless, Filli said: "Could be dangerous. The Empire might be on to those frequencies by now."

"Not if as many of us are dead as all of you seem to think," Shryne countered.

Bitters, Dix, and Archyr waited for Skeck to speak.

"Well, of course, we'd have to get the captain to agree," he said at last. "Anyway, I'm still waiting to hear the rest of the proposition—the part that makes it worth *our* while."

Everyone looked at Shryne.

"The Jedi have means of accessing emergency funds," he said, with a covert motion of his hand. "You don't have to worry about being paid for your services."

Skeck nodded, satisfied. "Then we don't have to worry about being paid for our services."

While Starstone was staring at Shryne in appalled disbelief and the crew members were talking among themselves about how best to slave the Jedi beacon transceiver to the communications suite, Brudi Gayn and a tall human woman entered the cabin space from the direction of the *Drunk Dancer*'s bulbous cockpit. The woman's black hair was shot through with gray, and her age showed there and in her face more than in the way she moved.

"Captain," Skeck said, coming to his feet, but she ignored him, her gray eyes fixed on Shryne.

"*Roan* Shryne?" she said.

Shryne looked up at her. "Last time I checked."

She forced an exhale and shook her head in incredulity. "Stars' end, it really is you." She sat down opposite Shryne, without once taking her eyes off him. "You're the image of Jen."

Baffled, Shryne said: "Do I know you?"

She nodded and laughed. "On a cellular level, at any rate." She touched herself on the chest. "I gave birth to you. I'm your *mother*, Jedi."

The Emperor's medical rehabilitation laboratory occupied the crown of Coruscant's tallest building. A room of modest size, the laboratory's antechamber closely resembled his former chambers in the Senate Office Building, and featured a semicircle of padded couch, three swivel chairs with shell-shaped backs, and a trio of squat holoprojectors shaped like truncated cones.

Palpatine sat in the center chair, his hands on his knees, the lights of Coruscant blazing behind him through a long arc of fixed windows. The cowl of his heavy robe was lowered, and the blinking telltales of an array of devices and control panels lit his deeply creased face, the face he kept concealed from his advisers and Senatorial guests.

For here he was not simply Emperor Palpatine, he was Darth Sidious, Dark Lord of the Sith.

On the far side of thick panels of transparisteel that separated the antechamber from a rib-walled operating theater, Vader sat on the edge of the surgical table on which he had been recalled to life and transformed. His flaring black helmet had been lifted from his head by servos that extended from the laboratory's ceiling, revealing the pasty complexion of his synthflesh face and the raised wounds on his head that might never fully heal.

The medical droids responsible for repairing what had remained of Vader's amputated limbs and incinerated body, some of which had observed and participated in the cyborg transformation of General Grievous on Geonosis a decade earlier, had been reduced to scrap by a scream that had torn from Vader's scorched throat on his learning of his wife's death. Now a 2-1B droid responding to Vader's voiced instruction was tending to an injury to Vader's left-arm prosthesis, the cause of which he had yet to explain.

"The last time you were in this facility, you were in no condition to supervise your own convalescence, Lord Vader," Sidious said, his words transmitted to the pressurized laboratory by the antechamber's sensitive enunciators.

"And I will remain ward of myself from this point forward," Vader said through the intercom system.

"Ward of yourself," Sidious repeated in an exacting tone.

"When it comes to overseeing modifications of this . . . shell, Master," Vader clarified.

"Ah. As it should be."

The humaniform 2-1B was in the midst of executing Vader's instructions when sparks geysered from Vader's left forearm, and blue electricity began to gambol across his chest. With an infuriated growl, Vader lifted the injured arm, hurling the med droid halfway across the laboratory.

"Useless machine!" he shouted. "Useless! Useless!"

Sidious watched his apprentice with rising concern.

"What is troubling you, my son? I'm aware of the suit's limitations, and of the exasperation you must be experiencing. But anger is wasted on the droid. You must reserve your rage for times when you can profit from it." He appraised Vader again. "I think I begin to understand the cause of your frustration . . .

Your rage owes little to the suit or the droid's ineptitude. Something disturbing occurred on Murkhana. Some occurrence you have elected to keep from me. For your good or mine? I wonder."

Vader took a long moment to reply. "Master, I found the three Jedi who escaped Order Sixty-Six."

"What of it?"

"The damage to my arm was done by one of them, though she is now dead, by my blade."

"And the other two?"

"They eluded me." Vader lifted his scarred face to regard Sidious. "But they wouldn't have if this suit didn't restrict me to the point of immobility! If the Star Destroyer you placed at my command was properly equipped! If Sienar had completed work on the starfighter I designed!"

Sidious waited until Vader was finished, then stood up and walked to within a meter of the room's transparent panels. "So, my young apprentice, two Jedi slip through your grasp and you scatter the blame like leaves blown about by a storm."

"Master, if you had been there—"

"Keep still," Sidious interrupted, "before you damage yourself all the more." He gave Vader a moment to compose himself. "First, let me reiterate that the Jedi mean *nothing* to us. In having survived, Yoda and Obi-Wan aren't exceptions to the rule. I'm certain that dozens of Jedi escaped with their lives, and in due time you will have the pleasure of killing many of them. But of greater import is the fact that their order has been crushed. *Finished,* Lord Vader. Do I make myself clear?"

"Yes, Master," Vader muttered.

"In burying their heads in the sands and snows of remote worlds, the surviving Jedi *humble* themselves before the Sith. So let them: let them atone for one thousand years of arrogance and self-absorption."

Sidious watched Vader, displeased.

"Once more your thoughts betray you. I see that you are not yet fully convinced."

Glancing at him, Vader gestured to his face and black-cloaked body, then gestured in similar fashion to Sidious. "Look at us. Are these the faces of victory?"

Sidious was careful to keep himself from becoming too angry, or too sickened by his pupil's self-pity.

"We are not this crude stuff, Lord Vader. Have you not heard that before?"

"Yes," Vader said. "Yes, I've heard it before. Too often."

"But from me you will learn the *truth* of it."

Vader lifted his face. "In the same way you told me the truth about being able to save Padmé?"

Sidious was not taken aback. For the past month he had been expecting to hear just such an accusation from Vader. "I had nothing to do with Padmé Amidala's death. She died as a result of your anger at her betrayal, my young apprentice."

Vader looked at the floor. "You're right, Master. I brought about the very thing I feared for her. I'm to blame."

Sidious adopted a more compassionate tone. "Sometimes the Force has other plans for us, my son. Fortunately I arrived at Mustafar in time to save you."

"Save me," Vader said without emotion. "Yes, yes, of course you did, Master. And I suppose I should be grateful." He got up from the table and walked to the panel to place himself opposite Sidious. "But what good is power without reward? What good is power without joy?"

Sidious didn't move. "Eventually you will come to see that power *is* joy. The path to the dark side is not without terrible risk, but it is the only path worth following. It matters not how we *appear*, in any case, or who is sacrificed along the way. We have won, and the galaxy is ours."

Vader's eyes searched Sidious's face. "Did you promise as much to Count Dooku?"

Sidious bared his teeth, but only briefly. "Darth Tyranus knew what he risked, Lord Vader. If he had been stronger in the dark side, *you* would be dead, and he would be my right hand."

"And if you should encounter someone stronger than I am?"

Sidious almost smiled. "There is none, my son, even though your body has been crippled. This is your *destiny*. We have seen to that. Together we are unconquerable."

"I wasn't strong enough to defeat Obi-Wan," Vader said.

Sidious had had enough.

"No, you weren't," he said. "So just imagine what Yoda might have done to you." He flung his words with brutal honesty. "Obi-Wan triumphed because he went to Mustafar with a single intention in mind: to kill Darth Vader. If the Jedi order had showed such resolute intention, if it had remained focused on what needed to be done rather than on fears of the dark side, it might have proved more difficult to topple and eradicate. You and I might have lost *everything*. Do you understand?"

Vader looked at him, breathing deeply. "Then I suppose I should be grateful for what little I have been able to hold on to."

"Yes," Sidious said curtly. "You should."

The crew of the *Drunk Dancer* was every bit as surprised by their captain's revelations as Shryne was. For most of them, though, the disclosure only explained why they had come to place so much trust in Jula's judgment and intuition.

Shryne and the woman who claimed to be his mother were sitting in a dark alcove off the main cabin, untouched meals between them and blue-tinted holoimages to one side, allegedly showing a nine-month-old Roan taking his first steps outside the modest dwelling that had been his home for just over three years. He had never enjoyed seeing likenesses of himself, and the images merely served to increase his embarrassment over the entire situation.

Master Nat-Sem had once told him that vanity was the cause of such uneasiness, and had ordered Shryne to spend a full week staring at his own reflection in a mirror, in an effort to teach Shryne that what he saw was no more who he was than a map of a place could be considered the territory itself.

Clear across the cabin, Eyl Dix, Filli Bitters, and Starstone were huddled around the ship's communications suite, into

which Filli had managed to patch Bol Chatak's beacon transceiver, and the *Drunk Dancer* was now transmitting on frequencies Jedi would scan in case of trouble, or if attempting to
establish contact with other Jedi. The talented young slicer,
whose face was nearly as colorless as his short spiked hair, was still
trying his best to engage Starstone's interest, but she was either
ignoring his attempts or simply too focused on awaiting a return
signal to be aware of them.

With her dark complexion and black curls, and Bitters's towheaded brilliance, they made for an interesting-looking couple,
and Shryne wondered if perhaps Starstone hadn't unwittingly
stumbled on a new path to follow.

Elsewhere in the main cabin, Brudi, Archyr, and Skeck were
playing cards at a circular table, labor droids whirring in to clean
up their dropped snacks and spilled drinks. All in all it was a
pleasant setup, Shryne decided. Almost like a family living room,
with the kids playing games, the adults watching competition
sports on the HoloNet, and the hired help in the kitchen preparing a big lunch for everyone.

As a Jedi, he had scant familiarity with any of it. The Temple
had been more like a huge dormitory, and one was constantly
aware of being in service to a cause greater than one's family or
oneself. Frequently there were classes or briefings to attend,
chores that needed completing as part of one's training, and long
meditative or lightsaber combat sessions with Masters or peers,
except for those rare days when one was allowed to wander about
Coruscant, sampling bits of a different reality.

In some ways the Jedi *had* led a life of royalty.

The order had been wealthy, privileged, entitled.

And that was why we didn't see it coming, Shryne thought.

Why so many of the Jedi had turned a blind eye to the
trap Palpatine had been setting. Because they had refused to accept that such entitlement could ever come to an end—could all

come crashing down around them. And yet even those who hadn't denied the possibility would never have believed that thousands of Jedi could be killed in one fell swoop, or that the order could be ended with one bold stroke, as if pierced through the heart.

We were played, he told himself.

And Skeck was right: knowing that you had been played was worse than losing.

But Roan Shryne—by a quirk of fate, circumstance, the will of the Force—had survived, been brought face-to-face with his mother, and was now at a loss as to what to make of it.

He had seen his share of mothers interacting with their children, and he understood what a child was *supposed* to feel, how he or she was *supposed* to behave. But all he felt toward the woman opposite him was an unspecific connection in the Force.

Shryne wasn't the first Jedi to have inadvertently encountered a blood relative. Over the years he had heard stories about Padawans, Jedi Knights, even Masters running into parents, siblings, cousins . . .

Unfortunately, he had never heard how any of the stories ended.

"I never wanted you to be found," Jula said when she had deactivated the holoprojector. "To this day I don't understand how your father could hand you over to the Jedi. When I learned he had contacted the Temple, and that Jedi agents were coming for you, I tried to talk your father into hiding you."

"That rarely happens," Shryne said. "Most Force-sensitive infants were voluntarily surrendered to the Temple."

"Really? Well, it happened to me."

Shryne regarded her with his eyes, and through the Force.

"Who do you think you inherited your abilities from?" Jula asked.

"Awareness does not always run in families." He smiled

lightly. "But I sensed the Force in you the moment you entered the cabin."

"And I knew you did."

Shryne exhaled and sat back in the chair. "So your own parents chose to keep you from joining the order."

She nodded. "And I'm grateful they did. I would never have been able to abide by the rules. And I never wanted you to have to abide by them, Roan." She considered something. "I have a confession to make: all my life I've known that I would meet you somewhere along the way. I think that's partly the reason I took up piloting after your father and I separated. In the hope of, well, bumping into you. It's because of our Force connection that I brought the *Dancer* to this sector. I *sensed* you, Roan."

For many Jedi, luck and coincidence didn't exist, but Shryne wasn't one of them. "What happened between you and your husband?" he asked finally.

Jula laughed shortly. "*You,* really. Jen, your father, simply didn't agree with me about the need to protect you—to hide you, I mean. We argued bitterly about it, but he was a true believer. He felt that I should never have been hidden; that I'd basically turned my back on what would ultimately have been a more fulfilling life. And, of course, that you would profit from being raised in the Temple.

"Jen had the strength—I guess you could call it strength—to forget about you after he handed you over to the Jedi. No, that's too harsh. He had confidence enough in his decision to believe that he had made the right choice, and that you were doing well." Jula shook her head. "I could never get there. I missed you. It broke my heart to see you leave, and know that I might never see you again. That's what eventually ruined us."

Shryne mulled it over. "Jen sounds like he was Jedi without the title."

"How so?"

"Because he understood that you have to accept what destiny sets in front of you. That you have to pick and choose your battles."

Her gray eyes searched his face. "What does that make me, Roan?"

"A victim of attachment."

She smiled weakly. "You know what? I can live with that."

Shryne glanced away, catching Starstone's look before she quickly turned back to the communications console. She was eavesdropping on their conversation, worrying that the efforts she had made to keep Shryne on the proper path were suddenly being undermined. Shryne could feel her wanting to tear herself away from the communications suite before it was too late, and Shryne was lost to the cause.

He looked at Jula once more. "I'll provide a confession in exchange for yours: I refused an assignment in the Temple's Acquisition Division. I'm still not sure why, except that I'd persuaded myself on some level that I didn't like the idea of kids being separated from their families." He paused briefly. "But that was a long time ago."

She took his meaning. "Long ago in years, maybe. But I'm guessing you still feel like you missed out."

"On what?"

"*Life*, Roan. Desire, romance, love, laughter, *fun*—all the things you've been denied. And children. How about that? A Force-sensitive child you could nurture and learn from."

He made his eyes dull. "I'm not sure how Force-sensitive a child of mine would be."

"Why is that?"

He gave his head a sharp shake. "Nothing."

Jula was willing to let the point drop, but she had more to say.

"Roan, just hear me out. From everything I've heard, the

Jedi order has been vanquished. Probably ninety-nine percent of the Jedi are dead. So it's not like you have a choice. Like it or not, you're in the real world. Which means you could get to meet and know your father, your uncles and aunts. All of them still talk about you. Having a Jedi in the family is a pretty big deal in some places. Or at least it was." She fell briefly silent. "When I heard what happened, I thought for a moment . . ." She laughed to push some memory aside. "I don't want to get into all that. Someday you can tell me the truth about what happened on Coruscant, and why Palpatine betrayed you."

Shryne narrowed his eyes. "If we ever learn the truth."

From the comm suite came a cheer of excitement, and a moment later Starstone was hurrying across the cabin toward them.

"Roan, we got a hit! From a group of Jedi on the run." She turned to Jula. "Captain, with your permission we'd like to arrange a rendezvous with their ship."

Filli appeared at Starstone's side to elaborate. "We'd have to divert from our course to Mossak. But the rendezvous wouldn't take us too far out of the way."

Shryne felt Jula's eyes on him. "I won't try to convince you," he said. "It's your ship, and I'm sure you have important business elsewhere."

Jula took a long moment to respond. "I'll tell you why I'm going to do it: just to have more time with you. With luck, enough time to persuade you to get to know us, and ultimately to stay with us." She cut her eyes to Starstone. "There's room for you, too, Olee."

Starstone blinked in indignation. "Room for me? I'm not about to abandon my Jedi oath to go gallivanting around the galaxy with a band of smugglers. Especially now that I know that other Jedi survived." She looked hard at Shryne. "We have contact, Roan. You can't be taking her offer seriously?"

Shryne laughed out loud. "Normally Padawans don't talk

like this to Masters," he said to Jula. "You can see how fast things have changed."

Starstone folded her arms across her chest. "You said I shouldn't call you 'Master.' "

"That doesn't mean you shouldn't respect your elders."

"I do respect you," she said. "It's your decisions I don't respect."

"Many Jedi have left the Temple to lead regular lives," Jula thought to point out. "Some have gotten married and had children."

"No," Starstone said, shaking her head back and forth. "Maybe apprentices, but not Jedi Knights."

"That can't be true," Jula said.

"It is true," Starstone said firmly, before Shryne could say a word. "Only twenty Jedi have ever left the order."

"Don't try to argue with her," Shryne advised Jula. "She spent half her life in the Temple library polishing the busts of those Lost Twenty."

Starstone shot him a gimlet look. "Don't even think about being number twenty-one."

Shryne let his sudden seriousness show. "Despite your claims for me, I'm not a Master, and there is no order. How many times are you going to have to hear it before you accept the truth?"

She compressed her lips. "That has no bearing on being a *Jedi*. And you can't be a Jedi and serve the Force if your attention is divided or if you're emotionally involved with others. Love leads to attachment; attachment to greed."

So much for Olee and Filli Bitters, Shryne thought.

At the same time, Jula was regarding Starstone as if the young Jedi had lost her mind. "They certainly did a bang-up job on you, didn't they." She held Starstone's gaze. "Olee, love is about all we have left."

Instead of reacting to the remark, Starstone said: "Are you going to help us or not?"

"I already said I would." Standing up, Jula gave Shryne a look. "But just so we understand each other, Roan? You and I both know that you don't have access to any 'secret funds.' You make one more attempt at using Force persuasion on any members of my crew, and I may forget that I'm your mother."

Darth Sidious had had most of his beloved Sith statues and ancient bas-reliefs removed from his ruined chambers in the Senate Office Building, where four Jedi had lost their lives and one had been converted to the dark side. Relocated to the throne room, the statues had been placed on the dais, the scuptures mounted on the long walls.

Swiveling his throne, Sidious gazed at them now.

As some Jedi had feared from the start, Anakin had been ripe for conversion when Qui-Gon Jinn had first brought him to the Temple, and for well over a decade all of Sidious's plans for the boy had unfolded without incident. But even Sidious hadn't foreseen Anakin's defeat by Obi-Wan Kenobi on Mustafar. Anakin had still been between worlds then, and vulnerable. The failure to defeat his former Master had worked to prolong that vulnerability.

Sidious recalled the desperate return trip to Coruscant; recalled using all his powers, and all the potions and devices contained in his medkit, to minister to Anakin's hopelessly blistered body and truncated limbs.

He recalled thinking: *What if Anakin should die?*

How many years would he have had to search for an apprentice even half as powerful in the Force, let alone one created by the Force itself to restore balance, by allowing the dark side to percolate fully to the surface after a millennium of being stifled?

None would be found.

Sidious would have had to discover a way to compel midichlorians to do his bidding, and bring into being one as powerful as Anakin. As it was, Sidious and a host of medical droids had merely restored Anakin to life, which—while no small feat—was a far cry from returning someone from death. For thousands of years, the ability to survive death had been pursued by Sith and Jedi alike, and no one had been successful at discovering the secret. Beings had been saved from dying, but no one had cheated death. The most powerful of the ancient Sith Lords had known the secret, but it had been lost or, rather, misplaced. Now that the galaxy was his to rule, there was nothing to prevent Sidious, too, from unlocking that mystery.

Then he and his crippled apprentice might hold sway over the galaxy for ten thousand years, and live *eternally*.

If they didn't kill each other first.

In large part because Padmé Amidala had died.

Sidious had deliberately brought her and Anakin together three years earlier, both to rid the Senate of her vote against the Military Creation Act and to put temptation in Anakin's path. Following the murder of Anakin's mother, Anakin had secretly married Padmé. When he had learned of the marriage, Sidious knew for certain that Anakin's pathological attachment to her would eventually supply the means for completing his conversion to the dark side.

Anakin's fears for her, in actuality and in visions—and especially after Padmé had become pregnant—had been heightened by keeping him far from her. Then it simply had been a matter of unmasking the Jedi for the hypocrites that they were, sacrificing Dooku to Anakin's rage, and promising Anakin that Padmé could be saved from death . . .

The latter, an exaggeration necessary for Anakin's turn from what the Jedi called right thinking; for opening his eyes to his true calling. But such was the way of the Force. It provided opportunities, and one needed only to be ready to seize them.

Not for the first time Sidious wondered what might have happened had Anakin not killed Padmé on Mustafar. For all she loved him, she never would have understood or forgiven Anakin's action at the Jedi Temple. In fact, that was one of the reasons Sidious had sent him there. Clone troopers could have dealt with the instructors and younglings, but Anakin's presence was essential in order to cement his allegiance to the Sith, and, more important, to seal Padmé's fate. Even if she had survived Mustafar, their love would have died—Padmé might even have lost the will to live—and their child would have become Sidious's and Vader's to raise.

Might that child have been the first member of a new Sith order of thousands or millions? Hardly. The idea of a Sith order was a corruption of the intent of the ancient Dark Lords. Fortunately, Darth Bane had understood that, and had insisted that only in rare instances should there exist more than two lords, Master and apprentice, at any given time.

But *two* were necessary for the perpetuation of the Sith order.

And so it fell to Sidious to *complete* Vader's convalescence.

As Emperor Palpatine, he had no need to reveal his Sith training and mastery to anyone, and for the moment Vader was his crimson blade. Let the galaxy think what it would of Vader: fallen Jedi, surfaced Sith, political enforcer . . . It scarcely mattered, since *fear* would ultimately bring and keep everyone in line.

Yes, Vader was not precisely what he had bargained for.

Vader's legs and arms were artificial, and he would never be able to summon lightning or leap about like the Jedi had been fond of doing. His dark side training was just beginning. But Sith power resided not in the flesh but in the *will*. Self-restraint was praised by the Jedi only because they didn't know the power of the dark side. Vader's real weaknesses were psychological rather than physical, and for Vader to overcome them he would need to be driven deeper into himself, to confront all his choices and his disappointments.

Powered by treachery, the Sith Master–apprentice relationship was always a dangerous game. Trust was encouraged even while being sabotaged; loyalty was demanded even while betrayal was prized; suspicion was nourished even while honesty was praised.

In some sense, it was survival of the fittest.

Fundamental to Vader's growth was the desire to overthrow his Master.

Had Vader killed Obi-Wan on Mustafar, he might have attempted to kill Sidious, as well. In fact, Sidious would have been surprised if Anakin *hadn't* made an attempt. Now, however, incapable of so much as breathing on his own, Vader could not rise to the challenge, and Sidious understood that he would need to do everything in his power to shake Vader out of his despair, and reawaken the incredible power within him.

Even at Sidious's own peril . . .

Alert to a mild disturbance in the Force, he swung toward the throne room holoprojector a moment before a half-life-size image of Mas Amedda resolved from thin air.

"My lord, I apologize for intruding on your meditation," the Chagrian said, "but an encrypted Jedi code transmission has been picked up and is being monitored in the Tion Cluster."

"More survivors of Order Sixty-Six," Sidious said.

"Apparently so, my Lord. Shall I summon Lord Vader?"

Sidious considered it. Would additional Jedi deaths be enough to heal Vader's wounds? Perhaps, perhaps not.

But not yet, in any case.

"No," he said finally. "I have need of Lord Vader on Coruscant."

"Right . . . *now*," Shryne overheard Filli tell Starstone.

The communications suite chimed and Filli, Starstone, and Eyl Dix leaned in to study a display screen. "The Jedi ship has reverted to realspace," Dix said, almost in awe, antennae twitching.

Filli stood to his full height, stretching his arms over his head in theatrical nonchalance and beaming. "I love it when I'm right."

Starstone glanced up at him. "I can tell that about you."

His frowned dramatically. "No put-downs in the main cabin."

"It's not a criticism," Starstone was quick to explain. "What I mean is that I was the same way at the Jedi Temple library. Someone would come in looking for data, and I would almost always be able to direct them right to the files they needed. I just had a sense for it." Her voice broke momentarily; then she continued in a confident tone. "I think you should be proud of doing what you do best, instead of hiding behind false humility, or"—she gave Shryne a furtive glance—"letting disillusion convince you that you need a new life."

Shryne got out of his seat. "I'll take that as my cue to leave."

A droid directed him to the corridor that led to the *Drunk Dancer*'s ample cockpit, where Jula and Brudi Gayn sat in adjacent chairs behind a shimmering sweep of instrument console. A crescent of red planet hung in the forward viewport, and local space was strewn with battle debris.

Shryne rapped his knuckles against the cockpit's retracted hatch. "Permission to enter, Captain?"

Jula glanced at him over her shoulder. "Only if you promise not to tell me how to pilot."

"I'll keep my mouth shut."

She patted the cushion of the acceleration chair behind hers. "Then take a load off."

Brudi gestured to a point of reflected light far to port. "That's them. On schedule."

Shryne studied the console's friend-or-foe display screen, in which a schematic of a sharp-nosed, broad-winged ship was rotating. "Republic SX troop transport," he said. "Wonder how they got ahold of that."

"I'm sure there's a story," Brudi said.

Shryne lifted his eyes to the viewports, and to the wreckage beyond. "What happened here?"

"Seps used this system as a staging area for reinforcing Felucia," Jula said. "Republic caught them napping and dusted them." She gestured to what Shryne had initially taken for marker buoys. "Mines. Command-detonated, but still a potential hazard. Better warn the transport to steer clear of them, Brudi."

He swiveled his chair to the comm unit. "I'm on it."

Shryne continued to gaze at the debris. "That's a docking arm of a TradeFed Lucrehulk. What's left of it, anyway."

When Jula finally spoke, she said: "Something's not right."

Brudi turned slightly in her direction. "Transport's registering the signature they transmitted before rendezvous."

She shook her head in uncertainty. "I know, but . . ."

"There are Jedi aboard the transport," Shryne said.

She glanced at him out of the corner of her eye. "Even I know that much. No, it's something else—"

A tone from the threat board cut her off, and Brudi swiveled again.

"Count six, make that eight bandits emerging from hyperspace," he said tersely. "Dead on the transport's vector."

Shryne watched the IFF transponder. "ARC-one-seventies."

"Affirmative," Brudi said. "Aggressive ReConnaissance starfighters."

Visual scanners caught the craft as their transverse wings were unfolding, splaying for battle and increased thermal stability. Jula's left hand made adjustments to the instruments while her right held tight to the yoke.

"Is the transport aware of them?"

"I'd say so," Shryne said. "It's going evasive."

Brudi pressed his headset tighter to his ear. "The transport's warning us away."

"Makes me like them already," Jula said. "Scramble our signature before the ARCs can get a lock on us."

"You may not be able to jam them," Shryne said. "They're not like V-wings. And they punch harder, too."

"Try anyway, Brudi," Jula said. "Last thing I want is the Empire chasing us all over the galaxy. And I am not about to get a new ship." She flipped an intercom switch. "Skeck, Archyr, are you there?"

Skeck's voice issued through the cockpit speaker. "Weapons are powering up, Captain. Just say when."

Jula looked at Shryne. "Any ideas, Jedi?"

Shryne swept his eyes over the display screens. "The ARCs are maintaining a wedge formation. They'll wait until they're within firing range of the transport, then they'll break formation and attempt to outflank it."

"Skeck," Jula said toward the audio pickup, "do you copy?"

"Loud and clear."

"Are the ARCs within range of your turbolasers?" Shryne asked.

"Almost," Skeck said.

"Anticipate the formation break. Lead them, and open up."

Brudi ran a fast calculation on the rate at which the Imperial starfighters were gaining on the transport. "You're good to go," he said.

"Firing!" Skeck announced.

Dense packets of scarlet light tore from the *Drunk Dancer*'s forward batteries, converging on their distant targets. A quartet of fiery blossoms lighted local space.

Archyr whooped. "Pursuit squadron reduced by half!"

"Nice," Jula said, grinning at Shryne. "What other tricks do you have up your sleeve?"

Shryne didn't answer her. On Murkhana, and despite everything that had happened, he had tried to avoid killing any clone troopers. Now here he was, lining them up to be blown to pieces.

"Roan," Jula said sharply.

"The remaining ARCs will regroup, forming up behind the squadron leader," he said at last. Tapping Brudi on the shoulder, he added: "Instruct the transport to nose up over the ecliptic. When the ARCs follow suit, Skeck and Archyr should have a clear shot at their bellies."

"Copy that," Brudi said.

Jula was studying one of the display screens. "Transport is outward bound. ARCs are up and away."

"Firing!" Skeck reported.

A fifth explosion blossomed over the red planet's north pole. Other laser beams went wide of their marks.

"They've figured us out," Shryne said. "They'll scatter now."

"Transport is angling for the mines," Brudi updated.

"Just what I'd do," Jula said.

The threat board loosed another alert tone.

Brudi tapped his finger on the long-distance scanner array screen. "Six more starfighters have emerged from hyperspace."

Jula forced a short exhale. "Tell whoever's piloting the transport to go to full throttle. He may not even be aware of the new players."

"He won't miss this," Brudi said somberly.

Shryne eased out of his seat to peer over Brudi's shoulder. "What?"

"Republic light cruiser," Jula said. "But don't worry, we can outrun it."

On the console's central screen, the scanners assembled a facsimile of the hourglass-shaped warship, highlighting its dozens of turbolaser and ion cannons.

"You won't outrun those guns," Shryne said.

Jula considered it. "Brudi, divert power to the forward deflectors. I'm going to try to take us behind that Lucrehulk arm." She took a moment to glance at Shryne. "Guess the Jedi are more important than I thought, if the Empire's sending cruisers after you."

"Cruiser's turbos are firing," Skeck said over the speaker.

"Hold tight," Jula warned.

Blinding light splashed against the viewports. Jolted, the *Drunk Dancer* lost power momentarily, then returned to life.

"We're okay," Brudi confirmed, "but the transport's in trouble."

"Instruct them to raise their aft shields and rendezvous with us behind the Lucrehulk arm," Jula said. "Tell them we'll hold off the cruiser and ARCs while they make a run for it."

Brudi relayed the instructions and waited for a response. "They'll try. But the transport's shields are heavily damaged. One more hit from the cruiser and they're dead in space."

Jula muttered a curse. The *Drunk Dancer* was just dropping behind the curved fragment of docking arm when she said: "I'm going to bring us back in the open. Rig for ion cannon fire. Let's see if we can surprise them."

The smugglers' ship sustained two powerful strikes as it was emerging from cover, but not enough to incapacitate it.

"Ion surprise," Archyr said.

"Laser chaser," Skeck chimed in.

White light flared in the distance, and blue current coruscated over the cruiser's dark hull.

Brudi bent to one of the screens. "Solid hit. And they definitely didn't see it coming. Their shields are dazed."

"Taking us back into cover," Jula said. "Where's the transport?"

Brudi spoke to it. "Weaving through the last of the mines."

"Archyr, get those ARCs off the transport's tail!"

"Will do, Captain."

Pulsed light streaked from the ship once more, and Shryne watched another starfighter come apart. But the remaining ARCs were gaining rapidly on the transport.

"Projected rendezvous in five-point-five," Brudi said. "Cruiser has come to, and is returning fire."

Jula firmed her lips. "We're not deep enough into cover. This is going to be a bad one."

Shryne hung on to the arms of the chair. Taking the brunt of the capital ship's enfilade, the docking arm vaporized. Tossed back by the blast, the *Drunk Dancer* lived up to its name. Klaxons blared deep within the ship, and the instrument console howled in alarm.

"Shuttle is still closing," Brudi said when he could.

Jula slammed her hand down on the intercom stud. "Prep the bay for emergency docking!" She swiveled to face Brudi. "Tell the transport we're done swapping punches with that

cruiser. Either they make their move now, or we're bowing out."
To Skeck, she said: "All power to the forward batteries. Fire at
will."

The ship rumbled as coherent light raced from the cannon
turrets.

"Transport is lined up for its approach," Brudi said.

Jula's right hand entered data into the navicomputer. "Calculating the jump to lightspeed."

Explosive light flashed outside the viewports, the *Drunk
Dancer* quaking as enemy fire ranged closer.

Brudi sighed in disappointment. "The transport fumbled its
first approach. They're reorienting for another try."

"Coordinates for the jump are in," Jula told him. "Count-
down commencing." She swung around to face Shryne. "I'm
sorry, Roan."

He nodded in understanding. "You did what you could."

The ship shook again.

"Transport is aboard," Brudi said suddenly.

Jula clamped her hands on the yoke. "Divert power to the
sublights. Give us all the distance you can."

"We're going to get our stern burned," Brudi warned.

"Small price to pay."

"Hyperspace engines engaged."

Jula reached for the control stick. "Now!"

And the distant stars became streaks of light.

Brudi hadn't said that the transport was *safely* aboard, and Shryne knew why the moment he and Starstone reached the docking bay. The wedge-shaped ship had skidded in on its port side, gouging the deck, destroying arrays of landing lights, reducing two labor droids to spare parts, and ultimately flattening its pointed bow against an interior bulkhead.

No one inside was injured in the crash, however.

Any more than they were already injured.

The six bedraggled Jedi who literally staggered down the transport's crumpled boarding ramp were a mix of alien, human, and humanoid. Neither Shryne nor Starstone knew any of them by sight, name, or reputation. Face and arms burned by blaster-fire, Siadem Forte was a short, thick-bodied human, older than Shryne but still a Knight. His Padawan was a young Togruta named Deran Nalual, who had been blinded during the same firefight in which Forte had been wounded. Klossi Anno, a Cha-lactan, was also a learner, her Master having died saving her life; where exactly the opposite had happened to Iwo Kulka, a bruised and limping Ho'Din Knight. Unranked human Jedi Jambe Lu and Nam Poorf were agricultural specialists who had been returning to Coruscant from a mission on Bonadan.

On board was a seventh Jedi, who had died during the transport's hyperspace jump to the rendezvous.

Med droids tended to the wounds of new arrivals. Then, after the Jedi had rested and been fed, everyone gathered in the main cabin, where Shryne, Starstone, and a few of the smugglers listened to accounts of savage engagements and close escapes on half a dozen worlds.

As Shryne had guessed, no other clone troopers were known to have refused to obey the Jedi execution order Palpatine was believed to have issued. Two of the Jedi had managed to kill the troopers who had turned on them. Another had escaped and survived by donning clone armor. The pair of Jedi from the Agricultural Corps hadn't been in the company of troopers, but had been fired on and pursued when a shuttle they were aboard had arrived at a Republic orbital facility.

Originally ten in number, they had gathered on Dellalt after receiving a 913 code transmitted by Forte, the eldest among them. It was on Dellalt that they had commandeered the transport, during a battle in which two of the Jedi had been killed and many of the others wounded—and seemingly from Dellalt that the light cruiser and ARC-170s had pursued them.

By the time all the stories had been told and endlessly discussed, the *Drunk Dancer* had emerged from hyperspace in a remote system of barren planets that had long served Jula and her crew as a hideout of sorts. Relieved of her pilot duties, she entered the main cabin and sat down next to Shryne just as talk was turning to HoloNet accounts of what had occurred on Coruscant following Palpatine's decree that the Grand Army had been victorious, and that the Republic was now an Empire.

"Some of the information released has to be false or exaggerated," the agronomist Jambe Lu said. "Holoimages we've seen thus far show that the Temple was certainly attacked. But I refuse to accept that *everyone* was killed. Surely Palpatine would have ordered the troopers to spare the younglings. Perhaps some instructors and administrators, as well."

"I agree," Lu's partner, Nam Poorf, said. "If Emperor Palpatine had wanted for some reason to exterminate the entire Jedi order, he could have done so at the start of the war."

Forte ridiculed the idea. "And who would have led the Grand Army—*Senators*? What's more, even if you're correct about the Temple, the best we can hope is that an untold number of Jedi are imprisoned somewhere. What we know to be true is that Masters Windu, Tiin, Fisto, and Kolar died in the attempt to arrest Palpatine; and that Ki-Adi-Mundi, Plo Koon, and other High Council members are reported to have been assassinated on Separatist worlds."

"Any word on Yoda or Obi-Wan?" Shryne asked Forte.

"Nothing more than HoloNet speculation."

"About Skywalker, as well," Nam Poorf said. "Although we heard rumors on Dellalt that he died on Coruscant."

The Ho'Din Jedi Knight glanced meaningfully at Shryne. "If Skywalker is dead, does that mean that the prophecy died with him?"

"What prophecy?" Forte's sightless Togruta Padawan asked.

Again, Iwo Kulka looked at Shryne. "I see no reason for secrecy now, Roan Shryne."

"An ancient prophecy," Shryne explained for the benefit of Nalual, Klossi Anno, and the two agronomists, "that a Chosen One would be born in the dark times to restore balance to the Force."

"And Anakin Skywalker was thought to have been this Chosen One?" Lu said in astonishment.

"Some members of the High Council believed there was justification for thinking so." Shryne looked at Iwo Kulka. "So in answer to your question, I don't know where the prophecy fits into all that's happened. Foretelling was never my area of expertise."

It came out more bluntly than Shryne had intended. But he was exasperated by the fact that everyone was talking around the real issues: that the Jedi were suddenly homeless and rudderless, and that important decisions had to made.

"What matters," he said into the silence that followed his sarcasm, "is that we—that *all* Jedi—are prey. Palpatine's initial actions might not have been premeditated. We'll leave that for the historians to determine. But he's intent on eliminating us now, and we're probably placing ourselves at greater risk by grouping together."

"But that's exactly what we have to do," Starstone argued. "Everything that has just been said is reason enough to remain together. Jedi being held prisoner. The younglings. The unknown fates of Masters Yoda and Kenobi . . ."

"To what end, Padawan?" Forte said.

"If nothing else, to prevent the Jedi flame from being extinguished." Starstone glanced around, in search of a sympathetic face. That she couldn't find one didn't prevent her from continuing. "This isn't the first time the Jedi order has been brought to the brink of extinction. Five thousand years ago the Sith thought that they could destroy the Jedi, but all their attempts failed, and the Sith Lords only ended up destroying one another. Palpatine might not be a Sith, but, in time, his greed and lust for power will be his undoing."

"That's a very hopeful attitude to take," Forte said. "But I don't see how it helps us now."

"Your best chance of surviving is in the Tingel Arm," Jula said suddenly, "while Palpatine's full control is still limited to the inner systems."

"Suppose we do go there," Starstone said while separate discussions were breaking out. "Sure, we can assume new identities and find remote worlds to hide on. We can mask our Force abilities from others, even from other Forceful individuals. But is that what you want to do? Is that what the *Force* wants for us?"

While the Jedi were considering it, Shryne said: "Have any of you heard the name *Lord Vader*?"

"Who is Vader?" Lu asked for all of them.

"The Sith who killed my Master on Murkhana," Starstone said before Shryne could speak.

Iwo Kulka looked hard at Shryne. "A Sith?"

Shryne lifted his eyes to the ceiling, then looked at Starstone. "I thought we agreed—"

"Vader fought with a crimson lightsaber," she interrupted.

Shryne took a calming breath and began again. "Vader assured the troopers on Murkhana that he wasn't a Jedi. And I'm not sure what he is. Possibly humanoid, but not fully organic."

"Like Grievous," Forte assumed.

"Again—possible. The black suit he wears appears to keep him alive. Beyond that, I don't know how much of Vader is cyborg."

Poorf was shaking his head in confusion. "I don't understand. Is this Vader an Imperial commander?"

"He's superior to the commanders. The troopers showed him the sort of respect they'd reserve for someone of very high rank or status. My guess is that he answers directly to Palpatine." Shryne felt exasperation surfacing once more. "What I'm getting at is that Vader is the one we need to worry about. He *will* track us down."

"What if we get to him first?" Forte said.

Shryne gestured broadly. "We're eight against someone who may be Sith, and one of the largest armies ever amassed. What does that tell you?"

"We wouldn't go after him immediately," Starstone said,

quickly picking up on Forte's question. "Palpatine isn't embraced by everyone." She looked at Jula. "You yourself said that his reach is limited to the inner systems. Which means we could work covertly to persuade Outer Rim Senators and military leaders to join our cause."

"You're neglecting the fact that most species are now convinced that we had a hand in starting and perpetuating the war," Shryne said strongly. "Even those who aren't convinced would risk too much by helping us, even by providing sanctuary."

Starstone was not deterred. "We were two yesterday, and we're eight today. Tomorrow we could be twenty or even fifty. We can keep transmitting—"

"I can't allow that," Jula cut her off. "Not from my ship, anyway." She looked at Forte and the others. "You say you were tracked from Dellalt. But just suppose the Empire is also monitoring Jedi frequencies for Nine Thirteen transmissions? All Palpatine would have to do is wait until you were all in one place, then send in the clones. Or this Vader character."

Starstone's silence lasted only a moment. "There's another way. If we could learn which worlds Jedi were assigned to, we could actively search for survivors."

Lu thought about it for a moment. "The only way to learn that would be by accessing the Temple's data banks."

"Not from the *Drunk Dancer,* you won't," Jula said.

"Couldn't happen anyway, Captain," Eyl Dix said. "Accessing the data banks would require a much more powerful hyperwave transceiver than we have, and one that would be very hard to come by."

Dix glanced at Filli for corroboration.

"Eyl's right," Filli said. Then, around a forming grin, he added: "But I know just where we can find one."

R ain was rare on weather-controlled Coruscant, but every
so often microclimatic storms would build in the bustling sky
and sweep across the technoscape. Today's had blown in from
The Works and moved east with great speed, lashing the abandoned Jedi Temple with unprecedented force.

Vader's enhanced hearing could pick up the sound of fat,
wind-driven raindrops spattering against the Temple's elegant
spires and flat roof, an eerie counterpoint to the sound of his
boot heels striking the adamantine floor and echoing in the dark-
ened, deserted corridors. Sidious had sent him here on a mission,
ostensibly to search the archives for certain Sith holocrons long
rumored to have been brought to the Temple centuries earlier.

But Vader knew the truth.

*Sidious wants to rub my masked face in the aftermath of the
slaughter I spearheaded.*

Though the corpses had been removed by stormtroopers and
droids, most of the spilled blood washed away, scorch marks on
the walls and ceiling attested to the surprise attack. Columns lay
toppled, heritage tapestries hung in shreds, rooms reeked of car-
nage.

But evidence of a less tangible sort also existed.

The Temple teemed with ghosts.

What might have been the wind wending into holed hallways never before penetrated sounded like the funereal keening of spirits waiting to be avenged. What might have been the resonance of the footfalls of Commander Appo's stormtroopers sounded like the beat of distant war drums. What might have been smoke from fires that should have gone out weeks earlier seemed more like wraiths writhing in torment.

Emperor Palpatine had yet to announce his plans for that sad shell of a place. Whether it was to be razed, converted into his palace, deeded to Vader as some sort of cruel joke, or perhaps left as a mausoleum for all of Coruscant to gaze on, a reminder of what would befall those who kindled Palpatine's disfavor.

Most of Vader's Anakin memories grew fainter by the day, but not Anakin's memories of what had happened here. They were as fresh as this morning's sunrise, glimpsed from the rooftop chamber in which Vader rested. True sleep continued to lie just out of reach, an object pursued in vain in an unsettling dream. He no longer had visions, either. That ability, that double-edged ability, seemingly had been burned out of him on Mustafar.

But Vader remembered.

Remembered being in thrall of what he had done in Palpatine's office. Watching the old man plead for his life; listening to the old man promising that only he had the power to save Padmé; rushing to his defense. Sith lightning hurling an astonished Mace Windu through what had been a window . . .

Anakin kneeling before Sidious and being dubbed Vader.

Go to the Jedi Temple, Sidious had said. *We will catch them off balance. Do what must be done, Lord Vader. Do not hesitate. Show no mercy. Only then will you be strong enough with the dark side to save Padmé.*

And so he had gone to the Temple.

Instrument of the same resolute intent that had carried Obi-Wan to Mustafar with one goal in mind: death to the enemy.

In his mind's eye Vader saw his and the 501st's march to the Temple gates, their wrathful attack, the mad moments of blood-lust, the dark side unleashed in all its crimson fury. Some moments he remembered more clearly than others: pitting his blade against that of swordmaster Cin Drallig, beheading some of the very Masters who had instructed him in the ways of the Force, and, of course, his cold extermination of the younglings, and with them the future of the Jedi order.

He had wondered beforehand: could he do it? Still new to the dark side, would he be able to call on its power to guide his hand and lightsaber? In answer, the dark side had whispered: *They are orphans. They are without family or friends. There is nothing that can be done with them. They are better off dead.*

But this recalling, weeks later, curdled his blood.

This place should never have been built!

In fact, he hadn't killed the Jedi to serve Sidious, though Sidious was meant to believe just that. In his arrogance Sidious was unaware that Anakin had seen through him. Had the Sith Lord thought he would simply shrug off the fact that, from the start, Sidious had been manipulating Anakin *and* the war?

No, he hadn't killed the Jedi in service to Sidious, or, for that matter, to demonstrate his allegiance to the order of the Sith.

He had executed Sidious's command because the Jedi would never have understood Anakin's decision to sacrifice Mace and the rest in order that Padmé might survive the tragic death she suffered in Anakin's visions. More important, the Jedi would have attempted to stand in the way of the decisions he and Padmé would have needed to make regarding the fate of the galaxy.

Beginning with the assassination of Sidious.

Oh, but on Mustafar she had worked herself into a state over what he had done at the Temple, so much so that she hadn't heard a word he was saying. Instead she had made up her mind that he had come to care more about power than he cared for her.

As if one matters without the other!

And then cursed Obi-Wan had shown himself, interrupting before Anakin could explain fully that everything he had done, in Palpatine's office and at the Temple, had all been for *her* sake, and for the sake of their unborn child. Had Obi-Wan not arrived he would have persuaded her to understand—he would have *made* her understand—and, together, they would have moved against the Sith Lord . . .

The rasp of Vader's breathing became more audible.

Flexing his artificial hands did nothing to waylay his rage, so he hunched his broad shoulders under the armor pectoral and heavy cloak, shuddering.

Why didn't she listen to me? Why didn't any of them listen to me?

His anger continued to build as he neared the Temple's archives room, where he parted company with Commander Appo and his stormtroopers, as well as with the members of the Internal Security Bureau who, Vader was given to understand, had their separate mission to perform.

He paused at the entrance to the library's vast and towering main hall, shaken not by memory but by memory's effect on his still-healing heart and lungs. The mask's optical hemispheres imparted a murkiness to the normally well-lighted hall, which had once boasted row after row of neatly arranged and cataloged holobooks and storage disks.

Blood let here still showed in maroon constellations that marred large areas of the floor and speckled some of the few still-standing sculpture-topped plinths that lined both sides of the long hallway.

Even if he had killed Sidious, even if he had won the war single-handedly for the Republic, the Jedi would have fought him to the bitter end. They might even have insisted on taking custody of his and Padmé's child, for their offspring would have been powerful in the Force indeed. Perhaps beyond measure! If only the High Council Masters hadn't been so set in their ways, so deceived by their own pride, they would have grasped that the Jedi *needed* to be brought down. Like the Republic itself, their order had grown stale, self-serving, corrupt.

And yet, if the High Council had seen fit to recognize his power, had granted him the status of Master, perhaps he could have abided their continued existence. But to call him the Chosen One only to hold him back; to lie to him and expect him to lie for them . . . What had they imagined the outcome would be?

Old fools.

He understood now why they had discouraged use of the dark side. Because they had feared losing the power base they enjoyed, even though enslavement to attachment was what had helped pull down the Sith! The Jedi had been conspirators in their own downfall, complicit in the reemergence of the dark side, and as important to its victory as Sidious had been.

Sidious—their *ally*.

Attachment to power was the downfall of all orders, because most beings were incapable of controlling power, and power ended up controlling them. That, too, had been the cause of the galaxy's tip into disorder; the reason for Sidious's effortless rise to the top.

Vader's heart pounded in his chest, and the respirator fed his heart's needs with rapid breaths. For his own health and sanity, he realized that he would have to avoid places that whipped his anger into such a frenzy.

The recognition that he would probably never be able to set foot on Naboo or Tatooine tore an anguished moan from him that toppled the rest of the plinths as if they were dominoes, leaving their crowning bronzium busts sliding and spinning across the polished, blood-flecked floor.

Hollowed by the mournful outpouring, he supported himself against a broken column for what seemed an eternity.

The chirping of the comlink on his belt returned him to the present, and after a long moment he activated it.

From the device's small speaker issued the urgent voice of the Internal Security Bureau chief, Armand Isard, communicating from the Temple's data room.

Someone, Isard reported, was attempting remote access of the Jedi beacon databanks.

In the dimly lighted corridor of a forlorn Separatist facility far across the stars, Shryne stopped to gaze at one of the niched statues that lined both walls.

Six meters high and exquisitely carved in the round, the statue was equal parts humanoid and winged beast. While it might have been modeled on an actual creature, the deliberate vagueness of its facial features suggested some mythical creature from antiquity. The indistinct visage was partly concealed by a hooded robe that fell to taloned feet. Identical statues stood in identical recesses for as far as Shryne could see in the wan light.

The complex of ancient, geometric structures the Separatists had converted into a communications facility had certainly stood on Jaguada's moon for thousands of standard years; perhaps tens of thousands of years. Scanners classified the metal used in the construction as "unidentifiable," and lightning fissures in the foundations of the largest buildings indicated that the complex had suffered the effect of the small satellite's every tectonic shift and meteor impact.

The light of Shryne's luma revealed details of the statue's intricately rendered wings. Locally quarried, the worked stone matched the striated rock of the sheer cliffs that walled the complex on two sides, from which had been carved statues thirty meters tall, the gaze of their time-dimpled faces directed not down the narrow valley over which they stood silent guard, but toward the moon's eastern horizon.

Based on similarities to holoimages she had seen of statuary on Ziost and Korriban, Starstone believed that the site could date to the time of the ancient Sith, and that the Separatists' reoccupation of the complex was in keeping with the fact that Count Dooku had become a Sith Lord.

The moon was arid Jaguada's sole companion in a desolate system slaved to a dying star, far from major hyperlanes. The fact that remote Jaguada should host a garrison of clone troopers in the desert planet's modest population center struck Shryne as something of a mystery. But the troopers' presence could owe to plans to salvage the Separatist war machines that had been left abandoned on the moon, as troopers were known to be doing in numerous Outer Rim systems.

This wasn't the first time Jula and her band of smugglers had visited the moon, but the secrecy that had attended the recent arrival had less to do with prior knowledge of the terrain than to the *Drunk Dancer*'s jamming capabilities. The ship had inserted into stationary orbit on the moon's far side without being detected by the Imperial troops on Jaguada, leaving Shryne, Starstone, and Jula, along with some of the crew members and Jedi, to ride down the well in the drop ship, slipping into the moon's thin atmosphere like a sabacc card up a gambler's sleeve.

Heaped with windblown sand, the facility's retrofitted landing platform appeared not to have seen use in several years. Shryne's estimate was borne out by the fact that the hundreds of deactivated droids that welcomed the drop ship party were early-generation Trade Federation infantry droids, of the sort controlled by centralized computers rather than super battle droids equipped with autonomous droid brains. As if the surfeit of silent war machines didn't render the place ghostly enough, there were the fanged carvings affixed to each doorway lintel, and the kilometers of parched corridors studded with gruesome statuary.

Access to the structure that housed the communications center hadn't been a problem, since whatever remote transmissions deactivated the droids had silenced the facility, as well. The power generators, however, were still functional, and Filli Bitters and Eyl Dix had been able to override the deactivation codes and bring some of the internal illuminators to life, along with the hyperwave transceiver the Jedi were intent on using to slice into the Temple beacon database.

Shryne had left the slicers, Starstone, and some of the other Jedi to what he regarded as their business, and had been wandering the aged corridors ever since, thinking through his dilemma.

Even this deep into the complex, the ceramacrete floors were covered with sand and bits of other inorganic debris carried in by the moon's constant, nerve-racking winds. To Shryne, the combination of wind and gloom couldn't have been more apropos to puzzling out whether his coming to Jaguada was in accord with the will of the Force, or merely symptomatic of a deep denial of the truth. Yet another attempt to convince himself that his actions had some import.

Perhaps if he hadn't recognized in Starstone and the other Jedi a powerful need to *believe*—a need to hold on to something in the wake of all that had been snatched from them—he might have tried harder to discourage them. But their need wasn't enough to keep him from asking himself whether this was the way he wanted to spend the rest of his days, hanging on to a dream that the Jedi order could be reassembled; that a handful of Jedi could mount an insurgency against as formidable an enemy as Emperor Palpatine. He couldn't escape the feeling that the Force had thrown him a curious curve once again. Just when he thought he was through with Jedi business, and that the Force had deserted him, he was in deeper than ever.

Roan Shryne, who had lost not one but *two* learners to the war.

Jula's words about reconnecting with family kept replaying themselves. Perhaps he wasn't so far gone that he couldn't actually benefit from attachment, if only as a means of making himself more human. But never to use the Force again . . . that was the bigger issue. His ability to sense the Force in others was so much a part of his nature that he doubted he would simply be able to set it aside, along with his robes and lightsaber.

He suspected that he would always feel like a freak among normal humans, and the idea of exiling himself among aliens with similar talents for telepathy held little appeal.

For the time being he was willing to remain with Starstone, if not mentor her. That was an entirely different problem: Starstone and the others were looking to him for leadership he simply couldn't provide, in part because leadership had never been his strength, but more because the war had eroded whatever measure of self-confidence he had once possessed. With any luck the attempts at locating surviving Jedi would lead eventually to a Jedi of greater Mastery than Shryne, to whom he could surrender the lead and gracefully bow out.

Or perhaps there would be no returns from the Temple beacon database.

Archived HoloNet images he had accessed while aboard the *Drunk Dancer* had showed smoke pouring from the Jedi Temple in the aftermath of the troopers' attack. So it was certainly conceivable that the beacon had been damaged or destroyed, or that the databases had been hopelessly corrupted.

Which would cause an abrupt end to the search.

And to the dreaming, as well.

He had begun to move deeper into the corridor when Jula appeared out of the gloom, a luma in hand, and fell into step beside him.

"Where are the guides when you need them?" she said.

"Just what I was thinking."

She had her jacket folded over her arm, a blaster holstered on her hip. Shryne wondered for a moment what her life might have been like had he remained in her care. Would her marriage to Shryne's father have endured, or would what seemed an unquenchable thirst for adventure have placed Jula just where she was now? Save with Roan at her side, part of her crew, her partner in crime.

"How are they doing back there?" he asked, nodding with his chin toward the communications room.

"Well, Filli's already sliced into the beacon. No surprises there. Now I suppose it's a matter of worming into the database itself." She regarded Shryne while they walked. "You're not interested in being there when they start downloading the names and possible whereabouts of your scattered confederates?"

Shryne shook his head. "Starstone and Forte can see to that. My credits aren't on their succeeding, anyway."

Jula laughed. "Then you won't get any side action from me." She looked at him askance. "Olee and Filli are two of a kind, don't you think?"

"I did for a while. But I figure she's already found her life partner."

"The Force, you mean." Jula forced an exhale. "That's dedication of a scary sort."

Shryne stopped walking and turned to her. "Why'd you say yes to taking us here, Jula?"

She smiled lightly. "I thought I'd made myself clear. I'm still hoping to convince you to join us." Scanning his face for clues, she asked: "Any movement at all on that front?"

"I don't know what I'm thinking."

"But you'll keep me updated?"

"Sure I will."

Shortly they reached the end of the corridor of winged statues and turned the corner into an intersecting corridor lined with smaller carvings.

In the bobbing light of the lumas, Shryne said: "How did Filli know about this place?"

"We made a couple of runs here six or so years back. Communications hardware for the hyperwave transceiver. And before you go all patriotic on me, Roan, we didn't realize that the facility would eventually be used to eavesdrop on Republic transmissions."

"That would have stopped you—knowing that a war against the Republic was brewing?"

"It might have. But you have to understand, we were hungry, like a lot of other freelancers in the outlying systems. It still amazes me that Coruscant remained in the dark about what was going on out here after Dooku formed the Separatist movement. Weapons buildup, Baktoid Armor Workshop installing foundries on dozens of worlds . . . Back then, there was a lot to be said for free and unrestricted trade."

"I would have figured that would be bad for business."

"Yes and no. Free trade invited competition, but it also meant we didn't have to worry about being chased by local system defense forces or Jedi Knights."

"Who hired you to bring in the comm hardware?"

"Someone named Tyranus, although none of us ever met him face-to-face."

"Tyranus," Shryne repeated, in uncertain recollection.

"Ring a bell?"

"Maybe. I'll have to run it by the librarian—Olee. So when did the Separatists pull up stakes?"

"Shortly after the Battle of Geonosis—"

Shryne came to a sudden halt in front of a tall, cloaked statue wearing a goggle-eyed mask.

"Gruesome," Jula started; then the corridor's regularly placed illuminators suddenly flooded the area with light. Squinting, she said, "I thought the idea was to avoid drawing too much attention to ourselves."

Distant rumblings overpowered Shryne's response. In one swift action, he drew and ignited the lightsaber clipped to his belt.

Jula raised her brows in surprise. "Where'd you come by that?"

"It belonged to the Master of one of the Padawans." Spinning on his heel, he began to race back toward the communications control room, Jula right behind him.

Shryne realized that the rumbling sounds were being made by doors and hatchways opening and closing. He hastened his pace, weaving through stands of deactivated battle droids.

In the control room Filli, his spiked hair matted to his skull, was doing furious input at a console, while Eyl Dix and Starstone paced behind him, Olee gnawing away at her lower lip. A few meters away Jedi Knights Forte and Iwo Kulka looked as if they were having second thoughts about what they had set in motion.

"Filli, what's going on?" Jula shouted.

The slicer's right hand pointed to Starstone, while his left continued to fly across the keys of a control pad. "She told me to do it!"

"Do what?" Shryne said, looking from Starstone to Filli and back again.

"Boost the transceiver with a burst from the power generator," Dix answered for Filli.

"We didn't have enough juice to download from the database," Starstone said. "I thought it would be fine."

Shryne's forehead wrinkled in confusion. "So what's the problem?"

"The generator wants to reactivate the entire facility," Filli said in a rush of words. "I can't get it to shut down!"

Slamming, hissing sounds began to replace the rumble of sliding doors.

Jula looked sharply at Shryne. "This entire place is sealing up."

A series of determined clicks and ready tones punctuated the din raised by descending hatches. All at once every battle droid in the control room powered up.

Swinging its thin head toward him and raising its blaster rifle, the battle droid standing closest to Shryne said: *"Intruders."*

Behind Armand Isard and the two Internal Security Bureau technicians seated at the Temple beacon control console, Vader stood with his arms folded across his chest, Commander Appo at his right hand.

"I want to know how the beacon was accessed," Vader said.

"By means of a Jedi transceiver, Lord Vader," the tech closest to Armand said.

"Cross-check the transceiver code with the identity database," the ISB chief said, anticipating Vader.

"The name should be coming up in a moment," the other tech said, eyes glued to rapidly scrolling text on one of the display screens. "Chatak," he added a moment later. "Bol Chatak."

The sound of Vader's breathing filled the ensuing silence.

Shryne and Starstone, he thought. Obviously they had been in possession of Chatak's beacon transceiver when they had evaded him at Murkhana. Now they were attempting to determine the location of other Jedi when Order Sixty-Six had been issued. Certainly they were hoping to establish contact with survivors, hoping to pick up the pieces of their shattered order.

And . . . what?

Devise their revenge? Unlikely, since that would entail calling on the dark side. Formulate a plan to kill the Emperor? Perhaps. Although, ignorant of the fact that Palpatine was a Sith, they would not plot an assassination. So perhaps they were contemplating an attack on the Emperor's enforcer?

Vader considered reaching out to Shryne through the Force, but rejected the idea.

"What is the source of the transmission?" he asked finally.

"The Jaguada system, Lord Vader," the first technician said. "More precisely, the moon of the system's only inhabited world."

A large holomap of the galaxy emerged from the console's holoprojector. Linked to myriad databases throughout the Temple, the map made use of a palette of colors to indicate trouble spots. Just now, in preservation of the moment Order Sixty-Six had been executed, more than two hundred worlds glowed blood red.

Perhaps this explained why Sidious hadn't had the Temple dismantled, Vader thought. So he could regard it from his lofty new throne room and *gloat*.

The holomap began to close tighter and tighter on a remote area of the Outer Rim. When, finally, the Jaguada system hung in midair, Vader strode into its midst.

"This moon," he said, gesturing with the forefinger of his black-gloved hand.

"Yes, Lord Vader," the tech said.

Vader glanced at Appo, who had already comlinked Central Operations on Coruscant.

"The moon is the site of an abandoned Separatist communications facility," Appo said. "Whoever is in possession of the Jedi transceiver must have brought the facility's hyperspace communications network online."

"Do we have any vessels in that sector, Commander?"

"No vessels, Lord Vader," Appo said. "But there is a small Imperial garrison on Jaguada."

"Instruct the garrison commander to scramble his troopers immediately."

"Capture or kill, Lord Vader?"

"Either would please me."

"I understand."

Vader cupped the holoimage of the tiny moon in his hand. "I have you now," he said quietly, and made a fist.

The lightsaber Klossi Anno had given Shryne felt foreign in his hand, but it was finely wrought, and its dense blue blade was perfect for deflecting the hail of blaster bolts the battle droids had unleashed. Beside him Jula was firing steadily and with impressive accuracy, dropping those droids Shryne's parried bolts didn't. Crouched behind the control console, Filli and Dyx were somehow managing to continue entering commands on the keyboards while the flashing lightsabers of Starstone, Forte, and Kulka provided cover.

In the control room and elsewhere in the facility, alert sirens were warbling, lights were flashing, and hatchways were sealing.

"Whatever you did, undo it!" Shryne said to Filli without missing a blaster bolt. "Deactivate the droids!"

A glance at display screens that had been sleeping moments earlier showed that scores of infantry droids and droidekas were hurrying toward the control center from all areas of the complex.

"Filli, hurry!" Jula added for emphasis. "More are headed this way!"

Shryne took a moment to look around the control room. The doorway through which he and Jula had entered was one of three, positioned 120 degrees from one another.

"Filli, can you seal us in here?" he shouted.

"Probably," the slicer yelled back. "But we may have bigger troubles."

"We can handle the droidekas," Forte assured him.

Filli raised his head above the console and shook it negatively. "Someone at the Temple knows that we've sliced in!"

Starstone whirled on him. "How do you—"

"We're getting an echo from the beacon," Eyl Dix explained.

Redirecting a flurry of bolts, Shryne reduced six droids to shrapnel. "How long before the Temple ascertains our location?"

"Depends on who's at the other end," Filli said.

"Then cancel the link!" Jula said.

"We're still downloading," Starstone said. "We need all the data we can get."

Shryne glowered at her. "What good is all the data in the Temple if we're not around to put it to use?"

She narrowed her eyes. "I knew you'd say that. Do it, Filli," she said over her shoulder. "Zero the link." Glancing apologetically at Forte and Kulka, she added: "We'll make the best of what we have."

"Done," Filli announced.

Shryne's deflection shot dismantled another droid. "Now shut the power down before we're shot to death or entombed in here!"

A moment later the droids returned to their inert status, and the control room was plunged into darkness. Five lumas provided just enough light to see by.

"I trust that someone knows the way out of here," Forte said.

"I do," Dix said, her antennae standing straight up.

"Then let's hope the exit's still open," Shryne said.

Filli nodded. "It is. I got a look at the security screen before we cut the power."

"Good job," Shryne started to say, when blasterfire erupted from somewhere outside the control room.

"You said you zeroed it, Filli," Jula snapped.

He spread his hands in confusion. "I did!"

Shryne listened closely to the distant discharges. "Those aren't droid blasters," he said after a moment. "Those are DC-fifteens."

Starstone stared at him. "Stormtroopers? Here?"

Jula's comlink chimed and she grabbed for it. "Archyr," she said for everyone's benefit.

"Captain, we've got company," Archyr said from the drop ship. "Troopers from the Jaguada garrison."

Shryne traded looks with Starstone.

"Whoever's at the Temple didn't waste any time," she said.

Shryne nodded. "They must have been monitoring us from the start."

"How many troopers?" Jula was asking Archyr.

"A couple of squads," he said. "Skeck and I are pinned down on the landing platform. But most of the troopers have headed inside."

"I can try to seal the entrances . . ." Filli said.

"No, don't," Shryne cut him off. "You think you can you rig a delay to the power generator?"

His luma grasped in his teeth, Filli began to riffle through his tool kit. "I'm sure I can cobble something together," he said.

Shryne turned to Jula. "How long will it take us to reach the front entrance, closest to the cliffs?"

She threw him a questioning look. "That'll dump us way downvalley, Roan. A good kilometer from the drop ship."

He nodded. "But we avoid engaging troopers on the way out."

Her brow continued to furrow. "Then why do you want Filli to—" She grinned in sudden revelation and turned to Filli. "Set it to power up in a standard quarter, Filli."

"That's cutting things pretty close, Captain."

"The closer, the better," she said.

By the time a holotransmission from the commander of the Jaguada garrison reached the Temple beacon room, Vader already knew that something had gone wrong.

"I'm sorry, Lord Vader," the helmeted stormtrooper was saying, "but we're trapped inside the facility with several hundred reactivated infantry and destroyer droids." The commander dodged blaster bolts and returned fire at something distant from the holocam's transmission grid. "All accesses sealed when the facility powered up."

"Where are the Jedi?" Vader asked.

"They left before the facility went online. We're trapped in here until we find a way to blow one of the doors."

"Did you destroy the ship the Jedi arrived in?"

"Negative," the commander said as bolts lanced the air around him. "The smugglers detonated a magpulse while the second squad was advancing. My troopers were expecting it, but in the time it took our hardware to reboot, the Jedi got their ship airborne."

Off cam a trooper said: "Fallback positions two and three have been overrun, Commander. We'll have to make a stand here."

"There's just too many of them!" the commander said as diagonal lines of noise began to interfere with the transmission.

Abruptly, it derezzed completely.

Armand Isard and the ISB technicians busied themselves at the beacon controls, if only to avoid having to look at Vader.

"Lord Vader," Appo said, "Jaguada base reports that jump points are limited in that system, and that they are scanning for vagrant traces of the Jedi ship. They may be able to calculate possible escape vectors."

Vader nodded.

Infuriated, he turned and stormed from the beacon room, wishing he had the power to simply reach out and pluck the Jedi from the sky.

Conclude their extermination.

Sidious was wrong, he told himself as he hurried through the empty hallways.

They are a threat.

he *Drunk Dancer* tore through mottled hyperspace, leaving
desolate Jaguada light-years behind. Skeck had sustained a nasty
blaster burn to his right arm during the troopers' attempt to disable the drop ship, but no one else had been hurt. Emerging
from the facility moments before Filli's time delay initiated the
power generator, Shryne and the others had raced upvalley to the
landing platform and had arrived in time to catch a squad of Imperials in a crossfire.

Sealed inside the facility, the remaining squads were up to
their T-visors in reactivated battle droids.

After Skeck's wound had been bandaged, Shryne had retired
to the dormitory cabin space Jula had provided for the Jedi. He
had always had a fondness for hyperspace travel—more, the sense
of being outside time—and was kneeling in meditation when he
sensed Starstone approaching the cabin. Simultaneous with her
excited entry he rose to his feet, eyes on the sheaf of flimsiplast
printouts she was holding.

"We have data on hundreds of Jedi," she said, rattling the
printouts. "We know where more than seventy Masters were at

the end of the war—when the clone commanders received their orders.”

Accepting the proffered flimsies, Shryne thumbed through them, then glanced at Starstone. “How many of these hundreds do you think might actually have survived the attacks?”

She gave her head a quick shake. “I’m not even going to try to guess. We can begin our search with systems closest to Mossak, and fan out from there toward Mygeeto, Saleucami, and Kashyyyk.”

Shryne shook the flimsies. “Has it occurred to you that if *we* have this information, then so does the Empire? What do you think our adversaries were doing in the Temple beacon room, playing hide-and-seek?”

Starstone winced at the harshness of his tone, but only briefly. “Has it occurred to you that our adversaries, as you call them, were there precisely because a good many Jedi survived? It’s crucial that we reach those survivors before they’re hunted down. Or are you proposing that we leave them to the Empire—to Vader and his stormtroopers?”

Shryne made a start at replying, then bit back his words and motioned to the edge of the nearest cot. “Sit down, and try for a moment to stop thinking like a HoloNet hero.”

When Starstone ultimately lowered herself to the cot, Shryne sat opposite her.

“Don’t misunderstand me,” he began. “Your goal couldn’t be more noble. And for all I know there are five hundred Jedi scattered throughout the Rim in need of rescue. *My* point is, I don’t want to see your name added to the casualty list. What happened at Jaguada is only a foretaste of what’s in store for us if we continue to band together.”

“I—”

Shryne stopped her before she could go on. “Think about the final beacon message we received at Murkhana. The message didn't tell us to gather together and coordinate a strike on Coruscant, or on Palpatine, or even on the troopers. It instructed us, each of us who received it, to *hide*. Yoda or whoever ordered the transmission knew that the Jedi were in a fight we couldn't win. The message was a way of saying just that—that the order is over and done with. That the Jedi are finished."

He hid his ruefulness. "Does that mean that you have to stop honoring the Force? Of course not. All of us will live out our lives honoring the Force. But not with lightsabers in hand, Olee. With right action, and right thinking."

"I'd rather die honoring the Force with my lightsaber," she said.

He had expected as much. "How is dying honoring the Force, when you could be out doing good works, passing on to others all that you've learned about the Force?"

"Is that what you plan to do—devote yourself to good works?"

Shryne smiled. "Right now I only know what I'm *not* going to do, and that's help rush you into a grave on some remote world." He held her gaze. "I'm sorry. But I've already lost two Padawans to this rotten war, and I don't want to lose you to it."

"Even though I'm not your learner?"

He nodded. "Even though."

She sighed with purpose. "I appreciate your concern for me, Master—and I *will* call you that because right now you're the only Master we have. But the Force tells me that we can make a difference, and I can't turn my back on that. Master Chatak instilled in me every day that I should follow the Force's lead, and that's exactly what I'm going to do."

She adopted an even more serious look. "Jula believes that you *can* turn your back. The Force is with her, but she's not a Jedi, Master. You can't unlearn overnight the teachings and practices of decades. Even if you should succeed, you'll regret it."

Shryne firmed his lips and nodded again. "Then you and I will be parting ways at Mossak."

Sadness pulled down the corners of her mouth. "I wish it didn't have to be this way, Master."

"That doesn't begin to say how I feel about it."

They stood, and he hugged her tenderly.

"You'll tell the others?" he said while she was gathering up the flimsies.

"They already know."

Shryne didn't watch her leave. But no sooner did she exit the cabin than Jula entered.

"Jedi business?"

Shryne looked at her. "You can probably figure it out."

Jula averted her gaze. "Olee's a fine young woman—they're all decent beings. But they're deluded, Roan. It's over. They have to realize that and get on with their lives. You told me that attachment is the root of many of our problems. Well, that includes being so attached to the Jedi order that you can't leave it behind. If being a Jedi means being able to accept what has happened and move on, then they honor the order best by letting go."

She looked at him now. "For some of them it's all about the loss of prestige, and the power to decide what's right or wrong. To believe that everything you do is motivated by the Force, and that you always have the Force on your side. But that's not always the way it works. I've no love for the order, you know that. Sometimes the Jedi caused as many problems as they solved. Now, for whatever reason, whether it's Palpatine or the fact that the Jedi couldn't accept the idea of taking second place to the Republic—the Force isn't necessarily your best ally."

She reached for his hands. "They took you from me once, Roan. I won't let you go a second time without a fight." She laughed lightly. "And that, ladies and gentlemen, concludes my little speech." Gazing at him, she said: "Join us."

"In crime, you mean."

A fire came into her eyes. "We're not criminals. All right, we've done some questionable things, but so have you, and that was in the past. If you come aboard, I promise we'll stick to taking contracts that will allow you to keep on doing good deeds, if that's what it's going to take."

"Such as?" Shryne said.

"Well, we already happen to have a good deed on deck. A contract to transport a former Senator from the Core to his home system."

Shryne allowed his skepticism to show. "Why would a former Senator have to be smuggled to his home system?"

"I don't have all the details. But my guess? The Senator doesn't share the ideals of the new regime."

"Is this a Cash Garrulan contract?"

Jula nodded. "And maybe that's another reason for you to say yes to accepting the offer. Because you owe him for arranging for your escape from Murkhana."

Shryne pretended scorn. "I don't owe Cash any favors."

"Okay. Then you'll do it to honor his memory."

Shryne stared at her.

"Imperial troopers caught up with him soon after all of you left Murkhana. Cash is dead."

From the high-backed chair that was his seat of power, Sidious watched Darth Vader turn and march from the throne room, long black cloak whooshing, black helmet burnished by the lights, anger palpable.

Atop a pedestal alongside the chair sat the holocrons Sidious had asked his apprentice to search out and retrieve from the Jedi archives room. Pyramidal in shape, as opposed to the geodesic Jedi version, the holocrons were repositories of recorded knowledge, accessible only to those who were highly evolved in the use of the Force. Arcane writing inscribed on the holocrons Vader had fetched told Sidious that they had been recorded by Sith during the era of Darth Bane, some one thousand standard years earlier. Sidious didn't have to imagine the content of the devices, because his own Master, Darth Plagueis, had once allowed him access to the *actual* holocrons. The ones stored in the Temple archives room were nothing more than clever forgeries—Sith disinformation of a sort.

Vader didn't realize that they were forgeries, of course, although he was certainly smart enough to have puzzled out that the holocrons were hardly the reason Sidious had ordered him to return to the Temple. But Vader's obvious anger hinted that something unexpected had occurred. Instead of helping Vader come to terms with his choices, the specious mission had muddled his emotions, and perhaps made matters worse.

What is to be done with him? Sidious thought.

Perhaps I will have to send him back to Mustafar, as well.

He mused on a strategy for a moment; then, depressing a button on the control panel set into the arm of the chair, he summoned Mas Amedda into the room.

The tall-horned Chagrian, now the Emperor's interface with sundry utterly dispensable Senatorial groups, moved cautiously between the Imperial Guards who flanked the door, inclining his head in a bow of respect as he approached Sidious.

Through the open door to the waiting room, Sidious glimpsed a familiar face. "Is that Isard outside?"

"Yes, my lord."

"Why is he here?"

"He asked that I inform you of an incident that occurred while he and Lord Vader were in the Temple."

"Indeed?"

"I'm given to understand that unknown parties accessed certain databases, by means of the beacon."

"Jedi," Sidious said, drawing out the word.

"None other, my lord."

"And Lord Vader was on hand to witness this remote infiltration?"

"He was, my lord. Once the source of the transmission was located, Lord Vader ordered a local garrison of troopers to descend on the Jedi responsible."

"The troopers *failed*," Sidious said, leaning forward in interest.

Mas Amedda nodded gravely.

More of his fugitive Jedi, Sidious thought. *He has not allowed himself to be done with them.*

"No matter," he said at last. "What business originally brought you here?"

"Senator Fang Zar, my lord."

Sidious interlocked the fingers of his fat hands and sat back in the chair. "One of the more vocal of the illustrious two thousand who wished to see me removed from office. Has he had a sudden change of heart?"

"Of a sort. You will recall, my lord, that following your announcement that the war had been won, Fang Zar and several other signatories of the Petition of the Two Thousand were briefly detained for questioning by Internal Security Bureau officers."

"Come to the point," Sidious snapped.

"Fang Zar was instructed not to leave Coruscant, and yet he did, managing to reach Alderaan, where he has been in residence at the Aldera Palace ever since. Now, however, the conflict that engulfed his home system has come to an end, and Fang Zar is apparently determined to return to Sern Prime without attracting the notice of the ISB or anyone else."

Sidious considered it. "Continue."

Mas Amedda spread his huge blue hands. "Our only concern is that his sudden return to Sern Prime might prompt dissension in certain outlying systems."

Sidious smiled tolerantly. "Some dissension should be encouraged. Better they rant and rave in the open than plot behind my back. But tell me, does Senator Organa know that Zar was questioned before he fled Coruscant?"

"Perhaps he does now, though it is unlikely he knew when he granted refugee status to Fang Zar."

Sidious grew interested once more. "How is Zar planning to reach Sern Prime without, as you say, attracting attention?"

"We know that he made contact wtih a crime lord on Murkhana—"

"Murkhana?"

"Yes, my lord. Perhaps he wishes to avoid involving Senator Organa in his predicament."

Sidious fell silent for a long moment, attuned to the currents of the Force. Currents linking Vader and Murkhana, and now Zar and Murkhana. And perhaps fugitive Jedi and Murkhana . . .

Into his thoughts came the words of Darth Plagueis.

Tell me what you regard as your greatest strength, so I will know how best to undermine you; tell me of your greatest fear, so I will know which I must force you to face; tell me what you cherish most, so I will know what to take from you; and tell me what you crave, so that I might deny you . . .

"Perhaps it would be more prudent for Fang Zar to remain on Alderaan awhile longer," he said finally.

Mas Amedda bowed his head. "Shall I inform Senator Organa of your wish?"

"No. Lord Vader should deal with the situation."

"To deflect his hunger for the Jedi," the Chagrian risked saying.

Sidious shot him a look. "To *sharpen* it."

Perhaps it was because Alderaan presented such a pleasant picture from deep space that it had enjoyed such a long history of peace, prosperity, and tolerance.

Even deeper into its intoxicating atmosphere, closer to its montage of alabaster clouds, blue seas, and green plains, the picture held. Coruscant's neighbor in the Core was a gem of a world.

The pacific impression didn't begin to diminish until one reached street level on the island-city of Aldera, and only then as a result of the day's activities, which demonstrated that for tolerance to endure, voice had to be granted to all, even when free expression challenged the perpetuation of peace.

Bail Organa understood this, as had his predecessors in the Galactic Senate. But Bail's compassion for those who had taken to Aldera's narrow streets was not a case of noblesse oblige, for he shared the concerns of the demonstrators and had deep sympathy for their cause. As many said of Bail, were it not for genetics, he might have been a Jedi. And indeed for most of his adult life he had been a valued friend of the order.

He stood in plain sight of the crowds, on a balcony of the

Royal Palace, in the heart of Aldera, which itself lay in the embrace of green mountains, their gentle summits sparkling with freshly fallen snow. Below him marched hundreds of thousands of demonstrators—refugees representing scores of species displaced by the war, bundled up in colorful clothing against the mountains' frigid downdrafts. Many of the refugees had been on Alderaan since the earliest days of the Separatist movement, living in housing Alderaan had provided; many more were recently arrived onplanet, to show their support. Now that the war had ended, almost all of them were eager to return to their home systems, pick up the pieces of their shattered lives, and reunite with members of their widely dispersed families.

But the Empire was attempting to thwart them.

Placards flashed and holoimages sprang from hand- and flipper- and tentacle-held devices as the throng moved past Bail's lofty perch in the north tower, behind the palace's high white walls and the arcs of reflecting pools that had long ago served as defensive moats.

PALPATINE'S PUPPET! one of the holoslogans read.

REPEAL THE TAX! read another.

RESIST IMPERIALIZATION! a third.

The first was a reference to the regional governor Emperor Palpatine had installed in that part of the Core, who had decreed that all refugees of former Confederacy worlds were required to submit to rigorous identity checks before being issued documents of transit.

The "tax" referred to the toll that had been levied on anyone seeking travel to outlying systems.

Already a catchphrase, the third slogan was aimed at any who feared the Emperor's attempts to bind all planetary systems, autonomous or otherwise, to Coruscant's rule.

While little of the angry chanting was directed at Alderaan's government or Queen Breha—Bail's wife—many in the crowd were looking to Bail to intercede with Palpatine on their behalf. Alderaan was merely their gathering place, after the demonstration's organizers had decided against holding the march on Coruscant, under the watchful gaze of stormtroopers, and with the memory of what had happened at the Jedi Temple fresh in everyone's mind.

Demonstrations were nothing new, in any case. Alderaanians were known throughout the galaxy for their missions of mercy and their unstinting support of oppressed groups. More important, Alderaan had been a hotbed of political dissent throughout the war, with Aldera University's Students of Collus—named for a celebrated Alderaanian philosopher—leading the movement.

With his homeworld thoroughly politicized, Bail had been forced to play a careful game in the galactic capital, where he was at once an advocate for refugee populations and a principal member of the Loyalist Committee; that is, loyal to the Constitution, and to the Republic for which it stood.

A reasonable man, one of a handful of rankled delegates who had found themselves caught between support for Palpatine and outright contention, Bail had understood that political wrangling was the only way to introduce change. As a result, he and Palpatine had engaged in numerous disputes, openly in the Rotunda as well as in private, on issues relating to Palpatine's rapid rise to incontestable power, and the subsequent slow but steady erosion of personal liberties.

Only with the war's sudden and shocking end had Bail come to understand that what had seemed political maneuvering on Palpatine's part had been nothing less than inspired machination—the unfolding of a diabolical scheme to prolong the war, and to so frustrate the Jedi that when they finally sought to hold him accountable for refusing to proclaim the war concluded with the deaths of Count Dooku and General Grievous, Palpatine could not only declare them traitors to the Republic, but also pronounce them guilty of having fomented the war to serve their own ends, and therefore deserving of execution.

Ever since, Bail had been forced to play an even more treacherous game on Coruscant—Imperial Center—for he now knew Palpatine to be a more dangerous opponent than anyone suspected; indeed a more dangerous foe than most could even begin to guess. While Senators such as Mon Mothma and Garm Bel Iblis were expecting Bail to join in their attempts to mount a secret rebellion, circumstance compelled him to maintain a low profile, and to demonstrate greater allegiance to Palpatine than he ever had.

That circumstance was Leia. And Bail's fears for her safety had only increased since his close encounter with Darth Vader on Coruscant.

He had spoken of the encounter only to Raymus Antilles, captain of the consular ship *Tantive IV.* Antilles had been given custody of Anakin's protocol and astromech droids, C-3PO and R2-D2. The former had undergone a memory wipe to safeguard the truth for as long as necessary, and to assure the continued protection of the Skywalker twins.

Could Vader actually be Anakin Skywalker? the two men wondered.

Based on Obi-Wan's account of what had occurred on Mustafar, Anakin's survival didn't seem possible. But perhaps Obi-Wan had underestimated Anakin. Perhaps Anakin's peerless strength in the Force had allowed him to survive.

Was Bail, then, raising the child of a man who was still alive?

What alternative was there? That Palpatine—that *Sidious*—had dubbed some other apprentice Darth Vader? That the black monstrosity Bail had seen on the landing platform was merely a droid version of Anakin, as General Grievous had been a cyborg version of his former self?

If that was true, would stormtroopers like Appo allow themselves to be commanded by a such a being, even if ordered to by Sidious?

The questions had gnawed at Bail without answer, and events such as the refugee march only served to place him at greater risk on Coruscant and heighten his concerns for Leia.

Unaided, Palpatine was capable of crushing any who opposed him. And yet he continued to allow others to do his dirty work, to preserve his image as a benevolent dictator. Palpatine used his regional governors to issue the harshest of his decrees, and his stormtroopers to enforce them.

The march's organizers had promised Bail that it would be a peaceful demonstration, but Bail suspected that Palpatine had infiltrated spies and professional agitators into the crowds. Riots could be used as an excuse by the regional governor to arrest dissidents and perceived troublemakers, and to announce new edicts that would make travel even more difficult and expensive for the refugees.

With so many ships arriving from nearby worlds, it had been impossible to screen for Imperial agents or saboteurs. Even if there had been some way to identify them, Bail would only have played into Palpatine's hands by issuing restrictions, thus alienating refugees and their ardent supporters alike, who viewed Alderaan as one of the last bastions of freedom.

Thus far, Alderaanian law enforcement units were doing a good job of confining the marchers to their preassigned circuit of the Royal Palace. Contingents of Royal Guards surrounded the palace, and the sky was filled with police skimmers and surveillance craft to ensure that the situation remained under control. On Bail's orders, active measures could only be used as a last resort.

Standing at the edge of the balcony, the object of shouts, appeals, chants, and flurries of raised fists, Bail ran his hand over his mouth, hoping that the Force was with him.

"Senator!" someone called from behind him.

Bail turned and saw Captain Antilles hurrying toward him from the direction of the palace's Grand Reception Room. Accompanying Antilles were two of Bail's aides, Sheltray Retrac and Celana Aldrete.

Antilles directed Bail's attention to a nearby holoprojector.

"You're not going to be pleased," the starship captain said by way of warning.

The holoimage of an enormous warship resolved in the projector's blue field.

Bail's brow wrinkled in confoundment.

"*Imperator*-class Star Destroyer," Antilles explained. "Hot off the line. And now parked in stationary orbit above Aldera."

"This is outrageous," Celana Aldrete said. "Even Palpatine wouldn't be so bold as to interfere in our affairs."

"Don't fool yourself," Bail said. "He would and he has." He swung to Antilles. "Comm the vessel," he ordered as Aldera's vizier and other advisers were hastening onto the balcony to gawk at the projected holoimage.

Before Antilles could activate his comlink, the holoprojector image faded and was replaced by the pinched, clean-shaven face of Palpatine's chief henchman, Sate Pestage.

"Senator Organa," Pestage said. "I trust you are receiving me."

Of all of Palpatine's advisers, Pestage came closest to being Bail's archnemesis. A thug, with no understanding of the legislative process, Pestage had no business being in a position of authority. But he had been one of Palpatine's chief advisers since Palpatine's arrival on Coruscant from Naboo, as that world's Senator.

Bail positioned himself on the projector's transmission grid and signaled for Antilles to open a link to Pestage.

"There you are," Pestage said after a moment. "Will you grant permission for our shuttle to land, Senator?"

"How unlike you to extend us the courtesy of a warning, Sate. What brings you to this part of the Core, in a Star Destroyer, no less?"

Pestage smiled without showing his teeth. "I'm merely a passenger aboard the *Exactor*, Senator. As to our business here . . . Well, let me say first how much I've enjoyed watching HoloNet feeds of your . . . political rally."

"It's a peaceful gathering, Sate," Bail fired back. "And it's likely to remain so unless your agitators succeed in doing what they do best."

Pestage adopted a surprised look. "My agitators? You can't be serious."

"I'm very serious. But suppose you get back to telling me why you are here."

Pestage tugged at his lower lip. "Now that I think about it, Senator, it might be more prudent for me to leave the explanation to the Emperor's emissary."

Bail stood akimbo. "That has always been your position, Sate."

"No longer, Senator," Pestage said. "I now answer to a superior."

"Who are you talking about?"

"Someone you've not yet had the pleasure of meeting. Darth Vader."

Bail froze, but only on the inside. He managed to keep from glancing at Antilles, and his voice belied none of his sudden dread when he said: "Darth Vader? What sort of name is that?"

Pestage smiled again. "Well, actually it's something of a title *and* a name." The smile collapsed. "But make no mistake, Senator, Lord Vader speaks for the Emperor. You would do well to bear that in mind."

"And this *Darth* Vader is coming here?" Bail said in a composed voice.

"Our shuttle should be setting down momentarily, assuming, of course, that we have your permission to land."

Bail nodded for the holocam. "I'll see to it that you receive approach and landing coordinates."

Pestage's holoimage had no sooner deresolved than Bail snatched his comlink from his belt and tapped a code into the keypad. To the female voice that answered, he said, "Where are Breha and Leia?"

"I believe they're already on their way to join you, sir," the Queen's attendant said.

"Do you know if Breha has her comlink with her?"

"I don't believe she does, sir."

"Thank you." Bail silenced the comlink and turned to his aides. "Find the Queen. She must be somewhere in the main residence. Tell her that she is not to leave the residence under any circumstances, and that she is to contact me as soon as possible. Is that understood?"

Retrac and Aldrete nodded, spun on their heels, and hurried off.

Bail swung to Antilles, eyes bulging in concern. "Are the droids on the *Tantive IV* or downside?"

"Here," Antilles said, exhaling. "Somewhere in the palace or on the grounds."

Bail tightened his lips. "They have to be located and kept out of sight."

Never was one for crowds, myself," Skeck said as he, Archyr, and Shryne were negotiating Aldera's throng of demonstrators.

"Is that what first took you to the Outer Rim?" Shryne asked.

Skeck mocked the idea with a motion of dismissal. "I just hang there for the food."

In addition to keeping out the cold, their long coats, hats, and high boots supplied hiding places for blasters and other tools of the smuggling trade. Jula, Brudi, and Eyl Dix had remained with the drop ship, which was docked in a circular bay a couple of kilometers west of the palace.

It was Shryne's first visit to Alderaan. From what little he had seen, the planet lived up to its reputation as both a beautiful world and an arena for political dissent, notwithstanding Alderaan's allegedly pacifist views. The mood of the enormous crowd, made up of war refugees and those who had arrived from countless worlds to demonstrate their solidarity, seemed to be in keeping with those views. But Shryne had already

zeroed in on scores of beings who clearly hoped to provoke the
marchers to violence, perhaps as a means of being assured extensive HoloNet coverage, and thus making their point with Palpatine.

Or maybe, just maybe, Alderaan had the Emperor himself to
thank for the rabble-rousers.

Judging by the way in which Aldera's police units were deployed, they had no interest in confrontation, and perhaps had
been ordered to exercise restraint at all costs. The mere fact that
the marchers were being allowed to voice their protests and display their holoslogans in such close proximity to the Royal Palace,
and that Senator Bail Organa himself would occasionally plant
himself in full view of the crowd, showed that the restraint was
genuine.

Alderaan really did care about the little guy.

For Shryne, the presence of such a huge crowd also suggested that Senator Fang Zar was more than a clever politi-
cian. While spiriting him off Alderaan would never have posed
an insurmountable challenge, the milling crowds combined
with Alderaan's deliberately lax policy toward orbital inser-
tions and exits was going to make the pickup as easy as one, two,
three.

Not bad for Shryne's first mission.

There might even be a small amount of good attached to it—
particularly if the rumors he had heard about Zar over the years
were true.

Now it boiled down to keeping the appointment with
him.

Shryne, Skeck, and Archyr had already circled the palace
twice, primarily to scope out potential problems at the south gate
entrance, where the prearranged meet was supposed to take
place. Shryne found it interesting that Zar's ostensible reason
for making a low-key departure was to keep from involving

Organa in his problems, but Shryne wasn't clear on just what those problems were. Both Zar and Organa had been outspoken members of the Loyalist Committee, so what could Zar have done to cause problems for himself that didn't already involve Organa?

Was he in a fix with Palpatine?

Shryne tried to convince himself that Zar's troubles were none of his business; that the sooner he accustomed himself to simply executing a job, the better—for him and for Jula. This, as opposed to thinking like a Jedi, which involved looking to the Force as a means of gauging possible repercussions and ramifications of his actions.

In that sense, the Alderaan mission was the first day of the rest of his life.

Olee Starstone was the only other issue he had to clear from his mind. His feelings for her didn't spring from attachment of the sort she would be the first to ridicule. In plain fact, he was worried about her to the point of distraction.

In response to Shryne's decision to follow his own path, she was about as angry as a Jedi was allowed to be, though some of the other Jedi had said that they understood.

All seven had taken the battered transport and gone in search of surviving Jedi. Shryne feared that it would just be a matter of time before they got themselves in serious trouble, but he wasn't about to serve as their watchdog. More to the point, they had seen the risks they were taking as flowing from the will of the Force.

Well, who knew for sure?

Shryne wasn't omniscient. Maybe they would succeed against all odds. Maybe the Jedi, in league with political protestors and sympathetic military commanders, could bring Palpatine to justice for what he had done.

Unlikely. But a possibility, nevertheless.

Jula had been generous enough to loan Filli to the Jedi, outwardly to help them sort through the data they had downloaded from the beacon databases. Shryne suspected, however, that Jula's real intent was to disable Starstone's reckless determination. The closer Starstone and Filli grew, the more the young Jedi would be forced to take a hard look at her choices. With time, Filli might even be able to lure her out of her attachment to the perished Jedi order, just as Jula had Shryne.

But then, Shryne had been halfway along before his mother had even entered the picture.

His mother.

He was still getting used to that development: that he was the son of this particular woman. Perhaps the way some of the troopers had had to adjust to the fact that they were all clones of one man.

Through his comlink's wireless earpiece, Shryne heard Jula's voice.

"I just heard from our bundle," she said. "He's in motion."

"We're working our way around to him now," Shryne said into the audio pickup fastened to the synthfur collar of his coat.

"You sure you're going to be able to recognize him from the holoimages?"

"Recognizing him won't be a problem. But finding him in this crowd could be."

"I'm guessing he didn't expect this big a turnout."

"I'm guessing no one did."

"Does that say something for the Emperor's days being numbered?"

"Someone's days, anyway." Shryne paused, then said: "Hold for a moment."

The palace's south gate entrance was within sight now, but in the time it had taken Shryne, Skeck, and Archyr to complete their third circuit, a mob had formed. Three human

speakers standing atop repulsorlift platforms were urging everyone to press through the tall gates and onto the palace grounds.
Anticipating trouble, a group of forty or so royal troops dressed
in ceremonial armor and slack hats had deployed themselves
outside the gates, armed with an array of nonlethal crowd
control devices, including sonic devices, shock batons, and stun
nets.

"Roan, what's going on?" Jula asked.

"Things are getting rowdy. Everyone's being warned away
from the south gate entrance."

The crowd surged, and Shryne felt himself lifted from his feet
and carried toward the palace. The cordon of troops issued a final
warning. When the crowd surged again, two front-line guards
sporting backpack rigs began to coat the cobblestone plaza with
a thick layer of repellent foam. The crowd surged back in response, but dozens of demonstrators closest to the front failed to
step back in time and were immediately immobilized in the
rapidly spreading goo. A few of them were able to retreat by
surrendering their footgear, but the rest were stuck fast. The
trio of hovering agitators took advantage of the situation, accusing Alderaan's Queen and vizier of attempting to hinder the
marchers' rights to free assembly, and of kowtowing to the Emperor.

The surges grew more powerful, with demonstrators trapped
in the center of the crowd taking the brunt of all the pushing and
shoving. Shryne began to edge toward the perimeter, with Skeck
and Archyr to either side of him. When he could, he enabled his
comlink.

"Jula, we're not going to be able to get to the gate."

"Which also means that our bundle won't be able to exit the
grounds that way."

"Do we have a substitute rendezvous?"

"Roan, I've lost voice contact with him."

"Probably temporary. When you hear from him, just tell him to stay put, wherever he is."

"Where will you be?"

Shryne studied the palace's curved south wall. "Don't worry, we'll find a way in."

Those poor beings, trapped in that terrible foam," C-3PO said as he and R2-D2 hastened for a narrow access door in the palace's south wall.

Close to the palace's underground droid-maintenance facility, where both droids had enjoyed an oil bath, the door was the same one they had used to exit the palace grounds earlier that day, when the protestors were just beginning their march.

"I think we'll be much better off inside the palace."

R2-D2 chittered a response.

C-3PO tilted his head in bafflement. "What do you mean we've been ordered inside anyway?"

The astromech chirped and fluted.

"Ordered to conceal ourselves?" C-3PO said. "By whom?" He waited for an answer. "Captain Antilles? How thoughtful of him to show concern for our well-being in the midst of this confusion!"

R2-D2 zithered, then buzzed.

"Something else?" C-3PO waited for R2-D2 to finish. "Don't tell me you *can't* say. It's simply that you *refuse* to say. I've every right to know, you secretive little machinist."

C-3PO fell briefly silent as the shadow of a low-flying craft passed over them.

His single photoreceptor tracking the flight of a midnight-black Imperial shuttle, R2-D2 began to whistle and hoot in obvious alarm.

"What is it now?"

The astromech loosed a chorus of warbles and shrill peeps. C-3PO fixed his photoreceptors on him in incredulity.

"Find Queen Breha? What *are* you going on about? A moment ago you said that Captain Antilles had ordered us into hiding!" Arms crooked, almost akimbo, C-3PO couldn't believe what he was hearing.

"*You* changed your mind. Since when do you get to decide what's important and what isn't? Oh, you're intent on getting us in trouble. I know it!"

By then they had reached the access door in the wall. R2-D2 extended a slender interface arm from one of the compartments in his squat, cylindrical torso and was in the process of inserting it into a computer control terminal alongside the doorway when the voice of a flesh-and-blood said: "Misplace your starfighter, droid?"

Turning completely about, C-3PO found himself looking at a human and two six-fingered humanoids wearing long coats and tall boots. The human's left hand was patting R2-D2's dome of a head.

"Oh! Who are you?"

"Never mind that," one of the humanoids said. Parting his coat, he revealed a blaster wedged into the wide belt that cinched his pants. "Do you know what this is?"

R2-D2 mewled in distress.

C-3PO's photoreceptors refocused. "Why, yes, it's a DL-Thirteen ion blaster."

The humanoid smiled nastily. "You're very learned."

"Sir, it is my fondest wish that my master recognize as much. Working with other droids has become so tiresome—"

"Ever see what an ionizer on full power can do to a droid?" the humanoid interrupted.

"No, but I can well imagine."

"Good," the human said. "Then here's the way it's going to work: you're going to lead us into the palace like we're all the best of friends."

While C-3PO was trying to make sense of it, the man added: "Of course, if you have a problem with that, my friend here"— he gestured to the other humanoid—"who happens to be very knowledgeable about droids, will just tap into this one's memory and retrieve the entry code. And then both of you will get to enjoy the effects of an ionizer firsthand."

C-3PO was too stunned to respond, but R2-D2 made up for the sudden silence by filling it with beeps and zithers.

"My counterpart says," C-3PO started to interpret, then stopped himself. "You certainly will *not* do as he says, you coward! These beings are not our masters! You should be willing to be disassembled rather than offer them the slightest help!"

But C-3PO's admonitions fell on deaf auditory sensors. R2-D2 was already unlocking the door.

"This is most unbecoming," C-3PO said sadly. "Most unbecoming."

"Good droid." The long-haired human patted the astromech's dome again, then threw C-3PO a narrow-eyed gaze. "Any attempts to communicate with anyone and you'll wish you'd never been built."

"Sir, you don't know how many times I've already wished that very thing," C-3PO said as he followed R2-D2 and the three armed organics through the door and onto the palace grounds.

Vader stood at the foot of the shuttle's boarding ramp, gazing at the white spires of the Royal Palace. Commander Appo and six of his stormtroopers spread out to flank him as Bail Organa and several others emerged from the ornate building. For a moment neither group moved; then Organa's contingent walked onto the landing platform and approached the shuttle.

"You are Lord Vader?" Organa asked.

"Senator," Vader said, inclining his head slightly.

"I demand to know why you've come to Alderaan."

"Senator, you are in no position to demand anything."

The vocoder built into his mask added menace to the remark. But, in fact, for perhaps the first time Vader felt as if he were wearing a disguise—a macabre costume, as opposed to a suit of life-sustaining devices and durasteel armor.

As Anakin, Vader hadn't known Bail Organa well, even though he had been in his company on numerous occasions, in the Jedi Temple, the corridors of the Senate, and in Palpatine's former office. Padmé had spoken of him highly and often, and Vader suspected that it was Organa, along with Mon Mothma, Fang Zar, and a few others, who had persuaded Padmé to withdraw her support of Palpatine prior to the war's finish. That, however, didn't trouble Vader as much as the fact that Organa, according to stormtroopers of the 501st, had been the first outsider to turn up at the Temple following the massacre, and was lucky to have escaped with his life.

Vader wondered if Organa had had a hand in helping Yoda, and presumably Obi-Wan, recalibrate the Temple beacon to cancel the message Vader had transmitted, which should have called all the Jedi back to Coruscant.

Aristocratic Organa was Anakin's height, dark-haired and handsome, and always meticulously dressed in the style of the Republic's Classic era, like the Naboo, rather than in the ostentatious fashion of Coruscant. But where Padmé had earned her status by being elected Queen, Organa had been born into wealth and privilege, on picture-perfect Alderaan.

Mercy missions or no, Vader wondered whether Organa had

any real sense of what it meant to live in the outlying systems, on worlds like sand-swept Tatooine, plagued by Tusken Raiders and lorded over by Hutts.

He felt a sudden urge to put Organa in his place. Pinch off his breath with a narrowing of his thumb and forefinger; crush him in his fist . . . But the situation didn't call for that—yet. Besides, Vader could see in Organa's nervous gestures that he understood who was in charge.

Power.

He had power over Organa, and over all like him.

And it was Skywalker, not Vader, who had lived on Tatooine. Vader's life was just beginning.

Organa introduced him to his aides and advisers, as well as to Captain Antilles, who commanded Alderaan's Corellian-made consular ship, and who tried but failed to conceal an expression of profound hostility toward Vader.

If Antilles only knew who he was dealing with . . .

From beyond the palace's walls came the sound of angry voices and chanting. Vader surmised that at least some of the turbulence owed to the presence of an Imperial shuttle on Alderaan. The thought entertained him.

Like the Jedi, the demonstrators were another group of deluded, self-important beings convinced that their petty lives had actual meaning; that their protests, their dreams, their accomplishments amounted to anything. They were ignorant of the fact that the universe was changed not by individuals or by mobs, but by what occurred in the Force. In reality, all else was unimportant. Unless one was in communication with the Force, life was only *existence* in the world of illusion, born as a consequence of the eternal struggle between light and dark.

Vader listened to the sounds of the crowd for a moment more, then turned to regard Organa.

"Why do you permit this?" he asked.

Organa's restless eyes searched for something, perhaps a peek at the man behind the mask. "Are such demonstrations no longer permitted on Coruscant?"

"Harmony is the ideal of the New Order, Senator, not dissension."

"When harmony becomes the standard for all, then protests will cease. What's more, by allowing voices to be heard here, Alderaan saves Coruscant any unmerited embarrassment."

"There may be some truth to that. But in due time, protests will cease, one way or another."

Vader recognized that Organa was in a quandary about something. Clearly he resented being challenged on his own world, but his tone of voice was almost conversational.

"I trust that the Emperor knows better than to end them by fear," he was saying.

Vader had no patience for verbal fencing, and having to match wits with judicious men like Organa only reinforced his growing distaste at being the Emperor's errand boy. When would his actual Sith training finally commence? Try as he might to convince himself, his was not real power, but merely the *execution* of power. He wasn't the swordmaster so much as the weapon; and weapons were easily replaceable.

"The Emperor would not be pleased by your lack of faith, Senator," he said carefully. "Or by your willingness to allow others to display their distrust. But I haven't come to discuss your little march."

Organa fingered his short beard. "What does bring you here?"

"Former Senator Fang Zar."

Organa seemed genuinely surprised. "What of him?"

"Then you don't deny that he's here?"

"Of course not. He has been a guest of the palace for several weeks."

"Are you aware that he fled Coruscant?"

Organa frowned in uncertainty. "It sounds as if you're suggesting that he wasn't permitted to leave of his own free will. Was he under arrest?"

"Not arrest, Senator. Internal Security had questions for him, some of which were left unanswered. ISB requested that he remain in Imperial Center until matters were resolved."

Organa shook his head once. "I knew nothing of this."

"No one is questioning your decision to house him, Senator," Vader said, gazing down at him. "I simply want your assurance that you won't interfere with my escorting him back to Coruscant."

"Back to—" Organa left the rest of it unfinished and began again. "I won't interfere. Except in one instance."

Vader waited.

"If Senator Zar requests diplomatic immunity, Alderaan will grant it."

Vader folded his arms across his chest. "I'm not certain that privilege still exists. Even if it does, you may find that refusing the Emperor's request is hardly in your best interest."

Again, Organa's confliction was obvious. *What is he hiding?*

"Is that a threat, Lord Vader?" he said finally.

"Only a fact. For too long the Senate encouraged political chaos. Those days are ended, and the Emperor will not permit them to resurface."

Organa showed him a skeptical look. "You speak of him as if he is all-powerful, Lord Vader."

"He is more powerful than you know."

"Is that why you've agreed to serve him?"

Vader took a moment to respond. "My decisions are my own. The old system is dead, Senator. You would be wise to subscribe to the new one."

Organa exhaled with purpose. "I'll take my chances that freedom is still alive." He fell silent for a moment, deliberating. "I don't mean to impugn your authority, Lord Vader, but I wish to consult with the Emperor personally on this matter."

Vader could scarcely believe what he was hearing. Was Organa deliberately attempting to obstruct him; to make him appear inept in the eyes of Sidious? Anger welled up in him. Why was he wasting his time chasing fugitive Senators when it was the Jedi who posed a risk to the New Order?

To the balance of the Force.

A nearby holoprojector chimed, and from it emerged the holoimage of a dark-haired woman with an infant in her arms.

"Bail, I'm sorry I've been delayed," the woman said. "I just wanted to let you know that I'll be there shortly."

Organa looked from Vader to the holoimage and back again. As the image faded he said: "Perhaps it's better if you spoke with Senator Zar in person." He gulped and found his voice. "I'll have him escorted to the conference room as soon as possible."

Vader turned and waved a signal to Commander Appo, who nodded. "Who is the woman?" Vader asked Organa.

"My wife," Organa said nervously. "The Queen."

Vader regarded Organa, trying to read him more clearly.

"Inform Senator Zar that I'm waiting," he said at last. "In the meantime, I would enjoy meeting the Queen."

More than seven centuries old, the palace was a rambling and multistoried affair of ramparts and turrets, bedrooms and ballrooms, with as many grand stairways as it had turbolifts. Without a map, its kilometers of winding corridors were nearly impossible to follow. And so where walking from the droid-maintenance room to the hallway that accessed the south gate had seemed a simple matter, it was in fact akin to negotiating a maze.

"The droid's more clever than it looks," Archyr said when it finally dawned on them that the two machine intelligences had been walking them in circles for the past quarter hour. "I think it's leading us on a wild gundark chase."

"Oh, he would never do that," C-3PO said. "Would you, Artoo?" When the astromech didn't answer, C-3PO slammed his hand down on R2-D2's dome. "Don't you even think about giving me the silent treatment!"

Skeck tugged the ion weapon from his belt and brandished it. "Maybe it forgot about this."

"No need to threaten us further," C-3PO said. "I'm certain

that Artoo isn't attempting to mislead you. We don't know the palace very well. You see, we've only been with our present master for two local months, and we're not very well acquainted with the layout."

"Where were you before two months ago?" Skeck asked.

C-3PO fell silent for a long moment. "Artoo, just where were we before that?"

The astromech honked and razzed.

"None of my business? Oh, here we go again. This little droid can be very stubborn sometimes. In any case, as to where we were . . . I think I recall acting as an interface with a group of binary loadlifters."

"Loadlifters?" Archyr said. "But you're programmed for protocol, aren't you?"

C-3PO looked as distressed as a droid could look. "That's true! However, I can't imagine that I'm mistaken! I know I have been programmed for—"

"Get ahold of yourself, droid," Skeck said.

Shryne brought the five of them to an abrupt halt. "This isn't the way to the south entrance. Where are we?"

C-3PO gazed around. "I believe that we have somehow ended up in the royal residence wing."

Archyr's pointed jaw dropped. "What the frizz are we doing here? We're a hundred and eighty degrees from where we want to be!"

Skeck aimed the ionizer at the astromech's photoreceptor. "You can navigate a starfighter through hyperspace and you can't get us to the south gate? Any more tricks and we're going to fry you."

Shryne stepped away from everyone and activated his comlink. "Jula, any word from—"

"Where in the galaxy have you three been? I've been trying to reach you for—"

"We got turned around," Shryne said. "We'll fix it. Any word from our bundle?"

"That's what I wanted to tell you. He *moved*."

"Where to?"

"The east gate."

Shryne blew out his breath. "All right, we'll get there. Just make sure you tell him to remain where he is." Silencing the comlink, he rejoined the others.

"*East* gate?" Skeck said when Shryne relayed the bad news. He turned himself through a circle and pointed. "That way, I think."

The astromech began to chitter. Shryne and the others looked to C-3PO for a translation.

"He says, sirs, that the quickest route to the east gate will involve our ascending one more level—"

"We're supposed to be going *down*!" Archyr said in exasperation.

"That's true," C-3PO continued. "But my counterpart advises that unless we go *up* first, we will be forced to detour around the upper reaches of the Grand Ballroom atrium."

"Enough," Shryne said, ending further argument. "Let's just get this over with."

With the astromech leading, rolling along on its three treads, the five of them filed into a turbolift and rode it up one floor. No sooner had they arrived than R2-D2 made a sudden left into the stately corridor and hurried off.

"What, all of a sudden it's in a rush?" Archyr said.

"Artoo, slow down!" C-3PO called, struggling to keep up.

The astromech disappeared around a bend in the corridor. Skeck muttered a curse and drew the ionizer again.

"I think it's trying to get away!"

The three of them began to race after their quarry, dashing around the same corner only to narrowly avoid colliding with a regally dressed woman cradling a sleeping baby in her arms.

Stopping suddenly, the astromech loosed an ear-piercing screech and extended half a dozen of its interface arms, waving them about like weapons.

Confronted with the sight, the woman pulled the baby closer to her with one hand while the other reached out to slap a security alarm stud set into the wall. Rudely awakened by the astromech's screech and the blare of alarms, the baby took a quick look at the droid and began wailing at the top of its lungs.

Exchanging the briefest of panicked looks, Shryne, Archyr, and Skeck about-faced and ran.

Bail's assured posture in one of the reception room's elegant chairs belied his sense of raw desperation.

A few meters away, standing at one of the tall windows, Darth Vader gazed out on crowds of demonstrators who were becoming more turbulent with every passing moment.

The cadence of his deep breathing filled the room.

This is Leia's father, Bail told himself, certain of it now.

Anakin Skywalker. Rescued somehow on Mustafar, and returned to life, though now confined to a suit that made manifest what Skywalker had become at the end of the war: betrayer, butcher of children, apprentice of Sidious, follower of the dark side of the Force. And soon Leia would be in his presence . . .

When Breha had comlinked him unexpectedly, Bail had come close to telling her to flee, fully prepared to suffer whatever consequences would descend on him. To ensure Leia's safety, he had even been ready to sacrifice Fang Zar.

Would Vader recognize Leia through the Force as his child? What would happen if he did? Would he compel Bail to reveal where Obi-Wan was; where Luke was?

No, Bail would die first.

"What's taking Senator Zar so long?" Vader asked.

Bail had his mouth open to reply that the palace's guest wing was some distance away when Sheltray Retrac entered the reception room, her expression alone making it clear that something was wrong. Approaching Bail, she leaned low to say in a quiet voice, "Fang Zar is not in the residence. We don't know where he is."

Before Bail could reply Vader swung to the two of them.

"Was Zar alerted of my coming?"

Bail came to his feet quickly. "No one was apprised beforehand of the reason for your visit."

Vader glanced at Commander Appo. "Find him, Commander, and bring him to me."

The words had scarcely left the black grille that concealed Vader's mouth than security alarms began to sound throughout the palace. Captain Antilles immediately moved into the transmission field of the reception room's holoprojector, where a half-life-size image of a security officer was already resolving.

"Sir, three unidentified beings have gained access to the palace. Their motive is unknown, but they are armed and were last seen in the residential wing, in the company of two droids."

Two droids! Bail thought, rushing across the room in an effort to beat Vader to the holoprojector.

"Do we have images of the intruders?" Retrac asked before Bail could silence her.

Bail's heart skipped a beat. If it was C-3PO and R2-D2—

"Only of the intruders," the security officer said.

"Show them," Antilles ordered.

The security cam image showed three males, one human and two humanoids, dashing down one of the corridors.

"Freeze the image!" Vader said from alongside the holoprojector. "Close in on the human."

Bail was as confused as everyone else. Did Vader know the intruders? Were they agitators dispatched by Coruscant to work the protestors into a frenzy?

"Jedi," Vader said, mostly to himself.

Bail wasn't sure he had heard Vader correctly.

"Jedi? That can't be possible—"

Vader whirled on him. "They've come for Fang Zar." He stared at Bail from inside the mask. "Zar is attempting to return to Sern Prime. Apparently he hoped to keep from implicating you in his flight."

The reception room fell silent, but only for a moment. From the holoprojector appeared an image of Breha, holding a distraught Leia in her arms.

"Bail, I won't be joining you, after all," she said, loud enough to be heard over the infant's crying. "We had a disturbing encounter with three trespassers and a couple of droids, who nearly frightened the baby to death. She's in no condition to be introduced to company. I'm trying to calm her—"

"That's probably best," Bail said in a rush. "I'll check back with you in a moment." Deactivating the holoprojector, he turned slowly to Vader, arranging his features to suggest a mix of mild disappointment at his wife's message, and deep concern for just about everything else that had occurred.

"I'm certain there'll be another time, Lord Vader."

"I look forward to it," Vader said.

With that, he turned and marched away.

Bail nearly collapsed. Exhaling in guarded relief, he dropped back into his chair.

"Jedi?" Antilles said, in obvious bewilderment.

Bail shook his head from side to side. "I don't understand, either. But that *is* Skywalker." Abruptly, he stood up. "We have to find Zar before he does."

"If I ever run into that astromech again . . . ," Skeck said as he, Archyr, and Shryne were racing for the palace's east entrance.

Archyr nodded in agreement. "Never a good feeling when you're tricked by an appliance."

His comlink enabled, Shryne was speaking with Jula.

"We're almost there. But that's no guarantee we can make it outside without being arrested."

"Roan, I'm going to reposition the ship. Close to our rendezvous there's a landing platform reserved for HoloNet correspondents."

"What makes you think you'll be allowed to set down?"

"No one's going be happy about it. But the good thing about Alderaan is that no one's going to blast us out of the sky, either."

"Parking ticket, huh?"

"Maybe not even."

"Then we'll see you there," Shryne said. "Out."

With the ornate east entrance in sight, the three of them slowed down to survey the situation. A pair of enormous doors opened on a broad staircase; from the last step, a paved footpath led to an arched bridge that spanned a crescent of reflecting pool. On the far side of the pool, the path led directly to a gated access in the high rampart. Perhaps a hundred meters beyond the wall was the media landing platform Jula had mentioned.

Shryne scanned the beings assembled on the narrow bridge and the green lawn between it and the rampart. Ultimately his gaze found a short, dark-complectioned man with a shock of long, white beard.

"That's Zar," he said, pointing out the Senator to Skeck and Archyr.

"And here comes trouble," Skeck said, indicating four Royal Guards who were hurrying for the gate, rifles slung over their shoulders.

"We need to make our move," Archyr said. "Before any more of them show up."

Skeck parted his long coat, reached around to the small of his back, and drew a blaster. "So much for pulling this off without a hitch."

Shryne placed his right hand on the weapon while Skeck was checking the power level. "You might not have to use it. Those long rifles are no match for even a hand blaster, and the guards know it. Besides, they probably haven't fired a round since the last royal funeral."

"Yeah, but can I quote you on that?" Skeck said.

Shryne took a step toward the doors, froze, then retreated, pressing himself to the wall.

Archyr regarded him in bafflement. "What—"

"Vader," Shryne managed.

Archyr's eyes widened. "The black stormtrooper? Let me see—"

Shryne restrained him from moving. "He's no stormtrooper."

Skeck was staring at Shryne, openmouthed. "Why's he here? For you?"

Shryne shook his head to clear it. "I don't know. He answers directly to the Emperor." He looked at Skeck. "He could be here for Zar."

"Doesn't really matter, does it," Archyr said. "Point being, he's *here*."

Shryne reached under his coat for his blaster. "If he is here for Zar, he's going to forget all about him when he sees me."

Skeck planted his hands on Shryne's shoulders. "You want to think this through?"

Shryne vouchsafed a thin smile. "I just did."

Vader hunted the hallways of the palace, the suit's array of sensors enhancing every sound and smell, every stray movement, his heavy cloak hooked around the hilt of his lightsaber.

The Emperor foresaw that this would happen, he told himself. *That is why he sent me. Despite what he says, he is concerned about the Jedi.*

Outside the palace, marchers continued to chant and circulate; inside, guards and others scurried about, stopping only to stare and move out of his path. Half of them were certainly in search of Fang Zar, and all of them were off course. But then, they lacked Vader's *sympathy* for those who were pushed and pulled and otherwise manipulated by the Force.

There was also the fact that Vader knew how Jedi *thought*.

Sensing a subtle presence, he stopped. At the same time, someone behind him shouted:

"Vader!"

Igniting his lightsaber, Vader turned completely around.

Hands by his sides, Shryne stood at the intersection of two corridors, one of which led to the palace's east portal, the other to the ballroom. Clearly, Zar had been found, was perhaps being moved out of the palace even then, or Shryne would not have shown himself.

"So you're the bait," Vader said after a moment. "It's an old ploy, Shryne. A ploy I've used. And it won't work this time."

"I have a backup plan."

Shryne flourished the blaster.

Vader focused on the weapon. "I see that you've abandoned your lightsaber."

"But not my commitment to justice." Shryne took a moment to glance down the hallway that led out of the palace. "You know how it is, Vader. Once a good guy, always a good guy. Then again, you probably don't know anything about that."

Vader advanced on him. "Don't be too sure of yourself."

"We're just trying to help Zar get home," Shryne said, retreating into the corridor. "Suppose we leave it at that."

"The Emperor has his reasons for recalling Zar to Coruscant."

"And you do whatever the Emperor tells you to do?"

In the intersection now, Vader could discern that Shryne was merely waiting for a chance to bolt through the doors. Well behind Shryne, on the far side of a footbridge that crossed a gentle curve of reflecting pool, one of Shryne's armed accomplices was holding four Royal Guards at bay while the other was all but dragging Fang Zar toward a gated breach in the palace's defensive wall, beyond which the conspirators surely had a getaway craft waiting.

Shryne fired a quick burst, then sprinted for the doorway. Behind him, his humanoid accomplices were also in motion, stunning the guards to unconsciousness and racing for the open gate.

Angling his blade, Vader deflected the bolts with intent, but by jinking and jagging Shryne managed to evade each parry.

Vader leapt, his powerful prosthetic legs carrying him to the top of a broad but short flight of steps in time to see Shryne sprint across the bridge at Jedi speed, motioning to his accomplices to move Zar through the gate.

Vader leapt again, this time to the bridge, and to within only a few meters of Shryne, who spun about, dropping to one knee and firing repeatedly. This time Vader decided to show Shryne whom he was dealing with. Holding his lightsaber to one side, he raised his right hand to turn the blaster bolts.

Clearly astonished, Shryne remained on one knee, but only briefly. In an instant he had passed through the gate and was shouldering his way through the crowd outside the wall.

Vader's final leap landed him just short of the rampart. Over the heads of the milling beings, at the forward edge of a landing platform, a woman with gray-laced black hair was gesturing frantically to Shryne and his cohorts, who were already hauling Fang Zar up the platform steps.

All too easy, Vader told himself.

Time to end it.

34

Bail and his two aides stood by the reception room holo-projector, awaiting some word of Fang Zar's whereabouts. From the direction of the residence wing came Antilles and the droids.

"Go ahead, Threepio, tell him," Antilles said when the three of them were within earshot of Bail.

"Master Organa, I hardly know where to begin," C-3PO said. "You see, sir, my counterpart and I were about to enter the palace grounds—"

"Threepio," Antilles said sharply. "Save the long story for another occasion."

R2-D2 communicated something in bleating tones.

C-3PO turned to the astromech. "Verbose? Tiresome? Just you mind your enunciator, you—"

"See-Threepio!" Antilles repeated.

The protocol droid fell silent. "I'm very sorry, sirs. I'm simply unaccustomed to so much excitement."

"That's all right, See-Threepio," Bail said. "Take your time."

"Thank you, Master Organa. I only wanted to report that the three intruders who held us captive were apparently intent on collecting some sort of 'bundle'—that was the word they used—at the palace's east gate."

"Quickly!" Bail said to his aides.

Aldrete bent to adjust the holoprojector's controls. An instant later an east gate security cam captured a holoimage of Fang Zar, seized in the grip of two humanoids who were running him toward a landing platform that had been designated for HoloNet personnel.

A second cam found Vader, crimson-bladed lightsaber in hand, fending off blasterfire from a long-haired human male who was also racing for the east gate.

"Sir," Sheltray Retrac said suddenly.

Following Asta's worried gaze, Bail saw Sate Pestage striding into the reception room.

"Senator, I have just learned that Senator Zar is at this moment being conducted from the palace," Pestage said, in what Bail sensed was almost theatrical spleen. "If this is your way of providing immunity—"

"We've only just discovered his whereabouts," Bail cut him off, motioning to the holoimages. "In any case, it looks as if the Emperor's 'emissary' has the situation well in hand."

Pestage dismissed Bail's anger with a superfluous wave of his hand. "Through no help of yours, Senator. I demand that you secure the palace before it's too late!"

Bail glanced at the holoimages of Vader, the long-haired man, Fang Zar . . .

"Seal it, I tell you!"

Bail took a final glance at the images, then complied.

Firing on the run, Shryne made a mad dash for the rampart gate. If his retreat struck Skeck, or Archyr, or even Fang Zar, as cowardly, then so be it. For it was clear that Vader wasn't going to be stopped by blaster bolts, and Shryne was a long way from the nearest lightsaber.

Shryne wasn't surprised that Vader knew him by name; that he did only reinforced the fact that Vader and the Emperor had full access to the Jedi Temple databases. For all Shryne knew, Vader had been at the Temple when Filli Bitters had sliced into the beacon.

Outside the gate now, he began to zigzag through the densely packed crowd. Catching sight of his weapon, many of the marchers hastened to open a path for him—an obvious berserker in their midst. Through gaps in the throng, Shryne could see Skeck, Archyr, Jula, and Zar on the landing platform, surrounded by what Shryne took to be irate HoloNet correspondents, yelling at them and gesticulating to the drop ship that had set down without permission.

Judging by her gestures, Jula was attempting to placate everyone, or at least assure them that the ship would soon be on its way—assuming that Vader didn't scuttle their plans with a single leap.

Midway up the stairway that led to the landing platform, Shryne came to a halt, to take what he hoped would be a last look at Vader, who was still on the palace grounds, a couple of meters shy of the rampart gate. Of greater interest to Shryne, however, was the fact that an alloy curtain, thick as a blast shield, was descending rapidly from the head jamb of the arched entrance.

The palace was being sealed shut, and Vader was in risk of not making it through the gate in time!

Understanding as much, the Emperor's executioner was moving faster now. A jump carried him to the rampart, just short of the lowering shield, where he did something so unexpected that it took Shryne a moment to make sense of what was happening.

Vader hurled his ignited lightsaber through the air.

For a split second Shryne thought that he had done so in anger. Then, in awe, he grasped that Vader had *aimed*.

Spinning out from under the lowering security grate, the crimson blade sailed high over the crowd, following a trajectory that took it north of the landing platform; then, on reaching the distal end of its arc, it began to boomerang back.

Shryne flew for the top of the stairway, his gaze fully engaged on the twirling blade, his heart hammering in his chest. Calling on the Force, he tried to influence the course of the lightsaber, but either the Force wasn't with him or Vader's Force abilities were overpowering his.

The blade was whipping toward the landing platform now, close enough for Shryne to hear it whine through the air, and spinning so swiftly it might have been a blood-red disk.

Passing within a meter of Shryne's outstretched hands, the lightsaber struck Fang Zar first, ripping a deep gouge across his upper chest and nearly decapitating him; then, continuing on, it struck an unsuspecting Jula across the back before completing its swift and lethal circle and slamming into the upper reaches of the fully lowered rampart gate, where it switched off and plummeted to the paving stones with a metallic clangor.

On the landing platform, Skeck was bent low over Fang Zar; Archyr, over Jula.

Rooted in place Shryne could sense Vader on the far side of the gate, a black hole of rage.

Shryne commenced a stiff-legged descent of the stairway, deaf to all sound, blind to color, scarcely in possession of his self.

He didn't come to his senses until he reached the foot of the stairs, where he turned and ran to help get his mother and Zar aboard the drop ship.

One by one Palpatine's military advisers appeared before him, standing in postures of obeisance below the throne room's dais, their eyes narrowed against the orange blaze of Coruscant's setting sun, delivering their reports and appraisals, their expert assessments of the state of his Empire.

Royal Guards stood to both sides of the high-backed chair; behind them sat Mas Amedda, Sly Moore, and other members of Palpatine's inner circle.

He listened to everyone without comment.

In some outlying systems, arsenals of Separatist weapons, in some cases entire flotillas of droid-piloted warships, had been commandeered by rogue paramilitary groups before Imperial forces could reach them.

In Hutt space, smugglers, pirates, and other scoundrels were taking advantage of the Emperor's need to consolidate power by blazing new routes for the movement of spice and other proscribed goods.

On many former CIS worlds, bounty hunters were tracking down former Separatist colluders.

In the Mid Rim, Imperial academies were filling with recruits obtained from flight schools throughout the galaxy.

In the Outer Rim, three new batches of stormtroopers were being grown.

Closer to the Core, capital ships were being turned out by Sienar, Kuat Drive, and other yards.

And yet at present there were simply too few battle groups or stormtroopers to deploy at every potential trouble spot.

Massive protests had been held on Alderaan, Corellia, and Commenor.

Progress was lagging on several of the Emperor's most cherished projects, owing to a lack of construction workers . . .

When the last of his advisers had come and gone, Palpatine dismissed everyone, including the members of his inner circle, and sat gazing over the western cityscape as it came to brilliant light in the deepening dusk.

Under the rule of the ancient Sith, the future of the galaxy had been in the able hands of many dark sovereigns. Now responsibility for maintaining order rested only with Darth Sidious.

For the moment it was enough that his advisers and minions respected him—for reestablishing peace, for eliminating the group that had posed the greatest threat to continued stability—but eventually those same advisers would need to fear him. To understand the great power he wielded, as both Emperor and Dark Lord of the Sith. And to that end, Sidious needed Vader.

For if someone as potent as Vader answered to the Emperor, then how powerful must the Emperor be!

After he had spent several hours drifting on the currents of possible futures, Palpatine summoned Sate Pestage. Swiveling his chair from the view of Coruscant when the most trusted of his advisers entered the throne room, Palpatine ordered Pestage to take a seat and appraised him.

"Events unfolded as you assured they would," Pestage said when Palpatine nodded for him to speak. "Organa was very predictable. My intervention was minimal."

"Senator Organa was willing to allow Fang Zar to escape, you mean."

"It certainly seemed that way."

Palpatine considered it. "He may bear watching in the future. But at present we won't make an issue of it. And Senator Zar?"

Pestage sighed with meaning. "Gravely wounded. Perhaps dead."

"Pity. Does Organa know?"

"Yes. He was very troubled by the outcome."

"And Lord Vader?"

"Even more troubled by the outcome."

Palpatine allowed a grin of satisfaction. "Even better."

Returned to its astral sanctuary, the *Drunk Dancer* drifted in space.

From the hatch to medbay, a 2-1B droid hovered out to report that it had been able to save Jula, but that Fang Zar had died on the operating table.

"Damage sustained by major vessels that supply the heart was too extensive to repair, sir," the droid told Shryne. "Everything that could be done, was done."

Shryne looked in on Jula, who was heavily sedated.

"I dragged you right back into it," she said weakly.

He pushed her hair off her forehead. "There might have been other forces at work."

"Don't say that, Roan. We just need to get farther away."

He smiled with effort. "I'll ask Archyr about outfitting the ship with an intergalactic drive."

He let her drift into sleep and went to his bunk. Whenever he shut his eyes, he would see the trajectory of Vader's blade; would see it slicing through Zar, through Jula . . . He didn't need to shut his eyes to recall how it had felt to be overwhelmed by Vader's ability to use the Force.

To use the power of the dark side.

A Sith.

Shryne was certain now.

A Sith in service to Emperor Palpatine.

That was the revelation he couldn't banish.

Count Dooku might as well have won the war, save for the fact that in place of independent systems, free trade, and the rest, the galaxy answered to the exclusive rule of Palpatine.

But how? Shryne asked himself. How had it happened?

Had Palpatine's alliance with Vader been brought about by the death of the Chosen One? Had Vader—*Darth* Vader—killed Anakin Skywalker? Had he struck a deal with Palpatine beforehand, promising Palpatine unlimited power in exchange for sanctioning Vader's murder of the Chosen One and the elimination of the Jedi, thus tipping the galaxy fully to the dark side?

Was it any wonder, then, that beings were fleeing for the far-flung reaches of known space?

And was it any wonder that Shryne had lacked the strength to alter the course of Vader's lightsaber? He had thought of his diminished abilities as a personal failure—owing to the fact that he had lost his faith in the Jedi order, allowed his two Padawans to die, grown thought-bound—when, in fact, it was the Force as the Jedi had known it that had been defeated.

The flame extinguished.

On the one hand, it meant that Shryne's transition into regular life could probably proceed more smoothly than he had thought; by contrast, that regular life meant existing in a world where evil had triumphed and ruled.

* * *

In the antechamber of his private retreat, Sidious, dressed in a dark blue cowled robe, paced in front of the curved window wall. Vader stood rigidly at the center of the room, his gloved hands crossed in front of him.

"It appears you attended to our little problem on Alderaan, Lord Vader," Sidious said.

"Yes, Master. Fang Zar need no longer concern you."

"I know I should feel some sense of relief. But in fact, I'm not entirely pleased with the outcome. Zar's death could arouse sympathy in the Senate."

Vader stirred. "He left me no recourse."

Sidious came to a halt and turned toward Vader. "No recourse? Why didn't you simply apprehend him, as I asked?"

"He made the mistake of attempting to flee."

"But *you* against someone like Fang Zar? It hardly seems an equitable match, Lord Vader."

"Zar was not alone," Vader said with venom. "What's more, if you don't like the way . . ."

Suddenly intrigued, Sidious moved closer. "Ah, what's this? Allowing your words to trail off—as if I can't see their destination." Anger showed in his yellow eyes. "As if I can't see the *thought* behind them!"

Vader said nothing.

"Perhaps you're not enjoying your new station in life, is that it? Perhaps you tire already of executing my commands." Sidious stared at him. "Perhaps you think you're better suited to occupy the throne than I am. Is that it, Lord Vader? If so, then admit as much!"

Breathing deeply, Vader remained silent for a moment more. "I am but an apprentice. *You* are the Master."

"Interesting that you refrain from calling me *your* Master."

Vader inclined his head to Sidious. "I meant nothing by it, my Master."

Sidious sneered. "Perhaps you wish you could strike me down, is that it?"

"No, Master."

"What stops you from doing so? Obi-Wan was once your Master, and you were certainly prepared to kill him. Even if you *failed*."

Vader clenched his right hand. "Obi-Wan did not understand the power of the dark side."

"And you do?"

"No, Master. Not yet. Not fully."

"And that's why you don't try to strike me down? Because I possess powers you lack?" Sidious lifted his arms, hands deployed like claws, as if to summon and hurl Sith lightning. "Because you know that I could easily overwhelm the delicate electrical systems of your suit."

Vader stood his ground. "I don't fear death, Master."

Sidious grinned maliciously. "Then why go on living, my young apprentice?"

Vader looked down at him. "To learn to become more powerful."

Sidious lowered his hands. "Then I ask you one final time, Lord Vader. Why not strike me down?"

"Because you are my path to power, Master," Vader said. "Because I need you."

Sidious narrowed his eyes and nodded. "Just like I needed my Master—for a time."

"Yes, Master," Vader said finally. "For a time."

"Good. Very good." Sidious smiled in satisfaction. "And *now* you are ready to release your anger."

Vader evinced confusion.

"Your fugitive Jedi, my apprentice," Sidious said. "They are traveling to Kashyyyk." He tipped his head to one side. "Perhaps, Lord Vader, they hope to lay a trap for you."

Vader clenched his hands. "That would be my most fervent wish, my Master."

Sidious clamped his hands on Vader's upper arms. "Then go to them, Lord Vader. Make them sorry they didn't hide while they had the chance!"

PART IV
Kashyyyk

Inside the battered transport that had once belonged to an Imperial garrison on Dellalt, Olee Starstone and the six Jedi who had joined her crusade waited to be granted clearance to continue on to Kashyyyk space. The commanders of the half dozen Imperial corvettes that made up the inspection-point picket answered not to distant Coruscant but to the regional governor, headquartered on Bimmisaari.

The Jedi had done all they could to make the ship look the part of a military-surplus transport. Thanks mostly to Jula's crew, the drives had been tweaked to produce a new signature, the ship's profile had been altered, the defensive shields and counter-measures suite repaired. To ensure that what remained conformed to Imperial standards, many of the advanced sensors and scanners had been eliminated, along with most of the laser cannons. The *Drunk Dancer*'s maintenance droids had given the ship a quick paint job and had helped remove some of the seats amidships, to create a common cabin space.

To Starstone, the vessel's fresh look matched the false identities the Jedi had adopted, as well as the clothes that made them look like a motley crew of struggling space merchants.

The transport's cockpit was spacious enough to accommo-date Starstone and Filli Bitters, in addition to Jambe Lu and Nam Poorf, late of the Temple's Agricultural Corps, who were doing the piloting, and still-sightless Deran Nalual, who was tucked into the cramped communications duty station.

No one had said a word since Nalual had transmitted the ship's authorization key to the picket array's cardinal corvette. Filli was confident that the transport's altered drive signature would pass muster, but—new to forging Imperial code—he was less certain about the authorization key.

Starstone placed her hand on Jambe's shoulder, as a way of saying: *Be ready to make a run for it.*

Jambe was centering himself behind the steering yoke when an officious voice issued from the cockpit speakers.

"*Vagabond Trader,* you are cleared for approach to Kashyyyk. Commerce Control will provide you with vector coordinates for atmospheric entry and landing."

"Understood," Deran said into the mouthpiece of her head-set.

Engaging the transport's sublight drive, Jambe and Nam began to edge the transport through the cordon.

Starstone heard Filli's eased exhalation and turned to him.

"You all right?"

"I am now," he said. "I was flying blind with that code."

"I guess we're both that good," Deran said from behind him.

Starstone touched Deran on the arm and smiled at Filli.

He smiled back. "Glad to help."

Starstone was still getting used to Filli's frequently awkward attempts at flirtation. But then, she wasn't even ranked a begin-ner. The idea that the towheaded slicer was on temporary loan from the *Drunk Dancer* was absurd. Shryne was merely using Filli as a means of keeping tabs on the Jedi, but she refused to let that bother her. If Filli's slicing skills could help locate fugitive

Jedi, so much the better, even if she did have to pretend to be flattered by his attention, as opposed to being embarrassed by it. She liked him more and more, but she had her priorities straight, and involvement wasn't among them.

She wasn't Shryne.

Initially she had been angry at him and at his ever-persuasive mother, but in the end she had realized that her anger was rooted more in attachment than anything else. Shryne had his own path to follow in the Force, despite his beliefs to the contrary, and despite the fact that she missed him.

The worst part about it was that she had somehow assumed the mantle of leader. Notwithstanding that both Siadem Forte and the Ho'Din, Iwo Kulka, were Jedi Knights, they had relinquished their due as higher-ranking Jedi without the issue ever being raised. For that matter, even Jambe and Nam outranked her. But because the search had been her idea, everyone had essentially granted her tacit approval to do most of the thinking.

Clear evidence of everyone's sense of dispossession, she thought.

On a mission that wasn't a Jedi mission, but was all about being a Jedi.

And thus far the crusade had come to nothing.

On every world they had visited between Felucia and Saleucami it had been the same: the Jedi had been revealed as traitors to the Republic and had been killed by the clone troopers they had commanded. None had survived, Starstone and the others had been told. And pity any who had survived, for anti-Jedi sentiment was widespread, especially in the Outer Rim, among populations that had been drawn into the war and now saw themselves as having been mere performers in a game the Jedi had been playing to assume control of the Republic.

Justification for Shryne to say *I told you so* when they next met.

Even in the few standard weeks since the war's end, a dramatic change had taken place. With the rapid diffusion of the symbols of the Empire, *fear* was radiating from the Core. On worlds where peace should have brought relief, distrust and suspicion prevailed. The war was over, and yet brigades of stormtroopers remained garrisoned on hundreds of worlds, formerly Separatist and Republic alike. The war was over, and yet Imperial inspection points dotted the major hyperlanes and sector jump points. The war was over, and yet the call was out for recruits to serve in the Imperial armed forces.

The war was over, and yet the HoloNet addressed little else.

Starstone believed she understood why: because in the depths of his black heart, the Emperor knew that the next war wouldn't be fought from the outside in, but rather from the inside out. That not a generation would pass, much less the ten thousand *years* Palpatine had predicted the Empire to endure, before the disease that had now taken root on Coruscant would infect every system in the galaxy.

Even so, as desperate as the quest seemed, she was still counting on the Wookiees to provide the Jedi with the hope they needed to carry on. From information gleaned from the Temple beacon database, they knew that three Jedi had been dispatched to Kashyyyk: Quinlan Vos, Luminara Unduli, and Master Yoda himself, who, according to Forte and Kulka, had enjoyed a long-standing relationship with the Wookiees.

If there was a planet where Jedi could have survived Palpatine's execution order, Kashyyyk would be it.

"Wookiee World," Nam said as he dropped the bow of the transport.

The planet rose into view, whitecapped, otherwise green and blue. Dozens of huge vessels hung in orbit, including the perforated hulks of several Separatist warships. Ferries and drop ships could be seen emerging from and disappearing into Kashyyyk's high-stacked clouds.

Jambe indicated a Separatist ship, tipped over on its starboard side, its underbelly heavily punctured by turbolaser bolts. Umbilicaled to it were a pair of craft that looked more like musical horns than space vessels.

"Wookiee ships," Jambe said. "They're probably cannibalizing whatever's useful."

Filli leaned toward the viewports for a better look. "They take immigrant technology and make it all their own. For enough credits, they could probably build us a wooden starship."

Starstone had heard as much. Inventive handiwork was the primary reason Wookiees frequently fell prey to slave traders, especially Trandoshans, their reptilian planetary neighbors. Skill, however, hadn't brought the Separatists to Kashyyyk, or the Trade Federation before them. The system was not only close to several major hyperlanes, but also an entry point for an entire quadrant of space. A Wookiee guild of cartographers known as the Claatuvac were said to have mapped star routes that didn't even appear on Republic or Separatist charts.

The communications console chimed a repeating series of tones.

"Vector routing from Commerce Control," Deran said.

"Make sure they understand we want to set down near Kachirho," Starstone said.

Deran nodded. "Transmitting our request. Relaying course coordinates to navigation."

Nam threw an excited look over his shoulder. "I've wanted to visit Kashyyyk for ten years."

"Half the Core would like to visit Kashyyyk," Filli said. "But the Wookiees don't cater to tourists."

"What, no luxury accommodations?" Jambe said.

Filli shook his head. "They *might* be willing to provide a tent."

"How many times have you been here?" Starstone asked him.

He thought about it, then shrugged. "Ten, twelve. In between regular jobs, we'd sometimes run scrap technology here."

"Can you speak the language?" Nam asked.

Filli laughed. "I once met a human who could bark a couple of useful phrases, but the best I could ever manage was a 'thank you,' and that worked only one out of ten times."

Starstone frowned. "Do we have a translator droid or some sort of emulator?"

"We won't need one," Filli said. "The Wookiees employ a mixed-species staff of go-betweens to help out with sales and trades."

"Who do we ask for?" Starstone said.

Filli took a moment. "Last time I was here, there was a guy named Cudgel . . ."

The *Vagabond Trader* began its descent into Kashyyyk's aromatic atmosphere, light fading as the ship dropped below the canopy of the planet's three-hundred-meter-tall wroshyr trees into an area of majestic cliffs crowned with vegetation. Adjusting course, Jambe and Nam guided the transport to a lakeshore landing platform made of wood. Towering majestically over the platform and the aquamarine lake rose the city of Kachirho, which consisted of a cluster of giant, tiered wroshyrs.

In his eagerness to fulfill a ten-year dream, Nam nearly botched the landing, but no one was hurt, despite being tossed about. As soon as everyone had exited the ship, Filli disappeared to find Cudgel.

Starstone gazed at the trees and sheer cliffs in wonderment. Her hopes for finding Yoda notwithstanding, the Wookiee world rendered other planets she had visited prosaic by comparison.

The scene at the exotic landing platform alone was impressive, with ships coming and going, and groups of Wookiees and their liaison crews haggling with beings representing dozens of different species. Outsize logs and slabs of fine-grained hardwoods were heaped about, and the air was rich with the heady smell of tree sap, and loud with the drone of nearby lumber mills. Protocol and labor droids supervised the loading and off-loading of cargo, which was moved by teams of hornless banthas or exquisitely crafted hoversleds. All of the activity shaded and dwarfed by trees that seemed to reach to the very edge of space . . .

Starstone had to catch her breath. The gargantuan size of everything made her feel like an insect. She was still gaping like a tourist when Filli returned, accompanied by a thickset male human dressed in short trousers and a sleeveless shirt. If he wasn't quite as hairy as a Wookiee, it was not for want of trying.

"Cudgel," Filli said, by way of introduction.

Cudgel smiled at everyone in turn, jocular but clearly dubious, and Starstone immediately saw why. While she and her band of fugitive Jedi could dress the part of merchants, even talk the part, they couldn't *stand* the part.

Literally.

Straight-backed, silent, hands clasped in front of them, they looked more like a group of vacationing meditators, which was not far from the truth.

"First time to Kashyyyk?" Cudgel said.

"Yes," Starstone answered for everyone. "Hopefully not our last."

"Welcome, then." Forcing a smile, he eyed the transport. "This is an L two hundred, isn't it?"

"Military surplus," Filli said quickly.

Cudgel cocked a flaring eyebrow. "Already? I was under the impression there wasn't any surplus." Before Filli could respond, he continued: "Can't be carrying much in the way of trade goods. Are you off a freighter up top?"

"We're not here to trade, exactly," Filli said. "More in the way of a fact-finding mission."

"We're in the market for an Oevvaor catamaran," Starstone explained.

Cudgel blinked in surprise. "Then your ship had better be filled with aurodium credits."

"Our client is prepared to pay a fair price," Starstone said.

Cudgel stroked his chest-length beard. "Not a question of price. More of availability."

"How bad were things here?" Forte asked abruptly. "The battle, I mean?"

Cudgel followed the Jedi's gaze to the tree-city. "Bad enough. The Wookiees are still cleaning up."

"Many killed?" Nam asked.

"Even one's too many."

"Were any Jedi involved?"

Jambe's question seemed to stop Cudgel cold. "Why do you ask?"

"We just came from Saleucami," Starstone said, hoping to put Cudgel at ease. "We heard that several Jedi were killed by clone troopers during the battle."

Cudgel appraised her. "I wouldn't know about that. I was in Rwookrrorro during most of it." He pointed. "Other side of the escarpment."

A short silence fell over everyone.

"Well, let's see if I can't find someone who knows catamarans," Cudgel said at last.

Starstone kept quiet until the hirsute middleman had moved off. "I don't think that went so well," she said to Forte and the others.

"Shouldn't matter," Iwo Kulka said. "Kashyyyk isn't Saleucami or Felucia. We're in Jedi-friendly territory."

"That's what you said on Boz Pity—" Starstone started to say when Filli cut her off.

"Cudgel's back."

With four rangy Wookiees in tow, Starstone saw.

"These are the folk I told you about," Cudgel was telling the Wookiees, in Basic.

Before Starstone could open her mouth to speak, the Wookiees bared their fangs and brandished the most bizarre-looking hand blasters she had ever seen.

The Star Destroyer *Exactor* and its older sibling, *Executrix*, drifted side by side, bow-to-stern, forming a parallelogram of armor and armament.

Vader's black shuttle navigated the short distance between them.

He sat in the passenger hold's forward row of seats, his cadre of stormtroopers behind him, and his thoughts focused on what awaited him on Kashyyyk, rather than on the imminent meeting, which he suspected was little more than a formality.

His last conversation with Sidious, weeks earlier but as if only yesterday, had made it clear that his Master was manipulating him now as much as he had before he had turned. Before and during the war Sidious's intention had been to entice him into joining the Sith; since, the goal was to transform him into a Sith. That was, to impress upon Vader that the power of the dark side did not flow from understanding but from appetite, rivalry, avarice, and malice. The very qualities the Jedi considered base and corrupt.

As a means of keeping their plucked pupils from exploring the deeper sides of their nature; as a means of reining them, lest they discovered for themselves the real power of the Force.

Anger leads to fear; fear to hatred; hatred to the dark side . . .

Precisely, Vader thought.

At Sidious's insistence, he had spent the recent weeks sharpening his ability to summon and make use of his rage, and felt poised at the edge of a significant increase in his abilities.

Deep space was appropriate to such feelings, he told himself as he gazed out the cabin's viewport. Space was more appropriate for the Sith than for the Jedi. The invisible enslavement to gravity, the contained power of the stars, the utter insignificance of life . . . Hyperspace, by contrast, was more suitable to the Jedi: nebulous, neither here nor there, incoherent.

When the shuttle had docked in the *Executor*'s hold, Vader led his contingent of stormtroopers out of the vessel, only to find that his host hadn't shown him the courtesy of being on hand to greet him. Waiting, instead, was his host's contingent of gray-uniformed crew members, commanded by a human officer named Darcc.

The games begin, Vader thought, as he allowed Captain Darcc to escort him deeper into the ship.

The cabin to which he was ultimately led was in the uppermost reaches of the Star Destroyer's conning tower. On entering, Vader found his host sitting behind a gleaming slab of desk, plainly debating whether to remain seated or to stand; whether to place himself on equal footing with Vader, or, by appearance, to continue to suggest superiority. Knowing, in any case, that Vader preferred to remain on his feet, his host was not likely to gesture him to a chair. Knowing, too, that Vader was capable of strangling him from clear across the cabin might also figure into his decision.

What to do? his host must have been thinking.

And then he stood, a slender, sharp-featured man, coming around from behind the desk with his hands clasped behind his back.

"Thank you for detouring from your course," Wilhuff Tarkin said.

The expression of gratitude was unexpected. But if Tarkin was intent on prolonging the game, then Vader would humor him, since in the end it amounted to nothing more than establishing status.

This was what the Empire would be, he thought. A contest among men intent on clawing their way to the top, to sit at Sidious's feet.

"The Emperor requested it," Vader said finally.

Tarkin pursed his thin lips. "I suppose we can attribute that to the Emperor's astute ability to bring like-minded beings together."

"Or pit them against one another."

Tarkin adopted a more sober look. "That, too, Lord Vader."

With a mind as sharp as his cheekbones, Tarkin had risen quickly through the ranks of Palpatine's newly formed staff of political and military elite, among whom naked ambition was highly prized. So much so that a new honorific had been created for Tarkin and ambitious men like him: *Moff.*

Vader had met him once before, aboard a *Venator*-class Star Destroyer, at the remote location where the Emperor's secret weapon was under construction. Vader, still new to his suit then; awkward, uncertain, between worlds.

Tarkin perched himself on the edge of his desk and smiled thinly. "Perhaps between the two of us, we can determine the reason the Emperor arranged this rendezvous."

Vader crossed his gloved hands in front of him. "I suspect that you know more about the purpose of this meeting than I do, Moff Tarkin."

Tarkin's smile disappeared, and in its place came a look of sharp attentiveness. "Surely you can guess, my friend."

"Kashyyyk."

"Bravo."

Tarkin activated a holoplate that sat atop his desk. In the cone of blue light that rose from it, a bruised transport of military design could be seen moving through a cordon of Imperial corvettes.

"This was recorded approximately ten hours ago, local, at the Kashyyyk system checkpoint. As you may have already guessed, the transport belongs to the Jedi. It appears to be a civilian model, but it isn't. It was hijacked on Dellalt some weeks ago, and was the object of a pursuit that ended in the destruction of several Imperial starfighters. We have, however, been successful at tracking its movements ever since."

"You've been tracking them," Vader said in genuine surprise. "Was the Emperor apprised of this?"

Tarkin smiled again. "Lord Vader, the Emperor is apprised of *everything*."

But his apprentice isn't, Vader thought.

"I ordered our checkpoint personnel to ignore the obvious fact that the transport's signature has been altered," Tarkin continued, "and to ignore, as well, the fact that whatever codes the transport furnished were likely to be counterfeit."

"Why weren't the Jedi simply taken into custody at the checkpoint?"

"We had our reasons, Lord Vader. Or perhaps I should say that the Emperor had his."

"They are on Kashyyyk now?"

Tarkin stopped the holoimage and nodded. "We thought they might be refused entry. Apparently, however, someone aboard the ship is familiar with Kashyyyk's trading protocols."

Vader considered it for a moment. "You said that you

had your reasons for clearing the transport through the check-point."

"Yes, I'm coming to that," Tarkin said, standing to his full height and beginning to pace in front of the desk. "I realize that you of all people require no assistance in . . . bringing the fugitive Jedi to justice. But I want to lay out a somewhat broader plan for your consideration. Should you accept the proposition, I'm in a position to provide you with whatever ships, personnel, and matériel you think necessary."

"What is the proposition, Moff Tarkin?"

Tarkin came to a stop and turned fully to Vader. "Simply this. The Jedi are your priority, as they should be. Certainly the Empire can't permit potential insurgents to run around loose. But—" He raised a bony forefinger. "—my plan allows for the Empire to profit even more substantially from your under-taking."

Reactivating the holoprojector, Tarkin turned his attention to an image of the Emperor's moonlet-size secret project, or-bitally anchored at its deep-space retreat. Vader had learned that the Emperor had placed Tarkin in charge of supervising certain aspects of construction.

Clearly, though, Tarkin was angling for more.

"How does my hunt for a few rogue Jedi figure into your scheme regarding the Emperor's weapon?" Vader asked.

"My 'scheme,' " Tarkin said, with a short laugh. "All right, then. Here's the truth of it. The project is already far behind schedule. It has been beset with engineering problems, delays in shipments, the unreliability of contractors, and, most important, a shortage of skilled laborers." He stared at Vader. "You must understand, Lord Vader, I wish nothing more than to please the Emperor."

This is Sidious's real power, Vader thought. *The ability to make others wish nothing more than to* please *him.*

"I accept that at face value," he said at last.

Tarkin studied him. "You would be willing to help me achieve this goal?"

"I see a possibility."

Narrowing his eyes, Tarkin nodded in a way that came close to being a bow of respect. "Then, my friend, our real partnership is just beginning."

They're interested in knowing why you're so interested in knowing whether any Jedi were here during the battle," Cudgel explained to Starstone and the others while the quartet of armed Wookiees glared down at them.

"Idle curiosity," Filli said, which only succeeded in eliciting rumbling growls from the four.

"They're not buying it," Cudgel said needlessly.

Starstone gazed up into the wide bronzium muzzles of weapons she suspected she would need the Force to heft, let alone fire. Peripherally she was aware that the confrontation had begun to draw the attention of other landing parties. Humans and aliens alike were suddenly interrupting their transactions with liaison staffers and Wookiees, and turning toward the transport.

Quickly she made up her mind to risk everything by simply telling the truth.

"We're Jedi," she said just loud enough to be heard.

From the way the Wookiees tilted their enormous shaggy heads, she grasped instantly that they had understood her. They kept their exotic weapons enabled and raised, but at the same time their expressions of wariness softened somewhat.

One of them brayed a remark to Cudgel.

Cudgel stroked his long beard. "Now, that's even harder to swallow than the idle-curiosity explanation, don't you think? I mean, considering the fact that the Jedi were wiped out."

The same Wookiee lowed and gobbled, and, again, Cudgel nodded, then centered his gaze on Starstone.

"Maybe if you'd said that *you* were a Jedi, then all of us on the happy side of these blasters would be convinced. But—" He counted heads. "—you can't be telling me all eight of you are Jedi. Seven anyway, 'cause I know Filli's almost as far from being a Jedi as it gets."

"I meant *me*," Starstone said. "I'm a Jedi."

"So it's just you, then?"

"She's lying," Siadem Forte said before she could respond.

Two of the Wookiees snarled in plain displeasure.

Cudgel looked from Forte to Starstone. "Lying? See, now you have everyone really confused, 'cause we always thought of the Jedi as truth tellers."

The Wookiees spoke among themselves, then one of them barked an outpouring at Cudgel.

"Guania, here, points out that you arrive in a military transport. You look as though you can handle yourselves. You start asking questions about Jedi . . . He's thinking that you might be bounty hunters."

Starstone shook her head back and forth. "Check the transport. Under the navicomputer console, you'll find six lightsabers—"

"Means nothing," Cudgel cut in. "You could have taken them off your quarries, just the way General Grievous did."

"Then how do we prove it?" Starstone said. "What do you want us to do, perform Force tricks?"

The Wookiees issued a yodeling warning.

Cudgel lowered his voice to say: "In the unlikely event that you are Jedi, that might not be such a good idea out here in the open."

Starstone forced an exhale, and looked up at the Wookiees. "We know that Masters Yoda, Luminara Unduli, and Quinlan Vos were here with brigades of troopers." When she saw in their deep brown eyes that she had their full attention, she continued. "We've risked a lot to come here. But we know that Master Yoda had good relations with you, and we're hoping that still counts for something."

The Wookiees didn't actually lower their weapons, but they did disable them. One of them lowed to Cudgel, who said: "Lachichuk suggests we continue this conversation in Kachirho."

Starstone asked Filli and Deran to remain with the ship; then she, Forte, Kulka, and the others began to follow Cudgel and the Wookiees toward the gargantuan wroshyr that stood at the center of Kachirho tree-city. No sooner had they left the landing platform than Cudgel's attitude changed.

"I heard that *none* of you survived," he said to Starstone as they walked.

"It's beginning to look like we're the only ones," she said sadly. Putting the edge of her hand to her brow, she gazed up at the huge balconies that tiered the tree, some of which showed evidence of recent damage.

"Do you know if any Jedi died here?"

Cudgel shook his head. "The Wookiees haven't told me anything. For a while it looked like Kashyyyk was going to have its own garrison of clone troopers, but after the Sep droids and war machines shut down, the troopers decamped. Ever since, the

Wookiees have been making good use of everything that was left behind."

"For weapons?"

"You bet, for weapons. Seps or no, they've still got enemies—species that want to exploit them."

Cudgel led everyone into the hollowed base of the tree, and finally to a turbolift that accessed Kachirho's upper levels.

Similar to everything she had seen since leaving the landing platform, the turbolift was an ingenious blend of wood and alloy, the technology that drove it artfully concealed. And at each tier, her astonishment only increased. In addition to the exterior platforms that grew like burls from the bole, the tree contained vast interior rooms, with shimmering parquet floors and curved walls inset with wooden and alloy mosaics. There didn't seem to be a straight line anywhere, and everywhere Starstone looked she saw Wookiees engaged in building, carving, sanding . . . as devoted to their work as Jedi had been in fashioning the Temple. Except the Wookiees hadn't enslaved themselves to symmetry or order; rather, they allowed their creations to emerge naturally from the wood. In fact, they seemed to invite a certain kind of imperfection—some detail to which the eye would be drawn, setting off an entire wall panel, or an expanse of floor.

Covered walkways and bridges crisscrossed the tree's interior shaft, and irregular openings brought verdant Kashyyyk *inside*. At every turn, every staircase spiral or turbolift stop, exterior views of the lake, the forest, and the sheer cliffs were framed by finely worked apertures and clefts. What Kachirho lacked in color, it made up for in luster and deep patina.

Fifty or so meters above the lake, the Jedi were ushered into a kind of central control room, which looked out over the glinting water and was perhaps the purest example yet of the Wookiees' ability to combine organic and high-tech elements. Console display screens and holoprojectors showed views of the landing platform, as well as loading operations in orbit.

There, their escorts exchanged muted growls and snorts, snuffs and rumbles, with two others, one of whom was certainly the tallest Wookiee Starstone had seen.

"This is Chewbacca," Cudgel said, introducing the shorter of the pair, "and this is one of Kachirho's war chiefs, Tarfful."

Starstone introduced herself and the rest of the Jedi, then lowered herself onto a beautifully carved stool built for human-size beings. Similar stools were rushed into the room, along with soft seat cushions and plates of food.

While all this was going on, Tarfful and Chewbacca were being briefed by Lachichuk. Bronzium bands gathered the chieftain's long hair into rope-thick tassels that fell to his belted waist. The shoulder straps of his baldric joined at an ornate pectoral. Chewbacca, whose black fur was cinnamon-tipped and nowhere near as long as Tarfful's, wore a simple baldric Starstone thought might double as an ammunition bandolier.

When everyone was seated and the Wookiees had finished conversing, Cudgel said: "Chieftain Tarfful understands and applauds the courage you've shown in coming to Kashyyyk, but it grieves him to report that he has nothing but sad tidings for you."

"They're . . . dead?" Starstone asked.

"Master Vos was presumed killed by fire from a tank," Cudgel explained, "Master Unduli by blasterfire."

"And Master Yoda?" she asked quietly.

Tarfful and Chewbacca fell into a long conversation—almost a debate—before expressing themselves to Cudgel, whose eyebrows shot up in surprise.

"Apparently, Yoda escaped Kashyyyk in an evacuation pod. Chewbacca, here, says he carried Yoda on his shoulders to the pod."

Starstone came to her feet, nearly tipping over a platter of food. "He's alive?"

"He could be," Cudgel said after a moment. "After the last of the clone troopers left, the Wookiees searched local space for the pod, but no distress-beacon transmissions were picked up."

"Was the pod hyperspace-capable?"

Cudgel shook his head.

"But it could have been retrieved by a passing ship."

The Wookiees conversed.

Cudgel listened attentively. "There's a chance it was."

Starstone looked at Tarfful. "What makes you think so?"

Cudgel ran his hand over his mouth. "Wookiee Senator Yarua reported that rumors circulating in the Senate claim Yoda led an attack on Emperor Palpatine in the Senate Rotunda itself."

"And?"

"Same rumor has it he was killed."

"Master Yoda doesn't lose," Siadem Forte said from his stool.

Cudgel returned a sympathetic nod. "Lots of us used to say that about the Jedi."

Starstone broke the silence that descended on the control room. "If Master Yoda *is* alive, then there's hope for all of us. He'll find us before we find him."

She felt renewed; hopeful once more.

"Tarfful asks what you plan to do now," Cudgel said.

"I suppose we'll continue our search," Starstone said. "Master Kenobi was on Utapau, and has yet to be heard from."

Tarfful issued what sounded like a sustained groan.

"He is honored to offer you safe haven on Kashyyyk, if you wish. The Wookiees can make it appear that you are valued customers."

"You would do that for us?" Starstone asked Tarfful.

His response was plaintive.

"The Wookiees owe the Jedi a great debt," Cudgel translated. "And debts are always honored."

A signal sounded from one of the consoles, and Cudgel and the Wookiees gathered around an inset screen. The human's expression was grave when he swung to the Jedi.

"An Imperial troop carrier is descending to the Kachirho platform."

Starstone's face lost color. "We shouldn't have come here," she said suddenly. "We've endangered all of you!"

By the time Cudgel returned to the landing platform the situation was already veering out of control. Blaster rifles raised and faced off with more than one hundred very indignant Wookiees, two squads of stormtroopers were deployed around the carrier that had delivered them to Kachirho, perhaps half a kilometer from where the Jedi transport was parked.

"Or are you going to tell us that your weapons are all the permission you need?" a human liaison staffer was saying to the troopers' commander as Cudgel hurried in.

The officer's armor was marked with green, and he wore a short campaign skirt. His sidearm was still holstered, but his enhanced voice was filled with menace. "Authorization was granted by Sector Three Command and Control. If you have any complaints, take them up with the regional governor."

"Commander," Cudgel said in a deferential tone, "how may I be of service?"

The officer gestured broadly to the gathered Wookiees. "Only if you can get these beasts to answer my questions."

High-decibel snarls and furious roars rose from the crowd.

"You might want to find a more politic way to refer to Kashyyyk's indigenes, Commander."

From behind the T-visored helmet, the trooper said: "I'm not here to be diplomatic. Let them howl all they want." He gazed at Cudgel. "Identify yourself."

"I'm known as Cudgel, far and wide."

"What are your duties here?"

"I assist with commerce. I can probably set you up with a nice selection of product, if you're interested."

"What would we want with wood?"

"What, you don't have campfires?"

The crowd woofed with laughter.

The commander put his gloved right hand on his blaster. "There'll be fires soon enough—*Cudgel*. Right where you can see them."

"I'm not sure I take your meaning, Commander."

The officer adjusted his stance, readying himself for action. "Kashyyyk is harboring enemies of the Empire."

Cudgel shook his head. "If there are enemies of the Empire here, the Wookiees are unaware of them."

"There are *Jedi* here."

"You mean you actually missed a few?"

The commander raised his left hand and poked Cudgel hard in the chest. "Either they are surrendered to us immediately, or we take this place apart, beginning with you." At the commander's wave, the stormtroopers began to spread out. "Search the landing area and the tree-city! All non-indigenes are to be seized and brought here!"

The Wookiees loosed a chorus of earsplitting yowls.

Cudgel backed out of range of the commander's armored fist. "They don't like it when people track dirt in."

Drawing his sidearm, the commander said: "I'm done with you."

But the words had scarcely left the officer's helmet enunciator when a Wookiee raced forward, knocking the blaster from his hand and hurling him into the troop carrier with such force that the commander's forearm and elbow armor remained in the Wookiee's grip.

At the same time, several Wookiee clarions roared in the distance.

The troopers turned, covering one another as the gathered crowd began to advance on them.

A ratcheting noise filled the western sky. Two gunships dropped from the treetops to reinforce the advance squads, stormtroopers descending from the open bay on rappel ribbons.

Rushing onto the landing platform, the new arrivals stopped short on hearing the familiar *snap-hiss* of igniting lightsabers.

Central to half a dozen blade-wielding Jedi stood a young raven-haired woman, with her weapon poised over her right shoulder.

"We hear you're looking for us," she said.

Standing on the bridge of the *Exactor,* Vader regarded distant Kashyyyk through the forward viewports. Commander Appo approached from one of the duty stations.

"Lord Vader, the conflict has begun. Theater commanders await your orders."

"Raise them, Commander, and join me in the situation room."

Leaving the bridge, Vader entered an adjacent cabin space just as holoimages were resolving above a ring of several holoprojectors. Appo came through the hatch behind him, waiting at the perimeter of the ring.

Members of the Emperor's new admiralty, the commanders were human, attired in formfitting jackets and trousers. Certainly each of them had been informed that Vader was to be treated with the same respect they showed the Emperor, but Vader could see in their ghostly faces that they had yet to make up their minds about him. Was he man, machine, something in between? Was he clone, apostate Jedi, *Sith*?

Kashyyyk would tell them all they needed to know, Vader thought.

I am something to be feared.

"Commanders, I want you to position your task forces to cover all major population centers." A holomap eddied from a holoprojector outside the ring, detailing Kashyyyk and the tree-cities of Kachirho, Rwookrrorro, Kepitenochan, Okikuti, Chena-chochan, and others. "Furthermore, I want Interdictor cruisers deployed to prevent any ships from jumping to hyperspace."

"Admiral Vader," one of the men said. "The Wookiees have no ranged weapons or planetary defense shields. Orbital bombardment would simplify matters greatly."

Vader decided not to make an issue of the misplaced honorific. "Perhaps, Commander," he said, "if this were an exercise in obliteration. But since it isn't, we'll adhere to my plan."

"I've had some experience with the Wookiees," another said. "They won't be taken into captivity without a fight."

"I fully expect a fight, Commander," Vader said. "But I want as many as possible taken *alive*—males, females, and younglings. Order your troops to drive them from their tree-cities into open spaces. Then use whatever means are at our disposal to disarm and subdue them."

"Kashyyyk hosts many merchants," a third said, leadingly.

"Casualties of war, Commander."

"Do you intend to occupy the planet?" the same asked.

"That is not my intention."

"Excuse me, sir, but what, then, are we supposed to do with tens of thousands of Wookiee captives?"

Vader faced the one who had challenged him. "Herd them into containment and keep them contained until they have accepted their defeat. You will then receive further orders."

"From whom?" the challenger said.

"From *me*, Commander."

The officer folded his arms in mild defiance. "From you."

"You seem to have a problem with that. Perhaps you wish to speak with the Emperor?"

The officer was quick to adopt a more military pose. "No, of course not . . . Lord Vader."

Better and better, Vader thought.

"Where will you be, Lord Vader?" the first asked.

Vader looked at all of them before answering. "My task needn't concern you. You have your orders. Now carry them out."

Try as she might to convince herself that her actions were justified, that the clone army had become the enemy not only of the Jedi but also of democracy and freedom, Starstone couldn't surrender herself fully to combat. Brought into being to serve the Republic, the troopers, like the Jedi, had fallen victim to Palpatine's treachery. And now they were dying at the hands of those who had helped create them.

This is wrong, all wrong, she told herself.

And yet, clearly, the notion of tragic irony hadn't been incorporated into the clones' programming. The troopers were out to kill her. Only the flashing blue blade of her lightsaber stood between her and certain death.

The stormtroopers who had been the first to land were already dead, from blaster rounds, bowcaster quarrels, lightsaber slashes, blows from war clubs and the occasional giant, shaggy fist. But more and more Imperial craft were dropping from the wan sky—gunships, troop carriers, scores of two-person infantry support platforms. Worse, word had it that the incursion wasn't confined to Kachirho, but was being repeated in tree-cites world-wide.

If the hearsay was true, then the Jedi weren't the priority. The Empire was merely using their presence to justify a full-scale invasion. And the fact that Imperial forces were refraining from launching orbital bombardments told Starstone that the ultimate goal was something other than speciecide.

The troopers had been ordered not to amass high body counts, but to return with prisoners.

Starstone held herself accountable. Inevitable or not, she had furnished the Empire with grounds to invade. Forte and Kulka were wrong to have deferred to her lead. She was not a Master. She should have listened to Shryne.

The surround of towering cliffs and trees made it difficult for large vessels to hover or land outside the perimeter of the landing platform. The lake that fronted Kachirho was expansive enough to accommodate a *Victory*-class Star Destroyer, but a subsequent offensive would entail storming the shoreline, as the Separatists had attempted to do, and Kachirho, at almost four hundred meters in height, presented a formidable battlement.

Natural fortresses, wroshyr trees not only deflected ordinary blaster bolts but also provided hundreds of defensive platforms. More important, trees that had endured for thousands of years were not easily burned, let alone uprooted or felled. Without employing turbolasers and resigning themselves to massive death tolls, Imperial forces faced a grueling battle.

Judging by the manner in which they had deployed the gunships and troop carriers, Kashyyyk's theater commanders were relying on the fact that the Wookiees had no ranged weapons and little in the way of anti-aircraft defense. But the Imperials had failed to take into account the thousands of war machines that had been abandoned by Separatist and Republic forces alike fol-

lowing the fierce engagement on the Wawaatt Archipelago—
tank droids, missile platforms, spider and crab droids, All Terrain
Walkers and juggernauts. And just now the Wookiees were putting all that they had salvaged to good use.

Imperial gunships were unable to descend below treetop
level without the risk of being blown from the sky by commandeered artillery that had been moved to Kachirho's loftiest platforms, or by fluttercraft retrofitted with laser cannons. Closer to
the ground, those gunships that succeeded in evading the fire
and flak found themselves set upon by flights of catamarans
mounted with rocket launchers and repeating blasters.

Troopers attempting to rappel from incapacitated ships were
picked off by hails of bowcaster quarrels, blaster bolts fired from
rifles taller than Starstone, sometimes bands of Wookiees swinging out from the tree-city platforms on braided vines. The few
troopers who survived the airborne barrages and reached the
ground faced focused fire from blaster nests high in the trees,
volleys of grenades, and showers of red-hot debris sizzling down
through the leafy canopy.

Fighting alongside Tarfful, Chewbacca, and hundreds of
Wookiee warriors, Starstone and the other Jedi were still involved
in the chaotic fray on the landing platform. Employing carved
shields and eccentric blasters, Wookiee females fought as fero-
ciously as the males, and many of the offworld merchants were
pitching in, recognizing that the Empire had no intention of
sparing them. Weapons cleverly concealed in drop ships and
transports were targeting anything the Wookiees missed, and
many ferries were racing up the well, intent on carrying entire
Wookiee families to safety.

In areas where there were lulls in the fighting, many Wookiee females and younglings were falling back toward the tree-city,
or evacuating Kachirho's lower levels for the refuge of the high
forest.

Starstone wondered just how much the Empire was willing

to risk at Kashyyyk. Had Palpatine's minions considered that, faced with captivity, the Wookiees might flee their arboreal cities and become a rebel force the likes of which the Grand Army had yet to confront?

The thought provided her with a moment of solace.

Then she glimpsed something that sent her heart racing.

Sensing her sudden distraction, Forte and Kulka followed her gaze to midlevel Kachirho, where a black Imperial shuttle was drifting in for a landing on one of the tree-city's enormous balconies.

"It's Vader," Starstone said when the two Jedi Knights asked.

"Are you certain?" Forte said.

At Starstone's nod, Kulka gestured broadly to the ongoing fight. "This is more about us than the Wookiees even know."

Starstone shut her eyes briefly and forced a determined exhalation. "Then it's up to us to make this about *Vader*."

Leading an exodus of women and younglings from Kachirho's lowest levels, Chewbacca thought about his own family in distant Rwookrrorro, which apparently was also under siege. Rwookrrorro was days away on foot, but only minutes by ship. He would get there one way or another.

Off to his left, the six Jedi who had been fighting alongside him for the better part of a local hour were suddenly racing back toward Kachirho's central wroshyr. Lifting his eyes, Chewbacca saw no significant threat, save for a *Theta*-class shuttle that was taking heavy fire as it attempted to fold its wings and settle on one of the tree-city balconies.

Higher up, the sky was crisscrossed by laserfire and contrails, and still filling with gunships, eerily reminiscent of what had happened only weeks earlier, when the Separatists had launched their invasion. Wookiee fluttercraft and an assortment of traders' vessels were engaging the Imperial ships, but the outcome was clear.

The sheer number of descending gunships gave evidence of a sizable flotilla of capital ships in orbit. For all the Wookiees' success in repelling the first wave, it was surely only a matter of time before the Star Destroyers would open fire. And then only a matter of time until Kashyyyk fell.

Anyone who thought that the Jedi were responsible for hav-ing brought the Empire down on Kashyyyk had no understand-ing of the nature of power. From the moment the troopers of Commander Gree's brigade had turned on Yoda, Unduli, and Vos, Chewbacca, Tarfful, and the elders of Kachirho had grasped the truth: that despite all the rhetoric about taxation, free trade, and decentralization, there was no real difference between the Confederacy and the Republic. The war was nothing more than a struggle between two evils, with the Jedi caught in the mid-dle, all because of their misplaced loyalty to a government they should have abandoned, and to a pledge that had superseded their oath to serve the Force above all.

If there was any difference between the Separatists and the newly born Imperialists, it was that the latter needed to *legiti-mize* their invasion and occupation, lest other threatened species rebel while they stood a fighting chance.

But a planet could fall without its species being defeated; a planet could be occupied without its species being imprisoned.

That was what separated Kashyyyk from the rest.

Back- and hip-packs bulging with survival food and rations, Wookiees were streaming down the city staircases, racing across the footbridges, and disappearing into the thick vegetation that surrounded the lake. Blazed as a defense against sneak attacks by Trandoshan slavers, hundreds of well-maintained evacuation routes cached with arms and supplies radiated from Kachirho and wove through the isolated rock outcroppings to the high forest beyond.

More to the point, Wookiees even as young as twelve, fresh from their coming-of-age hrrtayyk ceremonies, knew how to construct shelters from saplings, how to fashion implements from the stalks of giant leaves, and how to make rope. They knew which plants and insects were edible; the location of freshwater springs; the areas where dangerous reptiles or predatory felines lurked.

Despite all the elements of high technology they had incorporated into their lives, Wookiees never considered themselves separate from Kashyyyk's grand forest, which on its own could provide them everything they needed to survive, for as long as necessary.

Targeted by unexpected anti-aircraft fire, Vader's shuttle jinked for the largest of the Kachirho's arboreal balconies, its powerful defensive shields raised and its quad lasers spewing unrelenting fire at a pair of hailfire droids the Wookiees had hoisted into their massive tree-fortress. Bolts from the shuttle's forward weapons reduced the missile platforms to slagged heaps and chewed into the balcony's wooden columns and beams, filling the air with splinters hard as nails. The explosions flung the bodies of Kachirho's furry defenders far and wide. Hurled clear off the tier, some plummeted to the ground a hundred meters below.

In the cabin space of the shaken shuttle, Vader was being addressed by the holoimage of one of the task force commanders.

"Our circumspect attacks are being repulsed planetwide, Lord Vader. As I thought I made clear, Wookiees do not take lightly to the threat of captivity. Already they're abandoning the tree-cities for the high forests. If they penetrate deeply enough, we will need months, perhaps years to find and root them out. Even then, the cost to us will be great, in terms of matériel and lives."

Vader muted the holoprojector's audio pickup and glanced across the aisle to Commander Appo. "Do you concur, Commander?"

"As it is we're losing too many troopers," Appo said without hesitation. "Grant permission to the naval commanders to initiate surgical bombardment from orbit."

Vader mulled it over for a moment. He didn't like being wrong, much less admitting that he had been wrong, but he saw no way out. "You may commence bombardment, Commander, but make certain you save Kachirho for last. I have business to finish up here."

As the holoimage faded, Vader turned to the cabin's small porthole, meditating on the whereabouts of his Jedi quarries, and what nature of trap they had set for him. The thought of confronting them stirred his impatience and his anger.

Wings uplifted, the shuttle made a rough landing on the tier, bolts from Wookiee blasters careening from the fuselage. When the boarding ramp had extended, Appo and his stormtroopers hurried outside, Vader right behind him, his ignited blade deflecting fire from all sides.

Three troopers fell before they made it two meters from the ramp.

The Wookiees were dug in, shooting from behind makeshift barricades and from crossbeams high above the balcony. Raising the shuttle on repulsorlift power, the clone pilot took the craft through a 180-degree sweep, drenching the area with laserfire. At the same time, two Wookiees with satchel charges slung over their shoulders rushed from cover and managed to hurl the explosives through the shuttle's open hatch. A deafening explosion blew off one of the wings and sent the craft spinning and skidding to the very rim of the tier.

Counterattacking, Vader strode through fountaining flames to take the fight to the Wookiees. Crimson blade slashing left and right, he parried blaster bolts and amputated limbs and heads. Caterwauling and howling, showing their fangs and waving their long arms about, the Wookiees tried to hold their positions, but they had never faced anything like him, even in the darkest depths of Kashyyyk's primeval forest.

As tall as some of them, Vader waded in, his lightsaber cleaving intricately carved war shields, sending blasters and bowcasters flying, setting fire to shaggy coats, leaving more than a score of bodies in his wake.

He was waving Appo and the other troopers forward when flashes of refulgent blue light caught his eye, and he swung to the source.

Emerging from a covered bridge anchored distally to the bole of the giant tree rushed six Jedi, deflecting blaster bolts from the stormtroopers as they attacked, doing to Appo's cadre just what Vader had done to the Wookiees.

Forging through the offensive, three Jedi raced in to square off with Vader.

He recognized the petite, black-haired female among them, and tipped his blade in salute.

"You've saved me the trouble of looking for you, Padawan Starstone. These others must be the ones you gathered by accessing the Temple beacon."

Starstone's dark eyes bored into him. "You defiled the Temple by setting foot in it."

"More than you know," he told her.

"Then you'll pay for that, as well."

He angled the lightsaber in front of him, tip pointed slightly downward. "You're very much mistaken, Padawan. It is you who will pay."

Before Starstone could make a move, Siadem Forte and Iwo Kulka stepped in front of her and attacked Vader.

As was the case with many Jedi Knights, the two were familiar with accounts of what had happened on Geonosis when Obi-Wan Kenobi and Anakin Skywalker had gone after the Sith Lord, Count Dooku. And so Forte and Kulka went in as a team, each of them employing a radically different lightsaber style, determined to off-balance Vader.

But Vader merely stood like a statue, his blade angled toward the ground until the very instant the two Jedi unleashed their assault.

Then, as the three blades joined in scatterings of dazzling light and grating static sounds, he moved.

Forte and Kulka were skilled duelists, but Vader was not only faster than Starstone remembered him being on Murkhana against Master Chatak, but also more agile. He employed his awesome power to put a quick end to the fancy twirling of his opponents, who fell back against the hammering blows of Vader's bloodshine blade.

Time and again the two Jedi Knights attempted to alter their style, but Vader had an answer for every lunge, parry, and riposte. His style borrowed elements from all techniques of combat, even from the highest, most dangerous levels, and his moves were crisp and unpredictable. In addition, his remarkable foresight allowed him to anticipate Forte's and Kulka's strategies and maneuvers, his blade always one step ahead of theirs, notwithstanding the two-handed grip he employed.

Toying with the Jedi, he grazed Forte on the left shoulder, then on the right thigh; Kulka, he pierced lightly in the abdomen, then shaved away the flesh on the right side of the Ho'Din's face.

Seeing the two Jedi Knights drop to their knees, wincing in pain, Padawan Klossi Anno broke from where she was helping Jambe and Nam engage the stormtroopers and got to Vader one step ahead of Starstone.

Sidestepping, Vader slashed her across the back, sending her sprawling across the balcony; then he whirled on Forte and Kulka just as they were clambering to their feet and decapitated them. From behind Vader came Jambe and Nam, neither of whom was an experienced fighter and both of whom Vader immediately eliminated from the fight, amputating Jambe's right arm, and Nam's right leg.

To her horror, Starstone realized she was suddenly alone with Vader, who immediately signaled his stormtroopers to leave her to him, and to devote themselves to slaughtering the few Wookiees who remained on the tier.

"Now you, Padawan," he said, as he began to circle her.

Calling on the Force, Starstone fell on him in a fury, striking wildly and repeatedly, *and with anger.* Moments into her attack she understood that Vader was merely allowing her to vent, as the Temple's swordmaster had often done with students, allowing them to believe that they were driving him back, when in fact he was simply encouraging them to wear themselves out before disarming them in one rapid motion.

So she retreated, altering her strategy and calming herself.

Vader is so tall, so imposing . . . But perhaps I can get under or inside his guard as Master Chatak did—

"Your thoughts give you away, Padawan," he said in a flash. "You mustn't take the time to *think.* You must act on impulse. Instead of repressing your anger, *call on it!* Make use of it to defeat me."

Starstone feigned an attack, then sidestepped and slashed at him.

Shifting to a one-handed hold on his lightsaber, he parried her blade and lunged forward. She snapped aside in the nick of time, but he kept coming at her, answering her increasingly frantic strikes with harsher ones and driving her inexorably toward the rim of the balcony.

He flicked his blade, precisely, economically, forcing her back and back . . .

She felt as if she were fighting a droid, although a droid programmed to counter all her best stratagems. Ducking out from under a broad sweep of the crimson blade, she somersaulted to safety.

But only for a moment.

"You're skittish, Padawan."

Sweat dripped into her eyes. She tried to center herself in the Force. At the same time she was vaguely aware of a new sound in the air, cutting through the chaos of the battle below. And just then a familiar ship slammed down on the tier alongside the crippled shuttle, two equally familiar figures leaping from the hatch even while the ship was still in motion.

At once, and seemingly of its own accord, the blood-smeared hilt of Master Forte's lightsaber shot from the balcony floor, whizzing past Vader's masked face to snap into the hand of one

of the figures and ignite. A gurgled sound issued from somewhere close to the newly arrived ship and something metallic hit
the floor and began to roll forward.

His black cloak unfurling, Vader spun around to find the hel-
meted head of Commander Appo coming to a rocky rest at his
feet.

A few meters away Roan Shryne stood with his legs spread to
shoulder width, Forte's blue blade angled high and to one side.
Alongside him, blasters in both six-fingered hands, Archyr was
dropping every stormtrooper who approached.

"Get away from him!" Shryne yelled at Starstone.

She gaped at him. "How did you—"

"Filli was keeping us updated. Now move away—hurry!"

Vader made no effort to prevent her from slinking past him.
"Very touching, Shryne," he said after a moment. "Treating her
like your personal learner."

Shryne gestured broadly. "Olee, get the wounded into the
drop ship!" Advancing on Vader, he said: "I'm the one you want,
Vader. So here's your chance. Me for them."

"Shryne, no—" Starstone started.

"Take the wounded!" he cut her off. "Jula's waiting."

"I'm not leaving you!"

"I'll catch up with you when I'm done with him."

Vader looked from Shryne to Starstone. "Listen to your Master, Padawan. He has already lost two learners. I'm certain he
doesn't want to lose a third."

Coming back to herself, Starstone hurried to help Lambe,
Klossi, Nam, and some of the Wookiees get aboard the drop
ship. Determined to quiet her fears for Shryne, she forced herself
not to look at him, but she could feel him reaching out to her.

He is a Jedi again.

With gunships circling Kachirho like insects spilled from an aggravated nest, Skeck powered the drop ship over the edge of the balcony and dived for the beleaguered landing platform. Airbursts from Imperial artillery crawlers raked and scorched the ship, inside which Starstone sat slumped on her knees with her arm around Klossi Anno, who was going in and out of consciousness, the wound on her back like a blackened trench. Across the cramped passenger bay Lambe and Nam, white-faced with fear, were nursing their amputated limbs and calling on the Force to keep from going into shock.

Wookiees huddled, braying in anger or whimpering in pain. Two of those Starstone and Archyr had helped carry aboard were dead.

Who was Vader? she asked herself. *What* was he?

She looked again at Klossi's wound, then at the one in her upper arm she hadn't even felt herself sustain. Vader's way of marking them with a Sith brand.

Could even Shryne defeat him?

"Hold tight!" Archyr yelled from the drop ship's copilot's seat. "This'll be one to remember!"

Skeck was taking the ship in *fast*. While the impaired repulsors were managing to keep it airborne, the ship was tipped acutely to one side. As a result, the wing on that side made first contact with the platform, gouging a ragged furrow in the wooden surface and whipping the ship into a spin that sent it crashing into a parked ferry in even sorrier condition.

Starstone's head slammed against the bulkhead with such force that she saw stars. Setting Klossi down gently, she checked on Lambe and Nam. Then she stumbled through the drop ship hatch, with Archyr trailing while Skeck remained at the controls.

Daylight was fading and the air was filled with the smoke and grit of battle.

The sky wailed with ships and pulsed with strobing explosions. Wookiees and other beings were running every which way across the landing platform. Elsewhere, bands of Wookiees, including some of those the Jedi had met, were carrying the wounded to shelter. Many of the traders' ships had lifted off, but just as many had been savaged by gunship fire or were buried under debris that had fallen from Kachirho's uppermost limbs and branches.

Principal fighting had moved east of the platform, closer to the lake. There, several crashed gunships were in flames, and the ground was piled high with the bodies of dead Wookiees and clone troopers. Imperial forces were storming the tree-city from all sides, even from the far shore of the lake, arriving on swamp-speeders and other watercraft. Searing hyphens of blasterfire were streaming from fortified positions high up the trunk, but what with the circling gunships and mobile artillery, the Wookiees were slowly being driven toward the ground.

Her head swimming, Starstone steadied herself against the drop ship's tipped fin.

Out of billowing smoke came Filli, running in a crouch and leading Deran Nalual by her left hand. Converging on Starstone from another direction appeared Cudgel and a dozen or so

Wookiees, Chewbacca among them, some of them limping, some with blood-matted fur.

"Where are the others?" Filli asked her, loud enough to be heard above the maelstrom of smoke and fire.

She motioned to the drop ship. "Skeck, Lambe, Nam, and Klossi are inside."

"Forte?" Filli said. "Kulka . . . ?"

"Dead."

Deran Nalual hung her head and clutched on to Filli's arm. "Shryne?"

Wide-eyed she gazed up at the balcony, as if just recalling him. "Up there."

Filli's eyes remained on her. "The *Drunk Dancer*'s upside. You ready to leave?"

She stared at him. "Leave?"

He nodded. "Try to, anyway."

She looked around in naked dread. "We can't leave them to this! We brought this on!"

Filli firmed his lips. "What happened to your idea of perpetuating the Jedi order?" He reached for her hands, but she backed away. "If you want to die a hero here, then I'll stay and die with you," he said flatly. "But only if I'm convinced that you know our deaths aren't going to affect the outcome."

"Filli's right," Archyr said from behind her, shouting to be heard. "Punish yourself later, Olee. If we're gonna survive this, the sooner we're airborne, the better."

Starstone swept her eyes over the ruined landing platform. "We take as many as we can with us."

Overhearing her, Cudgel began gesticulating to the Wookiees with whom he had arrived. "Chewbacca, pack the drop ship and the transport! Get everyone you can inside."

Others heard her, as well, and it wasn't long before dozens of Wookiees began to press forward. Shortly the area was crowded with more Wookiees and traders than the two ships could possibly accommodate. But in the midst of the mad crush for space aboard the craft, Imperial gunships abruptly began to break off their attack on Kachirho.

The reason for the sudden withdrawal was soon made clear, as colossal turbolaser beams lanced from the sky, scorching areas of the surrounding forests into which thousands of Wookiees had fled. With great booming sounds, giant limbs broke from the wroshyrs, and hot wind and flames swept over the landing platform, setting fire to nearly everything flammable.

With explosive sounds rumbling, Wookiees ran screaming from the forest, fur singed, blackened, or ablaze.

It took Starstone a moment to realize that she was flat on her back on the landing platform. Picking herself up, hair blowing in a hot, foul-smelling wind, she struggled to her feet in time to hear Cudgel say: "Orbital barrage—"

The rest of his words were subsumed in a thunderous noise that commenced in the upper reaches of Kachirho as dozens of huge limbs fractured and fell, plummeting into the lake and flattening acres of shoreline vegetation.

Suddenly Archyr was tapping her on the shoulder.

"Olee, we're as full as we can be and still be able to lift off."

She nodded by rote.

Filli turned and started back toward the transport, only to stop, swing around, and show her an alarmed look. "Wait! Who's going to fly that thing?"

She gaped at him. "I thought—"

"I'm no pilot! What about Lambe or Nam?"

She shook her head back and forth. "They're in no shape." Scanning everyone, her gaze fell on Cudgel. "Can you pilot the transport?"

He gestured to himself in incredulity. "Sure. Providing you don't care about being shot out of the air as soon as we launch."

Her dread mounted, the rush of blood pounding in her ears. *I can't leave everyone here!* All at once Cudgel was calling to her and motioning Chewbacca forward.

"Chewbacca can pilot the transport!"

She shot the Wookiee a dubious glance, then looked to Cudgel for assurance. "Can he even *fit*?"

Chewbacca barked and brayed to Cudgel.

"He'll do the piloting in return for your allowing him to take the transport back down the well to Rwookrrorro," Cudgel explained. "His home village. He has family there."

Starstone was already nodding. "Of course he can."

"Everyone on board," Archyr yelled. "Seal 'em up!" Swinging to Starstone, he said: "Which one are you going up in?"

She shook her head. "I'm not. I'm waiting here for Shryne."

"Oh, no, you're not," he said.

"Archyr, you saw Vader!"

"And so did Roan."

"But—"

"We'll try to grab him on the way up." Archyr gestured to the transport. "Now get aboard, and tell Chewbacca to stick close. Skeck and I will provide cover fire."

I was rather fond of Commander Appo," Vader said, toeing the amputated head of the clone officer out of his path as he moved closer to Shryne.

Shryne tightened his grip on the hilt of Forte's lightsaber and sidestepped cautiously to the left, forcing Vader to adjust his course. "I felt the same about Bol Chatak."

"Tell me, Shryne, are *you* the trap the others hoped to spring on me?"

Shryne continued to circle Vader. "I wasn't even part of their plan. In fact, I tried to talk them out of doing something like this."

"But in the end you just couldn't stay away. Even if it meant abandoning what might have been a lucrative career as a smuggler."

"Losing Senator Fang Zar was a blow to our reputation. I figured I'd better eliminate the competition."

"Yes," Vader said, raising his blade somewhat, "I am your worst rival."

Lightsaber grasped in both hands, Vader took a single forward step and performed a lightning-fast underhand sweep that almost knocked Forte's lightsaber from Shryne's grip. Spinning, Shryne regained his balance and raced forward, feinting a diagonal slash from the left, then twisting the blade around to the right and surging forward. The blade might have gotten past Vader's guard, but instead it glanced off the back of his upraised left hand, smoke curling from the black glove. Shryne countered quickly with an upsweep to Vader's neck, but Vader spun to the right, his blade held straight out in front of him as he completed a circle, nearly cutting Shryne in half.

Folding himself at the waist, Shryne skittered backward, parrying a rapid series of curt but powerful slashes. Backflipping out of range, he twisted his body to the right, set the blade over his right shoulder, and rushed forward, hammering away. Vader deflected the blows without altering his stance or giving ground, but in the process left his lower trunk and legs unprotected.

In a blink Shryne dropped into a crouch and pivoted through a turn.

For an instant it seemed that the blade was going to pass clear through Vader's knees, but Vader leapt high, half twisting in midair and coming down behind Shryne. Shryne rolled as Vader's crimson shaft struck the floor at the spot he had just vacated. Scrambling to his feet, Shryne hurled himself forward, catching Vader in the right forearm.

Snarling, Vader took his left hand from the lightsaber hilt to dampen sparking at the site of what should have been a wound.

Astonishment eclipsed Shryne's follow-up attack.

"I know you don't have a heart," he said, taking stalking steps, "but I didn't realize that you're *all* droid."

Vader may have been about to reply when packets of blinding light speared through the balcony, opening holes ten meters across. The great wroshyr shook as if struck by the full force of a lightning storm, and branches and leaves rained down on what was left of the deck. With a loud splitting sound, a large section of the rim broke away, taking Vader's shuttle with it.

"There goes your ride home," Shryne said when he could. "Guess you're stuck here with me."

Vader was a good distance away, one hand and one knee pressed to the floor, his blade angled away from him. Slowly he stood to his full height, leaves falling around him, black cloak flapping in the downdrafts. Then, with determined strides, he advanced on Shryne, sweeping his blade from side to side.

"I wouldn't have it any other way."

Shryne took a quick look around.

With most of the tier behind him blown away, and gaping holes elsewhere, he began to back toward the hollowed trunk of the tree.

"Almost seems like your own people are trying to kill you, Vader," he said. "Maybe they don't like the idea of a Sith influencing the Emperor."

Vader continued his resolute march. "Trust me, Shryne, the Emperor couldn't be more pleased."

Shryne cast a quick glance over his shoulder. They were entering an enormous interior space of wooden ramps, walkways, bridges, and concourses. "He doesn't have enough experience with your kind."

"And you do?"

"Enough to know that you'll turn on him eventually."

Vader loosed what could have been a laugh. "What makes you think the Emperor won't turn on me first?"

"Like he turned on the Jedi," Shryne said. "Although I suspect that was mostly your doing."

Five meters away, Vader stopped short. "Mine?"

"You convinced him that with you by his side, he could get away with just about anything."

Again, Vader's exhalation approximated a laugh. "It's think-

ing like that that blinded the Jedi to their fate." He raised his
sword. "Now it's time for you to join them."

Vader closed the distance between them in a heartbeat, slashing left and right with potent vertical strokes, narrowly missing
Shryne time and again, but destroying everything touched by the
blade. No whirling now; no windmilling or deft lunges. He simply used his bulk and size to remain wedded to the floor. It was
an old style, the very opposite of what was said to have been
Dooku's style, and Shryne had no defense against it.

If I could see his face, his eyes, Shryne found time to think.

If he could knock that outsize helmet from Vader's head.

If he could lance his lightsaber through the control panel on
Vader's chest—

That was the key! That was the reason for Vader's antique
style—to protect his center, as Grievous had been forced to do.

If he could only get to that control panel . . .

44

The two craft lifted off into smoke and withering night, spiraling up through resuming enemy fire toward Kachirho's mid-level balconies. In the transport's cramped cockpit with Cudgel, Filli, and Chewbacca—wedged into his seat, his head grazing the ceiling—Starstone clenched her white-knuckled hands on the shaking arms of the acceleration chair.

She couldn't bring herself to lift her gaze to the viewports, for fear of what sights might greet her.

As if reading her mind, Cudgel said: "You can't save an entire planet, kid. And it's not like you didn't try."

Chewbacca reinforced the remark with a gutsy bass rumble, repeatedly slamming his huge hands down on the transport's control yoke for emphasis.

"The Wookiees knew that their days of freedom were numbered," Cudgel translated. "Kashyyyk will only be the first non-human world to be enslaved."

Chewbacca threw the weary transport through a sudden evasive turn, nearly spilling everyone from their chairs. Through the viewport, Starstone caught a glimpse of Vader's black shuttle, tumbling toward the ground. Firewalling the throttle, Chewbacca clawed for altitude, barely escaping the flames of the crashed shuttle's mushrooming fireball.

Archyr's voice issued through the cockpit enunciators as the drop ship appeared in the starboard panel of the viewport. "Close call!"

Growling irritably, Chewbacca ran a fast systems check.

"Tail singed," Cudgel told Archyr through the comlink. "But everything else is intact."

The drop ship remained in view to starboard.

"Half the balcony fell with the shuttle," Archyr continued. "There isn't much room to put down, even if you're still fool enough to risk it. Whatever Olee has in mind, she'd better be quick about it."

Cudgel swiveled to her. "You got that?"

She nodded as the ravaged balcony came into view, in worse shape than she had feared. Most of the rim was gone, and the few areas that still clung to the trunk of the wroshyr had been holed and crisped by turbolaser bolts. The bodies of Wookiees and stormtroopers sprawled in the spreading flames.

"I don't see any sign of Shryne *or* Vader," Archyr said over the comlink.

"Turbos could have killed them—" Cudgel started when Starstone cut him off.

"No. I would know."

Chewbacca directed a yodeling bray at her.

"He believes you," Cudgel translated.

Starstone leaned toward Chewbacca. "You think you can set us down?"

Chewbacca lowed dubiously, then nodded. Feathering the repulsorlift lever, he began to cheat the transport closer to the wroshyr. The craft was meters from landing when, without warning, what remained of the wooden tier sheared away from the massive trunk, taking several lower tiers with it as it disintegrated and fell.

Starstone sucked in her breath as Chewbacca pulled the ship sharply away from the bole. Half out of her chair, she focused her gaze on the cave-like opening to the tree's dimly lighted interior and stretched out with the Force.

"They're inside! I can feel them."

Filli pulled her back into her chair. "There's nothing we can do."

Archyr's voiced barked through the enunciator. "Gunships approaching."

Cudgel forced her to look at him. "What would Shryne want you to do?"

She didn't have to think about it. Blowing out her breath, she said: "Chewbacca, get us out of this."

Relieved sighs came from Filli and Cudgel, a melancholy rumble from the Wookiee, who lifted the transport's nose and accelerated.

"Steer clear of the lake," Archyr warned. Again the drop ship came alongside, warding off strikes from inrushing Imperial gunships. "We've only got a narrow escape vector, north-northwest."

Dodging fire, the two ships raced into a burnt-orange sunset and climbed for the stars, mingling with scores of escaping ferries and cargo haulers. Turbolaser bolts rained down from ships in orbit, and across the darkening curve of the planet, fires raged.

Lowing in anguish and pounding one giant fist on the instrument panel, Chewbacca pointed to a bright burning in the canopy.

"Rwookrrorro," Cudgel said. "Chewbacca's tree-village."

The stars were just losing their shimmer when the communications suite toned. Filli routed the transmission through the cockpit speakers.

"Glad to see you've come to your senses," Jula said. "Is Roan with either of you?"

"Negative, Jula," Filli said sadly.

Save for bursts of static, the enunciator remained silent for a long moment; then Jula's voice returned. "After Alderaan, there was nothing I could say . . ." Her words trailed off, but she wasn't finished. "None of us is out of this yet, anyway. Vader or whoever's in charge has Interdictor cruisers parked in orbit. No ships have been able to jump to hyperspace."

"Does the *Drunk Dancer* have enough firepower to take on the cruiser?" Cudgel asked.

"Filli," Jula said, "inform whoever asked that question that I'm not about to go to guns with a Detainer CC-twenty-two-hundred."

As the transport reached the edge of Kashyyyk's envelope, magnified views of local space showed hundreds of ships trapped in the artificial gravity well generated by the Interdictor's powerful projectors. Interspersed among the ensnared vessels drifted the blackened husks of Separatist warships that had been there since the end of the war.

"Too bad we can't start up one of those Sep destroyers," Cudgel lamented. "They have guns enough to deal with that cruiser."

Starstone and Filli looked at each other.

"We might know a way," he said.

On Kashyyyk, rapacious fires held night at bay. The shadows of running figures crisscrossed the ground. Spilled blood shone glossy black, as black as the charred bark of the wroshyr trees.

Safe inside their plastoid shells an occupying force of stormtroopers rappelled into the burning forests, flushing fleeing Wookiees back into the open, out onto the debris-strewn landing platform, the shore of the lake, the public spaces between the tree clusters that made up Kachirho.

Imperial war machines closed in from all sides; speeders and swift boats roaring up onto the sandy banks, gunships coiling down from the treetops, *Victory*-class Destroyers descending from the stars, their wedge-shaped armored hulls outlined by bright running lights.

Driven from tree-city and forest, the Wookiees found themselves surrounded by companies of troopers. Male and female alike, the largest were stunned into submission or killed. And yet the Wookiees continued to fight, even the youngest among them, and often with only tooth and nail, tearing scores of troopers limb from limb before succumbing to blasterfire.

Not all of Kachirho's tens of thousands were rounded up, but more than enough to satisfy the Empire's current needs. Should more be needed, the troopers would know where to look for them.

Herded to the center of the landing platform with countless others, Tarfful raised his long arms above his head and loosed a mournful, stentorian roar at the heavens.

Kashyyyk had fallen.

Shryne's slashing strike to Vader's lower left leg, owing as much to luck as to skill, released another shower of sparks.

Vader's enraged response was Shryne's only assurance that he was fighting a living being. Whatever had happened to Vader, by accident or volition, he had to be more flesh-and-blood than cyborg, or he wouldn't have raged or been able to call on the Force with such intensity.

High up in the smoke-filled latticelike room, they stood facing each other on a suspension bridge that linked two fully enclosed walkways, the gloom cut by shafts of explosive light from the continuing attack on Kachirho.

Shryne's determination to thrust his lightsaber into the control box Vader wore on his chest had forced the Sith to adopt a more defensive style that had left his limbs vulnerable. Throughout the fight that had taken them up the room's wooden ramps, Vader had kept his crimson blade straight out in front of him, manipulating it deftly with wrists only, elbows pressed tightly to his sides. Only when Shryne left him no choice did he shuffle his feet or leap.

"Artificial limbs and body armor seem a curious choice for a Sith," Shryne said, poised for Vader's riposte to his lucky strike. "Belittling to the dark side."

Vader adjusted his grip on the sword and advanced. "No more than throwing in with smugglers denigrates the Force, Shryne."

"Ah, but I saw the light. Maybe it's time you did."

"You have it backward."

Shryne was steeling himself for a lunging attack when, abruptly, Vader halted and withdrew the blade into the light-saber's hilt.

Before Shryne could begin to make sense of it, he heard a creaking sound from below, and something flew at him from one of the ramps. Only a last-instant turn of his sword kept the object from striking him in the head.

It was a plank—ripped from a ramp they had taken to the bridge.

Shryne gazed in awe at unreadable Vader, then began to race toward him, blade held high over his right shoulder.

He didn't make half the distance when a storm of similar planks and lengths of handrail came whirling at him. Vader was using his dark side abilities to dismantle the ramps!

Surrendering to the guidance of the Force, Shryne swung his lightsaber in a flurry of deflecting maneuvers—side-to-side, over-head, low down, behind his back—but the floorboards were coming in larger and larger pieces, from all directions, and faster than he could parry them.

The butt end of a board struck him on the outer left thigh.

The face of a wide plank slammed him across the shoulders.

Wooden pegs flew at his face; other speared into his arms.

Then a short support post hit him squarely in the forehead, knocking the wind out of him and dropping him to his knees.

Blood running into his eyes, he fought to remain conscious,

extending the lightsaber in one shaking hand while clamping the other on the bridge's handrail. Five meters away Vader stood, his hands crossed in front of him, lightsaber hanging on his belt.

Shryne tried to keep him in focus.

Another board, whirling end-over-end, came out of nowhere, hitting him in the kidneys.

Reflexively the hand that was grasping the railing went to the small of his back, and he lost balance. Trying but failing to catch himself, he fell through space.

Give in the wooden floor saved his life, but at the expense of all the bones in his left arm and shoulder.

Above him Vader jumped from the bridge, dropping to the floor with a grace he hadn't displayed before and alighting just meters away.

Ignoring the pain in his shattered limb, Shryne began to propel himself in a backward crawl toward the opening through which he and Vader had entered the wroshyr's trunk, a hot wind howling at him, whipping his long hair about.

The balcony was gone. Fallen.

There was nothing between Shryne and the ground but gritty air filled with burning leaves. Far below, Wookiees were being herded onto the landing platform. The forests were in flames . . .

Vader approached, drawing and igniting his Sith blade.

Shryne blinked blood from his eyes; lifted his lightsaber hand only to realize that he had lost the sword during his fall. Slumping back, he loosed a ragged, resigned exhalation.

"I owe you a debt," he told Vader. "It took you to bring me back to the Force."

"And you to firm my faith in the power of the dark side, Master Shryne."

Shryne swallowed hard. "Then tell me. Were you trained by Dooku? By Sidious?"

Vader came to a halt. "Not by Dooku. Not yet by Sidious."

"Not yet," Shryne said, as if to himself. "Then you're his apprentice?" His eyes darted right and left, searching for some means of escape. "Is Sidious also in league with Emperor Palpatine?"

Vader fell silent for a moment, making up his mind about something. "Lord Sidious *is* the Emperor."

Shryne gaped at Vader, trying to make sense of what he had said. "The order to kill the Jedi—"

"Order Sixty-Six," Vader said.

"*Sidious* issued it." Pieces to the puzzle Shryne had been grappling with for weeks assembled themselves. "The military buildup, the war itself . . . It was all part of a plan to eliminate the Jedi order."

Vader nodded. "All about this." He gestured to Shryne. "About you and me, you could say."

Shryne's stomach convulsed, and he coughed blood. The fall hadn't only broken his bones, but ruptured a vital organ. He was dying. Backing farther out the opening, he gazed into the night sky, then at Vader.

"Did Sidious turn you into the monstrosity you've become?"

"No, Shryne," Vader said in a flat voice. "I did this to myself—with some help from Obi-Wan Kenobi."

Shryne stared. "You knew Obi-Wan?"

Vader regarded him. "Haven't you guessed by now? I was a Jedi for a time."

Shryne let his bafflement show. "You're one of the Lost Twenty. Like Dooku."

"I am the twenty-first, Master Shryne. Surely you've heard of Anakin Skywalker. The Chosen One."

47

The Commerce Guild ship Starstone and the others had chosen to infiltrate grew larger in the transport's cockpit viewports. Just over a thousand meters in length and bristling with electromagnetic sensor antennas and point-defense laser cannons, the *Recusant*-class support destroyer had taken a turbolaser bruising during the Battle of Kashyyyk, but its principal cannons and trio of aft thrust nozzles appeared to be undamaged.

Elsewhere local space was dotted with Imperial landers and troop transports, along with hundreds of freighters that had fled the surface of the tormented planet. Central to the latter craft, and a good distance from the support destroyer, floated the Interdictor cruiser that was preventing the traders' ships from jumping to hyperspace.

Those trapped ships are the reason I was spared, Starstone thought.

The reason she had been rescued by Shryne . . .

"Any response from the droid brain?" she asked over Filli's shoulder.

"Well, we're chatting," the slicer said from the cockpit's

comm suite. "It recognized the code we used to activate the facility at Jaguada, but it refuses to accept any remote commands. My guess is that it was rudely shut down during the battle, and wants to run a systems check before bringing the destroyer fully online."

"Be best if we can keep from announcing ourselves," Cudgel said from the copilot's chair. "You think you can keep the brain from lighting up the entire ship?"

Chewbacca woofed in agreement.

"Not initially," Filli said. "The brain will probably restore universal power gradually as part of its diagnostic analysis. Once that's over and done with, I can task it to kill all the running lights, except for those around the forward docking bay."

A sudden growl from Chewbacca called Starstone's attention to the forward viewports.

Fore-to-aft, the pod-like warship was coming to life.

Cudgel muttered a curse. "The Interdictor's scanners are bound to pick that up."

"Just a couple of moments more," Filli said.

Everyone waited.

"Done!" Filli announced.

In reverse order the destroyer's running lights began to blink out, save for an array of illuminators that defined the rectangular entrance to the docking bay.

Filli flashed Starstone a grin. "The brain's being very cooperative. We're good to dock."

Chewbacca brayed an interrogative.

"Any atmosphere?" Cudgel translated.

Filli did rapid input at the keyboard.

"The ship originally carried several squadrons of vulture and droid tri-fighters," he said. "But unless the Gossams converted it fully to droid operation I'd expect there be atmosphere and artificial gravity in some areas . . ." His eyes darted to the display screen. "Looks like a bit of both: Gossam and droid crew."

"Battle droids?" Starstone said.

Filli nodded. " 'Fraid so."

"You can't shut them down?"

"Not without shutting down the command bridge."

Starstone frowned and turned to Cudgel. "Gather up as many blasters as we've got aboard. And while you're at it, you'll find some rebreathers in the main cabin—just in case there's no atmosphere."

"You want a blaster," he asked as he stood up, "or are you sticking with a lightsaber?"

"This is an occasion that calls for both," she said.

"Archyr, Skeck, are you copying all this?" Filli said toward the audio pickup.

"Affirmative," Archyr responded from the drop ship. "But we'll precede you into the docking bay. We're better armed and better shielded. After that there's nothing to do but fight our way to the command bridge."

Filli displayed a schematic of the destroyer on one of the suite's monitor screens. "Most of the habitable areas are amidships, but the command bridge is in the outrigger superstructure above the bow."

"Lucky break for us," Archyr said. "It's closer to the bay."

Starstone was studying the destroyer when the drop ship came alongside the transport. Without having to be told, Chewbacca decelerated and fell in behind the smaller craft.

Starstone slipped into the vacant copilot's chair to watch the drop ship glide into the bay. Almost immediately blaster bolts crisscrossed the darkness. By the time the transport nosed through the opening, battle droids were dropping like targets in a shooting gallery, and the deck was strewn with spindly body parts.

Rebreathers strapped to their faces, lumas to their foreheads, Starstone, Cudgel, and Filli were standing at the boarding ramp hatch when Chewbacca set the transport down. Shortly the

Wookiee joined them there, the bowcaster he carried over his shoulder assembled and gripped in his hands.

As the transport's outer hatch slid open, the harsh sibilance of blasterfire infiltrated the ship. Starstone and the others hurried out into the thick of the fighting, their headlamps casting long shadows all over the bay. Archyr and several well-armed Wookiees were off to one side, clearing a path through battle droids toward a hatch in the bay's forward bulkhead.

Firing on the run and hurtling pieces of disintegrated droids, Starstone, Filli, Cudgel, and Chewbacca made a desperate dash for the hatch. The corridor beyond was crowded with battle droids marching in to reinforce those in the docking bay.

Explosive quarrels from Chewbacca's bowcaster combined with blasterfire and deflections from Starstone's lightsaber dropped a dozen droids at a time. But for every dozen destroyed, another dozen appeared. Archyr and some of the Wookiees brought up the rear, ultimately allowing Starstone's contingent to shoot their way into a turbolift that accessed the destroyer's outrigger arm.

Prepared for the worst, the four of them burst onto the command bridge, only to find a group of befuddled humaniform technical droids, outfitted with power studs at the backs of the heads that allowed them to be quickly and methodically shut down.

Realizing that the bridge had oxygen, everyone removed their rebreathers. Chewbacca dogged the hatch to the corridor while Filli centered himself at the ship's control console and activated the bridge's emergency lights.

"Gossams have longer fingers than I have," he said in the scarlet glow of the illuminators. "This could take some time."

"We're running short as it is," Cudgel said. "Just get the main cannons enabled."

Battle droids on the far side of the sealed hatch were already trying to pound their way onto the bridge.

Filli went back to work, but a moment later said: "Uh-oh."

Chewbacca loosed a trolling roar at him.

"Uh-oh, what?" Starstone asked.

Abruptly the destroyer lurched and began to nose about toward Kashyyyk's crescent of bright side.

"The brain wants to complete the task it was in the middle of when the ship was shut down," Filli said.

Starstone turned to him. "What was the task?"

"It thinks that the Separatists are losing Kachirho. It's converting itself into a giant bomb!"

"Can't you retask it?"

"I'm trying. It won't listen!"

Cudgel muttered to himself, and Chewbacca issued a sound that was somewhere between a growl and a groan.

"Filli!" Starstone said sharply. "Let the brain think what it wants. Just assign it a new target."

His blank stare yielded slowly to a grin of comprehension. "Can do."

Starstone returned the smile, then glanced at Cudgel. "Comlink the *Drunk Dancer* to prepare to receive guests."

As soon as Jula received word that the drop ship and transport had exited the Commerce Guild warship, she left the *Drunk Dancer* in the capable hands of Brudi Gayn and Eyl Dix and headed for the docking bay. Her eagerness sabotaged by the lightsaber gash she had suffered on Alderaan, she moved slowly and carefully, arriving just as the two craft were drifting through the hatch. Forewarned that both were carrying injured, she had ordered the ship's med droids to rendezvous with her there.

Forewarned.

But not thoroughly enough to prepare her for the number of wounded evacuees who hobbled from the ships, Wookiees squeezing out like circus performers from an absurdly cramped vehicle, and many of them in grave condition.

As for the Jedi, only five of the original seven had survived, and just barely, from the look of them. Jambe Lu, Nam Poorf, and Klossi Anno especially were in a lot worse shape than when they had first come aboard the *Drunk Dancer*, weeks earlier.

Even the ship's med droids were dismayed. "This may prove overwhelming, Captain," one of them said from behind Jula.

"Do all you can," she told the droid.

It was an unnerving sight, however, and she felt a bit pan-icked. But the tears she had been holding back since learning of Roan's sacrifice didn't gush forth until she set eyes on Filli and Starstone. Seeing her standing distraught, crying into the palms of her hands, Starstone hurried over to wrap her in a comforting embrace.

Jula allowed herself to be held for a long moment. But when she finally stepped out of the embrace, she saw that Starstone's cheeks were slick with tears, and that only got her crying again. Gently she stroked the young woman's face.

"What happened to avoiding attachment?" Jula said, snif-fling.

Starstone backhanded tears from her cheeks. "I've lost the skill. It doesn't seem to fit well with the Emperor's New Order, anyway." She held Jula's searching gaze. "Your son saved our lives. We tried to go back for him, but . . ."

Jula averted her eyes. "Someone had to try to stop Vader."

"I don't know that Vader can be stopped," Starstone said.

Jula nodded. "Maybe if I'd raised Roan, he wouldn't have turned out to be so stubborn." She frowned in distress. "Some people can't be talked out of being a hero."

"Or a Jedi."

Jula nodded. "That's what I meant."

Starstone smiled sadly, then turned to regard a Wookiee and a bearded human who were standing at the foot of the trans-port's boarding ramp, speaking with Filli, Archyr, and Skeck. Taking Jula by the hand, Starstone led her over to the unlikely pair, whom she introduced as Chewbacca and Cudgel.

Clearly in distress, the Wookiee was leaning against the ship, resting his head on his folded arms, and slamming his paws against the hull.

"We saw Chewbacca's tree-city in flames," Cudgel explained. "There's no way to know whether his family escaped in time."

"I promised him the transport," Starstone told Jula.

Jula looked at Cudgel. "We'll get it refueled as quickly—"

"No need," Cudgel cut her off. "Chewie knows that it's too late. He figures he can do more for his people as a fugitive than he could as a captive."

The Wookiee affirmed it with a melancholy roar.

"You're speaking for all of us, Chewbacca," Starstone said.

"So," Cudgel continued, "we're wondering, Chewie and I, if we could ride out of this with you."

Jula's comlink toned while she was nodding yes.

"Captain, we're T-ten for the jump to hyperspace," Brudi said from the bridge, almost casually. "Assuming everything goes according to plan."

"Have you been able to notify the other ships?" Jula asked.

"As best I could. And I'm trusting that that Interdictor isn't eavesdropping on every comlink frequency."

"See what jump options the navicomputer provides," Jula said. "I'll join you in a moment."

She moved away from Starstone and the others to gaze at Kashyyyk's waning crescent of bright side. Tears streaming down her face, she said in a quiet voice: "I love you, Roan. I thank the Force that I got to know you for a time. But I'll miss you more now than I ever did."

In command of the Detainer parked above Kachirho, Captain Ugan normally refused to allow himself to be disturbed when he was on the bridge. But Ensign Nullip was so insistent about seeing him that he finally granted permission for the young technician to be escorted onto the command deck.

A swarthy man with blunt features, Ugan remained seated in his chair, his dark gaze shifting between projected holoimages of the invasion on Kashyyyk and the viewport panorama of the planet itself.

"Be quick about it," he warned Nullip.

"Yes, sir," the ensign promised. "It's simply that we've been monitoring some unusual readings from one of the Separatist ships that was left in orbit after the battle here. Specifically, a Commerce Guild *Recusant*-class support destroyer. I've tried repeatedly to convince someone in tactical to bring this to your attention, sir, but—"

Ugan cut him off. "What makes these readings 'unusual,' Ensign?"

"They are initiation readings, sir." In response to the captain's dubious look, Nullip continued: "I know, sir. I was puzzled, too. That's why I took it upon myself to check the scanner recordings. Much to my surprise, sir, I learned that the destroyer's central control computer had been remotely enabled to run a diagnostic, and then to bring several of the ship's systems online."

When Ugan's expression of perplexity deepened, Nullip activated a small holoplate he had placed on the palm of his right hand. A grainy recording shone from the device.

"You can see two craft entering the destroyer, just here, at the forwardmost docking bays." Nullip's forefinger fast-forwarded the recording. "Here, you can see the craft leaving. We're still trying to determine their destination."

Ugan glanced from the recording to Nullip. "Salvagers?"

"That was my first thought, sir. But, in fact, when the craft exited, the destroyer itself was in motion."

Ugan stared at him. "In motion? What's its heading?"

"That's just it, sir. It's heading toward us." Turning to the forward viewports, Nullip indicated a dark shape moving through the greater darkness. "Just there, you see?"

Ugan swiveled to an officer at the tactical duty station. "A Separatist ship is approaching our port side. Scan it, immediately!" Rising from his chair, he walked to the viewport, Nullip a step behind him.

"Captain," the tactical officer said, "the ship is a Confederacy droid-piloted support destroyer—"

"I already know that!" Ugan said, whirling around. "Does it pose any risk to us?"

"Checking, sir."

The officer spent a moment studying the duty station's array of display screens, then turned toward Ugan, ashen-faced.

"Captain, the destroyer's main reactor is in critical failure. The ship is effectively a massive bomb!"

Shryne sprawled in the wroshyr's cavernous opening, the wind tugging at his clothing, blood trickling from the corners of his mouth, clearly struggling with the revelation he had been granted.

Vader stood over him, his right hand resting on the hilt of the lightsaber, though he had no intention of drawing it from his belt again. One strong gust could topple Shryne to his final resting place.

It is enough to let him die knowing that the order was betrayed by one of its own.

More important, Vader's bloodlust had been appeased; replaced by self-possession of a sort he had never before experienced. It was as if he had crossed some invisible threshold to a new world. He could feel the power of the dark side surging through him like an icy torrent. He felt invulnerable in a way that had nothing to do with his durasteel prostheses, his suit of armor and gadgets, which now seemed little more than an outfit. And it had taken a Jedi—yet *another* Jedi—to usher him over that threshold.

He gazed down at Shryne, emblematic of the defeated Jedi order, as Obi-Wan should have been. He recalled the way Dooku had gazed down at him on Geonosis, and the way Anakin had gazed down at Dooku in the General's quarters aboard the *Invisible Hand*.

Someday he would gaze down at Sidious in the same way.

After he took an apprentice, perhaps. Someone with the same rebellious spirit that Shryne demonstrated.

Shryne coughed weakly. "What are you waiting for, Skywalker? Strike me down. You're only killing a Jedi."

Vader planted his fists on his hips. "Then you do accept the truth."

"I accept that you and Palpatine are a perfect match—" Shryne began, when without warning an immense explosion turned a small region of the western sky bright as day. Eclipsing stars, a roiling ball of fire blossomed high over Kashyyyk, expanding and expanding until the vacuum of space suffocated it.

When Vader looked at Shryne again, the Jedi appeared to be grinning.

"Would that be one of your ships? Your Interdictor cruiser, maybe?" He coughed blood and a laugh. "They've escaped you again, haven't they."

"If so, they will be found, and killed."

Shryne's expression suddenly changed, from smug to almost rapturous.

"I've seen this," he uttered, mostly to himself. "I envisioned this . . ."

Vader pressed closer to hear him. "Your death, you mean."

"An explosion bright as a star," Shryne said. "A forest world, intrepid defenders, escaping ships, and . . . *you*, I think, somehow at the center of it all." His bloodstained lips formed themselves into a sublime smile, and a tear ran from his right eye. "Skywalker, it won't matter if you find them. It won't matter if you

find and kill every Jedi who survived Order Sixty-Six. I understand now . . . the Force will never die."

Vader was still gazing down at Shryne's inert body when several
stormtroopers emerged from one of the Wookiees' ingenious
turbolifts and hurried over to him.

"Lord Vader," the officer among them said. "The Interdictor
positioned over Kachirho has been destroyed. As a result, hundreds of evacuation ships succeeded in jumping to hyperspace."

Vader nodded. "Inform the group commanders that they are
to continue their orbital bombardment," he said angrily. "I want
every Wookiee flushed out of hiding, even if that means burning
these forests to the ground!"

Epilogue

Two there should be; no more no less.
One to embody power, the other to crave it.

—Darth Bane

A half-life-size holoimage of Wilhuff Tarkin shone from one of the cone-shaped holoprojectors that studded the lustrous floor of the throne room.

"The planet suffered more damage that I might have anticipated," the Moff was saying, "especially given the military resources I placed at Lord Vader's disposal. Although I suppose I shouldn't be surprised by the Wookiees' intractability."

The Emperor gestured negligently. "What is one world, more or less, when the galaxy is being reordered?"

Tarkin took a moment to reply. "I will bear that in mind, my lord."

"What of the Wookiees themselves?"

"Some two hundred thousand were rounded up and placed in containment camps on the Wawaatt Archipelago."

"Can you accommodate that many?"

"We could accommodate twice that number."

"I see," the Emperor said. "Then you have my permission to transport the slaves to the weapon."

"Thank you, my lord."

"Be certain to inform the regional governor of your activities, but make no mention of the Wookiees' final destination. Oh, and see to it, Moff Tarkin, that you cover your tracks well. Questions are already being asked." The Emperor paused, then leaned forward to add: "I don't want any problems."

Tarkin inclined his head in a bow. "I appreciate the need for utmost secrecy, my lord."

"Good." The Emperor sat back. "And, tell me, what is your opinion of Lord Vader's handling of the occupation of Kashyyyk?"

"He proved very capable, my lord. No one involved in the operation will soon forget his . . . sense of commitment, shall we say?"

"Do the fleet commanders concur with your assessment?"

Tarkin stroked his high-cheekboned face. "May I speak candidly?"

"I suggest you make it a practice, Moff Tarkin."

"The commanders are not pleased. They don't know who Lord Vader is under his mask and armor. They have no inkling of the true extent of his power, or how he came to be your liaison with the regional governors and the fledgling Imperial Navy. There are rumors, my lord."

"Continue to speak freely."

"Some are convinced that Lord Vader is a former Jedi who assisted you in your counterstrike against the order. Others believe that he was an apprentice of the late Count Dooku."

"Who is spreading these rumors?"

"From what I have been able to ascertain, the rumors began among the special ops legions that attacked and secured the Jedi Temple. If you wish, my lord, I could pursue the matter further."

"No, Tarkin," the Emperor said. "Let the rumors persist. And let the regional governors and naval officers think what they will of Lord Vader. His identity shouldn't concern them. I am interested only in their obeying his commands, as they would mine."

"If nothing else, my lord, they understand that much. Word of what happened at Kashyyyk is spreading quickly through the ranks."

"As I knew it would."

Tarkin nodded. "My lord, I wonder if I might call on Lord Vader's . . . expertise from time to time, if only in the interest of enhancing his reputation among the fleet commanders."

"You may, indeed. Both you and Lord Vader will profit from such a partnership. When the battle station is completed, your responsibilities will be manifold. Lord Vader will relieve you of the need to oversee every matter personally."

"I look forward to that day, my lord." Tarkin bowed once more, and the holoimage disappeared.

Sidious was pleased. Vader had done well. He had sensed the change in him, even in the brief conversation they had had following the events on Kashyyyk. Now that Vader had begun to tap deeply into the power of the dark side, his true apprenticeship could begin. The Jedi were incidental to him. He was covetous of the power Sidious wielded, and believed that one day they would be equals.

You must begin by gaining power over yourself; then another; then a group, an order, a world, a species, a group of species . . . finally, the galaxy itself.

Sidious could still hear Darth Plagueis lecturing him.

Envy, hatred, betrayal . . . They were essential to mastering the dark side, but only as a means of distancing oneself from all common notions of morality in the interest of a higher goal. Only when Sidious had understood this fully had he acted on it, killing his Master while he slept.

Unlike Plagueis, Sidious knew better than to sleep.

More important, by the time Vader was capable of becoming

a risk to his Mastery, Sidious would be fully conversant with the secrets Plagueis had spent a lifetime seeking—the power of life over death. There would be no need to fear Vader. No real reason to have an apprentice, except to honor the tradition Darth Bane had resurrected a millennium earlier.

The ancient Sith had been utter fools to believe that power could be shared by thousands.

The power of the dark side should be shared only by two; one to embody it, the other to crave it.

Vader's transformation meant that Sidious, too, was able to focus once more on important matters. With Vader in his place, Sidious could now devote himself to intensifying his authority over the Senate and the outlying star systems, and to rooting out and vanquishing any who posed a threat to the Empire.

He had brought peace to the galaxy. Now he meant to rule it as he saw fit—with a hand as strong and durable as one of Vader's prostheses. Crushing any opponents who rose up. Instilling fear in any who thought to obstruct or thwart him.

Vader would prove to be a powerful apprentice, at least until a more suitable one was found.

And a powerful weapon, as well, at least until a more powerful one was readied . . .

For some time, Sidious sat, musing on the future; then he called for Sate Pestage to join him in the throne room.

The time had come to give the rest of the galaxy a look at Darth Vader.

O h, Bail, Breha, what a precious child," Mon Mothma said while she rocked Leia in her arms. "And such a feisty one!" she added a moment later as Leia worked one arm, then the other, out from under her swaddlings, curled her hands into tiny fists, and let out a wail that echoed in the palace's great room. "Ah, you want your mom and dad, don't you, Princess Leia?"

Queen Breha was already hurrying over to relieve Mon Mothma of a now gesticulating and kicking Leia.

"That's her *feed-me* cry," Breha said. "If you'll excuse me, Senator . . ."

"Of course, Your Majesty," Mon Mothma said, rising to her feet. She watched Breha leave the room, then swung to Bail, who was seated by the room's gaping fireplace. "I'm so happy for the two of you."

"We couldn't be happier ourselves," Bail said.

He wished he could tell Mon Mothma the truth about the child she had just held in her arms, but he couldn't risk it; not yet, perhaps never. Particularly with "Darth Vader" on the loose.

Picking up on Bail's moment of introspection, Mon Mothma returned to her chair and adopted a more serious look.

"I hope you understand why I couldn't trust this conversation to the usual means, Bail," she said. "Are we secure here?"

"Of course, I understand. And yes, we can speak freely here."

Mon Mothma closed her eyes briefly and shook her head in dismay. "Most of the Senate is actually willing to accept that Fang Zar was under suspicion for committing acts of sedition on Coruscant, and that he came to Alderaan only to rally anti-Imperial sentiment."

Bail nodded. "I've heard the reports. There's no truth to any of them. He was fleeing for his life."

"Has Palpatine remarked on the fact that you granted him refuge?"

"I honestly didn't know that he'd been questioned by Internal Security and ordered to remain on Coruscant. When Palpatine's . . . *agents* told me as much, I said I would grant him diplomatic immunity if he asked for it—though I doubt he would have asked, knowing that Alderaan would suffer the repercussions."

"Even so, Palpatine's silence is curious." She looked hard at Bail. "Perhaps he's trusting that you won't reveal the truth about what went on here."

Bail nodded in agreement. "Something like that. Although it could work to our long-term advantage to have him believe that I'm willing to support even his lies."

Mon Mothma compressed her lips in doubt. "That's probably true. But I'm concerned about the message your silence sends to our allies in the Senate. Sern Prime is in an uproar over this incident. The president-elect has threatened to recall the entire delegation from Coruscant. This could provide just the impetus we need."

Bail stood up and paced away from his chair. "Palpatine wanted to make an example of Fang Zar. He won't hesitate to make an example of Sern Prime itself, if the president-elect isn't careful."

"How did Zar die?" Mon Mothma said, watching him pace.

"Vader," Bail said sharply.

Mon Mothma shook her head in ignorance. "Who is Vader? One of Armand Isard's agents?"

Bail finally sat down, resting his elbows on his knees. "Worse, far worse. He's Palpatine's right hand."

Mon Mothma's expression of uncertainty intensified. "Closer to him than Pestage?"

Bail nodded. "Closer to Palpatine than any of them."

"Out of the blue? I mean, how is it that none of us encountered Vader before now?"

Bail grasped for words that would reveal enough, without revealing too much. "He . . . came to prominence during the war. He wields a lightsaber."

Mon Mothma's eyes widened in surprise.

"No, he's not a Jedi," Bail said, before she could ask. "His blade is crimson."

"What does the color have to do with anything?"

"He's a Sith. A member of the same ancient order to which Dooku swore allegiance."

Mon Mothma loosed a fatigued exhalation. "I've never understood any of this, about the Siths' involvement in the war."

"You only need to understand that Vader is Palpatine's executioner. He's powerful almost beyond belief." Bail studied his hands. "Fang Zar was not the first person to feel the wrath of Vader's blade."

"Then Vader is all the more reason for us to act while there's still time," Mon Mothma said in a forceful voice. "Palpatine's plan to kill a few to instill fear in the rest is already working. Half the signatories of the Petition of the Two Thousand are all but recanting the demands we issued. I understand that you want to honor Padmé Amidala's advice to you about biding our time. But what did she know, really? She supported Palpatine almost to the very end.

"Bail, he's assembling a vast navy. Half the budget is going to the production of these enormous new Star Destroyers. He's having new stormtroopers grown. And that's not the worst of it. The Finance Committee can't even account for some of the spending. Rumor has it that Palpatine has some secret project in the works."

She fell silent, then continued in a quieter tone. "Think back to what happened three years ago. If it wasn't for the secret army the Jedi created, the Republic wouldn't have had a hope of defending itself against Dooku's Confederacy. Granted, Palpatine took advantage of the situation to crown himself Emperor. But consider what's happening now. We don't have an army of insurgents waiting in the wings, and we'll never have one if we don't begin to marshal support. Palpatine's military will rule by the sword. He'll do as he wishes, whatever he wishes, in the name of keeping the Empire intact. Don't you see?"

The question hung in the air, but only for a moment.

Raymus Antilles appeared in the wide doorway to say: "Senators, there's something the two of you need to see."

Antilles hastened to the HoloNet receiver and switched it on.

". . . At this moment, details remain sketchy," a celebrated commentator was saying, "but reliable sources have stated that the Wookiees were allowing a band of rogue Jedi to use Kashyyyk as a base for rebel strikes against the Empire. The police action is believed to have begun with a demand that the Jedi be surrendered. Instead, the Wookiees resisted, and the result was a battle that left tens of thousands dead, including the Jedi insurgents, and perhaps hundreds of thousands imprisoned."

Bail and Mon Mothma traded looks of astonishment.

"On Coruscant," the commentator continued, "Kashyyyk Senator Yarua and the members of his delegation were placed under house arrest before any statements could be issued. But on the minds of many just now is the identity of this person, captured by holocam on a landing platform normally reserved for the Emperor himself."

"Vader," Bail said, on seeing the tall figure in black, leading a cadre of stormtroopers into the Emperor's building.

"HoloNet News has learned that he is known in the highest circles as Lord Vader," the commentator said. "Beyond that, almost nothing is known, save for the fact that he led the action on Kashyyyk.

"Is he human? Clone? The Emperor's own General Grievous? No one seems to know, but everyone wants to—"

"Switch it off," Bail said to Antilles.

"Kashyyyk," Mon Mothma said in incredulity. She ran her hands down her face and stared at Bail. "We're too late. A dark time has begun."

Bail didn't respond immediately. Into the silence stepped Breha, holding Leia against her shoulder, and into Bail's rattled mind came thoughts of Yoda, Obi-Wan, and Leia's twin brother, Luke.

"All the more reason to keep hope hidden," he said softly.

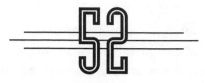

The *Drunk Dancer* was home, parked in the cold gloom, light-years from any inhabited systems. This far from the Core, HoloNet broadcasts were standard days, sometimes weeks, behind and always degraded, but clear enough just now for Starstone, Jula, and everyone else—Jedi and crew members alike—to identify the bodies of Iwo Kulka and Siadem Forte.

". . . All the Jedi who took part in the battle were killed," a correspondent was saying when Starstone asked Filli to mute the recorded feed. Everyone had already seen the original reports, which had since been embellished with exaggerations and out-right lies.

Gazing around the cabin space at Jambe, Nam, Deran Na-lual, and Klossi Anno, Starstone couldn't help but think that the five of them made up what could be thought of as the final Jedi Council. With herself having called for the meeting, as master of ceremonies, without ever having passed the trials, let alone been dubbed a teacher.

But she could remember Shryne saying on Murkhana that the war was *trial enough for anyone*.

"What I'm about to say was already said by Master Shryne,"

she began at last. "He warned us that by gathering together we would make ourselves a larger target for the Empire, and that we would end up drawing others into our predicament. We can't risk fomenting another Kashyyyk. The Empire will have to come up with justifications that don't rely on the presence of Jedi.

"Because there are no more Jedi.

"That much is clear to me now, and I'll never forgive myself for not having had sense enough to recognize it sooner. Maybe then I wouldn't have to think of what happened at Kashyyyk as further diminishing the legacy of the Jedi among those who never doubted that Palpatine betrayed us. But if we can't be Jedi, we can at least continue to honor that legacy in our own way."

Starstone looked at Chewbacca. "Just before we jumped from Kashyyyk, Chewbacca said that he believed he could be of greater help to his people from afar. I feel the same, and I know that some of you do, as well."

She took a breath before continuing. "I've decided to remain aboard the *Drunk Dancer* with Jula, Filli, Archyr, and the rest of this mad crew." She smiled weakly. "Chewbacca and Cudgel are also going to remain aboard for a time. Our priority will be to learn where so many of Chewbacca's people were taken, and to help liberate them, if at all possible. I'm hoping that by finding them, we'll also be able to learn why the Empire was so intent on invading Kashyyyk to begin with.

"Along the way . . ." Starstone shrugged. "Along the way we're going to keep our eyes open for any Jedi survivors who surface on their own, or are forced into the open by Imperial spies. Not to repeat the mistakes we made at Kashyyyk, but to get them to safety. Gradually, other smugglers will spread word of what we're doing, and of the safe routes we'll establish, and maybe some Jedi will actually come looking for us.

"Beyond that, we'll undermine the Empire at every opportunity, any way that we can."

"We're going to keep my son's memory alive," Jula said.

The cabin fell silent for a moment.

"I know this may sound like I've gone over to the enemy," Jambe Lu said, "but I plan to sign up with a flight school somewhere, and try to finagle my way into one of the Imperial academies. Once inside, I'm going to foster whatever dissent I can."

"We have something similar in mind," Nam said, speaking for himself, Klossi Anno, and Deran Nalual. "But by getting ourselves attached to Imperial agricultural or construction projects, and engineering what flaws we can into the Empire's designs."

Starstone's eyes brightened.

"I trust that all of you understand there can be no contact among us—ever again. That's going to be the hardest part for me." She sighed deeply. "I guess I've grown attached to all of you. But I'm certain of this much: Palpatine's Empire will rot from the inside out, and eventually someone will cast him from his throne. I only hope that all of us are alive to witness that day."

She drew her lightsaber from her belt. "We need to say good-bye to these, as well." She ignited the blade briefly, then summoned it back into the hilt and placed it at her feet on the deck.

Regarding everyone, she said: "May the Force be with all of us."

Lord Vader," the gunnery officer said, nodding his head in salute as Vader passed by his station.

"Lord Vader," the communications officer said, saluting in similar fashion.

"Lord Vader," the *Exactor*'s captain said, in crisp acknowledgment.

Vader continued on to the end of bridge walkway, thinking: *This is how I will be greeted from now on, wherever I set foot.*

Standing at the forward viewports, he scanned the stars with his reconstructed eyes.

He had guardianship of all this, or at least joint custody of it. The Jedi no longer mattered; they were no different from others who would interfere with his and Sidious's realm. Their mission was to maintain order, so that the dark side could continue to reign supreme.

Anakin was gone; a memory so deeply buried he might have dreamed rather than lived it. The Force as Anakin knew it was interred with him, and inseparable from him.

Just as Sidious promised, he was now married to the order of the Sith, and needed no other companion than the dark side of the Force. He embraced all that he had done to bring balance to the Force, by dismantling the corrupt Republic and toppling the Jedi, and he reveled in his power. It could all be his, anything he wished. He needed only the determination to take it, at whatever cost to those who stood in his way.

But . . .

He was also married to Sidious, who doled out precious bits of Sith technique as if merely lending them—just enough to increase his apprentice's power, without making him supremely powerful.

There would come a day, however, when they would be equals.

He scanned the stars, looking forward to a time when he could find an apprentice of his own and, together with that one, topple Darth Sidious from his throne.

It gave him something to live for.

54

Another glass, stranger?" the cantina owner asked Obi-Wan Kenobi.

"What will it cost me?"

"Ten credits for refills."

"That's as much as a shot of one of your imported brandies."

"The price of staying hydrated on Tatooine, my friend. Yes or no?"

Obi-Wan nodded. "Fill it."

Gathered by the cantina's single moisture vaporator, the water was somewhat cloudy and had a metallic taste, but it was of a higher quality than that gathered by Obi-Wan's own vaporator. If he was to survive in the hovel he had found, he would need to have the vaporator repaired, or somehow obtain a newer one from the Jawa traders who occasionally passed through the region he now called home.

If it hadn't been for the kindness of the maroon-cloaked creatures, he would still be walking to Anchorhead rather than sitting in the scant shade of the cantina's veranda, sipping water. A wind-scoured settlement close to Tatooine's Western Dune

Sea, Anchorhead was little more than a trading post frequented
by the moisture farmers who made up the Great Chott salt flat
community, or by merchants traveling between Mos Eisley and
Wayfar, in the south. Anchorhead had a small resident population, a dozen or so pourstone stores, and two small cantinas. But
it was known mainly for the power generator located at the edge
of town.

Named for its owner, Tosche Station supplied energy to the
moisture farms and served as a recharge depot for the farmers'
landspeeders and other repulsorlift vehicles. The station also
boasted a hyperwave repeater, which—when it functioned—
received HoloNet feeds relayed from Naboo, Rodia, and, occasionally, Nal Hutta, in Hutt space.

Tosche was working today, and The Weary Traveler's handful
of afternoon customers were catching up on news and the outcome of sports events that had taken place standard weeks earlier.
Obi-Wan—known locally as Ben—had taken possession of an
abandoned home on a bluff in the Jundland Wastes. He glanced
at the HoloNet display from time to time, but the focus of his interest was a provisions store across the street from the cantina.

In the months since he had arrived on Tatooine his hair and
beard had grown quickly, and his face and hands had turned nut
brown. In his soft boots and long robe, its cowl raised over his
head, no one would have taken him for a former Jedi, let alone a
Master who had sat on the High Council. In any case, Tatooine
wasn't a world where questions were asked. Residents wondered,
and they gossiped and theorized, but they rarely inquired about
the reasons that brought strangers to remote Tatooine. Coupled
with the fact that the world was still largely under the sway of the
Hutts, the prevailing frontier etiquette had made Tatooine a
refuge for criminals, smugglers, and outlaws from star systems
galaxywide.

Many of the locals were just learning that the former Republic was now an Empire, and most of them didn't care one way or another. Tatooine was on the fringe, and fringe worlds might as well have been invisible to distant Coruscant.

Months earlier, when he and Anakin had been in pursuit of clues they had hoped would lead them to Darth Sidious, Obi-Wan had told Anakin that he could think of far worse places to live than Tatooine, and he still felt that way. He took in stride the ubiquitous sand that had so rankled Anakin. Tatooine's double-sunset skies were always a marvel to behold.

And the isolation suited him.

All the more because Anakin had been subverted by Palpatine and, for a brief time, had served this new Emperor.

Given everything that had happened since, the one image Obi-Wan knew he would never be able to erase from his memory was that of Anakin—Darth Vader, as Sidious had dubbed him—kneeling in allegiance to the Dark Lord, after having gone on a murderous spree in the Jedi Temple. If there was a second image, it was of Anakin burning on the shore of one of Mustafar's lava flows, cursing him.

Had he been wrong to let Anakin die there? Could he have been redeemed, as Padmé had believed to the last? These were questions that plagued him, and pained him more deeply than he would ever have thought possible.

And now, all these months later, here he was on Tatooine, Anakin's homeworld, watching over Anakin's infant son, Luke.

Obi-Wan's reason for living.

Watching from afar, at any rate. Today was as close as he had come to the child in weeks. Just across the street, Luke sat in a front carrier worn by Beru while she purchased sugar and blue milk; neither she nor her husband, Owen, was aware of Obi-Wan's presence on the cantina veranda, his vigilant though covert gaze.

As Obi-Wan brought the water glass to his mouth and

sipped, a HoloNet news report caught his ear and he swung to the cantina's display, simultaneous with a torrent of static that interrupted the feed.

"What was she saying?" Obi-Wan asked a human seated two tables away.

"Band of Jedi were killed on Kashyyyk," the man said. Close to Obi-Wan's age, he wore utilities of the sort affected by docking bay workers in Mos Eisley spaceport.

Had the HoloNet reporter been referring to Jedi who had been on Kashyyyk with Yoda—

No, Obi-Wan realized when the feed suddenly returned. The reporter was talking about more recent events! About Jedi who had obviously survived Order Sixty-Six and been discovered on Kashyyyk!

He continued to listen, growing colder and colder inside.

The Empire had accused Kashyyyk of plotting rebellion . . . Thousands of Wookiees had died; hundreds of thousands more had been imprisoned . . .

Obi-Wan squeezed his eyes shut in dismay. He and Yoda had recalibrated the Temple beacon to warn surviving Jedi *away* from Coruscant. What could the ones discovered on Kashyyyk have been thinking, banding together like that, drawing attention to themselves instead of going to ground as they had been ordered to do? Did they think they could gather enough strength to go after Palpatine?

Of course they did, Obi-Wan realized.

They hadn't realized that Palpatine had manipulated the war; that a Sith occupied the throne; that like everyone else, the Jedi had failed to grasp a truth that should have been evident years earlier: the Republic had never been worth fighting for.

The ideals of democracy hadn't been stamped out by Palpatine. The Jedi had carried out missions of dubious merit for any

number of Supreme Chancellors, but always in the name of safe-
guarding peace and justice. What they had failed to understand
was that the Senate, the Coruscanti, the citizens of countless
world and star systems, grown weary of the old system, had *allowed* democracy to die. And in a galaxy where the goal was
single-minded control from the top, and wherein the end justified the means, the Jedi had no place.

That had been the final revenge of the Sith.

When Obi-Wan lifted his gaze, the intermittently garbled
HoloNet was displaying an image of someone outfitted in
what almost seemed a costume of head-to-toe black. Human or
humanoid—the being's species wasn't mentioned—the masked
Imperial had apparently played a role in tracking down and executing the "insurrectionist" Jedi, and enslaving their Wookiee
confederates.

The burst of static that accompanied the reporter's mention
of the figure's identity might have surged from Obi-Wan's brain.
Still chilled by the earlier announcement about the Jedi, he was
now paralyzed by sudden dread.

He couldn't have heard what he thought he heard!

He whirled to the spaceport worker. "What did she say? Who
is that?"

"Lord Vader," the man said, all but into his glass of brandy.

Obi-Wan shook his head. "No, that's not possible!"

"You didn't ask if I thought it was possible, sand man. You
asked me what she said."

Obi-Wan stood up in a daze, knocking over his table.

"Hey, take it easy, friend," the man said, rising.

"Vader," Obi-Wan muttered. "Vader's alive."

The cantina's other customers turned to regard him.

"Get ahold of yourself," the man told Obi-Wan under his
breath. He called for the cantina owner. "Pour him a drink—a
real one. And put it on my tab." Righting the table, he urged

Obi-Wan back into his chair and lowered himself onto an adjoining one.

The cantina owner brought the drink and set it down in front of Obi-Wan. "Is he all right?"

"He's fine," the man from Mos Eisley said. "Aren't you, friend?"

Obi-Wan nodded. "Heatstroke."

The cantina owner seemed satisfied. "I'll bring you some more water."

Obi-Wan's new friend waited until they were alone to say, "You really all right?"

Obi-Wan nodded again. "Really."

The man adopted a conspiratorial voice. "You want to remain all right, you'll keep your voice down about Vader, understand? You'll keep from asking questions about him, too. Even in this Force-forsaken place."

Obi-Wan studied him. "What do you know about him?"

"Just this: I have a friend, a trader in hardwoods, who was on Kashyyyk when the Imperials launched their attack on a place called Kachirho. I guess he was lucky to get his ship raised and jumped. But he claims he got a glimpse of this guy Vader, ripping into Wookiees like they were stuffed toys, and going to lightsabers with the Jedi who were onworld." The spaceport worker glanced furtively around the cantina. "This Vader, he *toasted* Kashyyyk, friend. From what my friend says, it'll be years before a piece of wroshyr goes up the well."

"And the Wookiees?" Obi-Wan said.

The stranger shrugged forlornly. "Anyone's guess." Placing a few credits on the table, he stood up. "Take care of yourself. These desert wastes aren't as remote as you may think they are."

When the water arrived, Obi-Wan downed it in a gulp, shouldered his rucksack, and left the cool shade of the veranda for the harsh light of Anchorhead's principal street. He moved in a daze that had little to do with the glare or the heat.

As impossible as it seemed, Anakin had survived Mustafar and had resumed the Sith title of Darth Vader. How could Obi-Wan have been so foolish as to bring Luke *here,* of all worlds? Anakin's homeworld, the grave of his mother, the home of his only family members . . .

Obi-Wan gripped the lightsaber he carried under his robe.

Had he driven Anakin deeper into the dark side by abandoning him on Mustafar?

Could he face Anakin again?

Could he kill him this time?

From the far side of the street, he shadowed Owen and Beru as they moved from store to store, stocking up on staples. Should he warn them about Vader? Should he take Luke away from them and hide him on an even more remote world in the Outer Rim?

His fear began to mount. His and Yoda's hopes for the future, dashed, just as the Chosen One had dashed the Jedi's hopes of bringing balance to the Force—

Obi-Wan.

He came to an abrupt halt. It was a voice he hadn't heard in years, speaking to him not through his ears, but directly into his thoughts.

"Qui-Gon!" he said. "Master!" Realizing that the locals were quickly going to brand him a madman if they heard him talking to himself, he ducked into the narrow alley between two stores. "Master, is Darth Vader Anakin?" he asked after a moment.

Yes. Although the Anakin you and I knew is imprisoned by the dark side.

"I was wrong to leave him on Mustafar. I should have made *sure* he was dead."

The Force will determine Anakin's future. Obi-Wan: Luke must not be told that Vader is his father until the time is right.

"Should I take further steps to hide Luke?"

The core of Anakin that resides in Vader grasps that Tatooine is the source of nearly everything that causes him pain. Vader will never set foot on Tatooine, if only out of fear of reawakening Anakin.

Obi-Wan exhaled in relief. "Then my obligation is unchanged. But from what Yoda told me, I know that I have much to learn, Master."

You were always that way, Obi-Wan.

Qui-Gon's voice faded, and Obi-Wan's fears began to dissipate, replaced by renewed expectation.

Returning to the dazzling light of Tatooine's twin suns, he caught up with Owen, Beru, and Luke, and kept silent watch over them for what remained of the day.

If you enjoyed *Star Wars: Dark Lord—The Rise of Darth Vader*
and would like to delve further into the stories that paved the way
for the original *Star Wars* movies,
pick up a copy of *Star Wars: Outbound Flight*
by #1 *New York Times* bestselling *Star Wars* author Timothy Zahn!
Coming in February 2006 from Del Rey